THE UNIT
SEEK AND DESTROY

THE **UNIT**

SEEK AND DESTROY

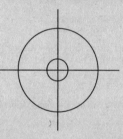

PATRICK ANDREWS

A SIGNET BOOK

SIGNET
Published by New American Library, a division of
Penguin Group (USA) Inc., 375 Hudson Street,
New York, New York 10014, USA
Penguin Group (Canada), 90 Eglinton Avenue East, Suite 700, Toronto,
Ontario M4P 2Y3, Canada (a division of Pearson Penguin Canada Inc.)
Penguin Books Ltd., 80 Strand, London WC2R 0RL, England
Penguin Ireland, 25 St. Stephen's Green, Dublin 2,
Ireland (a division of Penguin Books Ltd.)
Penguin Group (Australia), 250 Camberwell Road, Camberwell, Victoria 3124,
Australia (a division of Pearson Australia Group Pty. Ltd.)
Penguin Books India Pvt. Ltd., 11 Community Centre, Panchsheel Park,
New Delhi - 110 017, India
Penguin Group (NZ), 67 Apollo Drive, Rosedale, North Shore 0632,
New Zealand (a division of Pearson New Zealand Ltd.)
Penguin Books (South Africa) (Pty.) Ltd., 24 Sturdee Avenue,
Rosebank, Johannesburg 2196, South Africa

Penguin Books Ltd., Registered Offices:
80 Strand, London WC2R 0RL, England

First published by Signet, an imprint of New American Library,
a division of Penguin Group (USA) Inc.

First Signet Printing, September 2008
10   9   8   7   6   5   4   3   2   1

This book is dedicated to the memory of my father

Lieutenant Colonel Clyde Andrews
82nd Airborne Division, World War II

The first of three generations of paratroopers.

The aim of war must always be the overthrow of the enemy; this is the fundamental idea from which we set out.

—Clausewitz

PROLOGUE

The Hotel Rizzo, just off La Strada Elisa near the Renaissance Wall, was a small establishment hidden away from the mainstream traffic of the city. The neighborhood with its narrow streets and ancient apartment buildings and shops was never visited by tourists or even casual locals. Only people with special reasons went there; and the motives behind the visits were as varied as they were shady. The clerks who worked the desks of the down-at-the-heels hostelry were used to serving a quiet clientele who demonstrated a sharp sense of propriety. These individuals, who never engaged in small talk, registered quickly, then went quietly up to their rooms, generally without much more luggage than small valises. Their stays were only for short periods, never more than three days; and the people who visited their rooms had conspiratorial and suspicious appearances about them.

But two of the latest guests seemed entirely different. They were dressed reasonably well and each had a couple of nice roller bags when they checked in. But the pair were tough-looking individuals with features that bespoke hard lives in arduous environs, no doubt about that. One was tall with heavy shoulders and thinning hair that was cut short. A slash of a mouth sat under a nose that looked like it had been broken several times, and his muscular neck flowed down into thick shoulders. He had registered and produced documents that identified him as Karl Baroudeur. His companion had a Slavic look about him, and was short and stocky. His shaven head glistened in the lobby lights, and he peered out of pale blue eyes with a dull gaze. His name was Vlad Krashchenko.

Both spoke a crude manner of Italian with undeterminable accents. They took adjoining rooms, living in one and rearranging the furniture in the other. They moved the bed and bedstead over to one side, and requested a small table be sent up. This they put in the rear center of the room with a chair behind it, so that whoever sat in it faced the door like a business executive in his office.

After a couple of days passed, they began having visitors, and this was what made them truly stand out from the other guests. All the callers were male, athletic in appearance, and they moved in a fluid, almost graceful way, somewhat like martial artists or professional pugilists. Each had a healthy, robust demeanor, staying anywhere from half to three-quarters of an hour, then leaving quietly, never to return.

Although the room clerks were slightly curious about the goings-on, they minded their own business. This behavior was not only for courtesy, but it guaranteed a great degree of physical safety in such situations. The pair of lodgers promptly paid the bills for their rooms on a daily basis—an unusual practice that was greatly appreciated by the management. It was hoped they remained as guests for a long time.

15 MARCH
1400 HOURS LOCAL
1300 HOURS ZULU

The only visitors to the hotel room scheduled for that day had come in the morning, leaving the afternoon free for Baroudeur and Krashchenko to do as they pleased for a change. They wandered out of the neighborhood over to the tourist spots along the Via Paolino to stretch their legs and get something to eat besides the limited fare of the small café next to the hotel. They took an outdoor table at a *trattoria,* ordering an *agnolotti* pasta dish, bread, and a couple of liters of the local Tuscany wine. The two ate and drank slowly, gazing indolently at the tourists passing by, appreciating the scanty apparel worn by the women.

Karl Baroudeur's name was not the one he had been born with; but it was legal and proper. It had been given him in 1982 on the day when he enlisted in the French Foreign Legion in the city of Aubagne, France. It was the Legion's tradition to let a recruit start his life over with a new name. He could wipe the proverbial slate clean, and build a new existence, making whatever he could of it. Baroudeur did not waste that unique opportunity. He did well, and after a decade he had earned the rank of *major*, the highest warrant officer grade in the French Army. During his career he served in Lebanon, the Gulf War, Mogadishu, and Bosnia. Now retired and a citizen of France, he had turned to another form of soldiering— one that had brought him to the beautiful Italian city of Lucca that spring season.

It was about the same story for Vlad Krashchenko, although he had chosen the name rather than take one offered him by the Legion upon enlistment. It was his mother's maiden name, and using it seemed to close the gap somewhat between who he presently was and who he had once been. He served many years with Barou-deur, in fact meeting him at the *Centre de Recrutement* in Aubagne. But Krashchenko was not as anxious for authority and responsibility as his friend. He ended his Legion career holding the rank of *caporal-chef*—chief corporal—and that particular grade matched his personality perfectly. This was strictly a French noncommissioned rating that is unknown in any other army. When Krashchenko accepted the rank, he indicated he wanted no further promotions. He would never be a *sergent* or *sergent-chef,* but as a *caporal-chef,* he would have less responsibility than they, but some of the same perks, such as permission to own a car, eating in a special mess hall with his peers, and not having to do grunt work around the garrison. And after following Baroudeur around the different postings offered in the French Foreign Legion, Krashchenko shared these new activities in Italy with him in a military organization without legalized regulations, standard uniforms, or a national flag to serve.

Now, in the tourist section of Lucca, Baroudeur pushed his empty plate away and took a sip of wine. "How many are coming for interviews tomorrow?"

Krashchenko reached into his shirt pocket and pulled out a small notebook, flipping it open. "Three in the morning and four in the afternoon. A busy day."

"I suppose things are going well, but I am impatient," Baroudeur said.

"We already have eighty-two in the operational area," Krashchenko remarked as he replaced the notebook. "Another twenty or twenty-five should do it. They are coming faster now, so we shall be finished here soon."

"*C'est bon,*" Baroudeur said. "That's good. I need some time campaigning to sharpen old habits and instincts that have dulled over the last couple of years."

CHAPTER ONE

The five Unit operators walked at a slow but steady pace down the hall toward the Isolation Area. They were formed up as if they were consciously aware of their individual ranks and status, but the semi-formation was more instinctive than protocol for the professional soldiers. Sergeant Major Jonas Blane occupied the right front. The African-American was well-groomed and clean-shaven with an air of quiet dignity about him. On his immediate left, Master Sergeant Mack Gerhardt walked almost in step with him. Mack had a craggy handsomeness about him, looking soldierly even though he needed a shave. Staff Sergeant Bob Brown was a couple of paces behind the two senior NCOs. He was as martial as Mack, but had a more youthful appearance. Sergeants Charles "Carlito" Grey and Lance Matoskah brought up the rear.

The group's apparel was of the most laid-back civilian type: T-shirts, jeans, and light footgear. They looked more like a group of friends heading down to the corner bar for an afternoon of tossing back brews and watching sports on TV than members of an elite and very clandestine military organization.

Their presence in that Spartan building was in response to a serious and unexpected summons sent to them with a strong implication of "immediately if not sooner." They had given quick goodbye kisses to the women in their lives, grabbed some prepacked items of preferred gear from bedroom and hall closets, then driven from the Belleau Wood Post Housing Area to the 303rd Logistical Study Unit. This designation was the cover for an outfit referred to only as "the Unit" by the handpicked men assigned to it.

Their destination was the area where all premission briefings, logistical chores, administrative matters, and other necessary activities were carried out. Once a team went into Isolation, they did not come out until it was time to be deployed. They had a full latrine, bunks, tables and chairs, lockers, and other military amenities as they went through this vital preparation stage prior to insertion into some of the most violent locales on the face of the earth. There was also one individual—and one individual only—who was allowed to communicate with the internees. In the case of the Unit, it was their commanding officer, Colonel Tom Ryan.

They reached a guard who stood at his post beside a small desk in the hallway. Although the sentry knew them all, he required each to produce the proper ID before allowing them to proceed. With that taken care of, the quintet continued in silence, pushing whatever apprehension they felt to the back of their minds. This was a practice that gave the operators at least a semblance of self-control in circumstances where they had no idea what the immediate future held for them.

When the five turned into the short corridor leading to the Isolation Area, they came to an abrupt halt. Colonel Ryan stood waiting for them, his arms folded across his chest. He gazed at them in his usual manner, meaning that his rugged features were inscrutable but rather grim.

"Chill!" Ryan muttered.

"Sir?" Jonas Blane asked, puzzled.

"I said, 'Chill,' " Ryan said. "When you go through that door, I don't want to hear a word spoken, see a frown, or notice anybody displaying that all-American gesture of the middle finger of the hand extended."

The five Unit operators exchanged glances of bafflement. But when the colonel spoke, he was to be explicitly obeyed, no questions asked nor comments uttered. Ryan opened the door and stepped through as the others followed. Once more they stopped in their tracks. Delmar Munger, a controller-at-large from the CIA, sat in a chair looking back at them with his eyes narrowed and his mouth set in a half smile, half sneer. This was one individual the Unit men hated with an intensity bordering on religious fervor. They smothered their immediate reactions in accordance with the Colonel's one-word order, and went to a row of benches arranged in a semicircle, facing a podium.

"Sit!" Ryan said.

The five men settled down, taking notice of the two men flanking Munger. One was an effeminate softy in a well-tailored business suit, and the other a muscular black man dressed casually in a shirt and slacks.

Ryan went to the podium and leaned against it, looking at his operators. "You have been alerted for a special mission. This, of course, is nothing new, but this one has the potential to be long-term, so I hope you gave your lovely ladies some good loving last night, 'cause you ain't gonna roll in the hay with 'em for a month or so. And that's a minimum estimate. The maximum could run six or seven times that." He nodded toward Munger. "Our ol' buddy is here and I know how pleased you are to see him."

"Not half as much as I am to see these cowboys," Munger snorted. He was a bald, fat man who pictured himself as a lean, mean James Bond. In actuality he did his spying and espionage work from behind a desk at CIA Headquarters in Washington, D.C.

Ryan frowned. "Let's not get insulting, Munger. You keep your personal observations to yourself, and I'll see to it that these guys do the same." He turned back to the team. "You're headed for Africa. The Democratic Republic of the Congo, as a matter of fact. That's about all I know right now, so I'll invite Mr. Munger to give you the SITREP."

Munger stood up, pulling some notes from his pocket as he walked toward the podium. When he was in position, he spoke deliberately and slowly. "I'll use one- and two-syllable words as much as possible so as not to confuse you."

Mack Gerhardt spoke up with a wide grin. "Up yours, Munger."

Ryan yelled at him. "I told you to chill, Sergeant! Are you gonna have a problem with that?" He didn't wait for a reply, but whipped his eyes around to Munger. "As for you, I'm gonna insist on dignified decorum or I'll clean your clock myself." He walked up to the CIA man, putting his face close to his. "You just remember that anytime you're here at Fort Griffith, you're on thin ice. So don't stomp your feet." He went to the back of the room and leaned against the wall to observe the proceedings. He noted the little guy who had come with Munger was visibly shaken by the angry exchanges. He had an expression on his face that fairly shouted, "What the hell have I gotten myself into?"

Munger, impassive, continued. "There is a growing insurgency in the Democratic Republic of the Congo.

It is a fetus of a revolution right now, but has the potential of growing into a gigantic, mischievous big boy who could be the terror of the international neighborhood. The movement is financed by a clandestine organization of European industrialists and financiers who refer to themselves as the Consortium. They have turned their greedy eyes on that nation's natural resources. They are particularly interested in the mining operations involving gold, silver, and copper. These enterprises are badly managed presently and are producing far below acceptable levels."

Bob Brown, who had been taking notes like the others, raised his hand. "If that Consortium is so clandestine, how'd it get discovered?"

"It was detected because there are skillful CIA operatives who let nothing escape their attention," Munger said, stretching the truth. "And that's all you need to know."

"Just a minute," Mack Gerhardt said. "I noticed you used the word 'detected.' Would I be correct in assuming this Consortium is not 'compromised'?"

"You would be correct," Munger admitted. "At any rate, there are elements in the Congolese National Army who have sided with the rebellion, but so far they are scattered and not well organized. It is a matter of fact that neither the bulk of the local military nor the population care much one way or the other about the outcome of this situation. The Consortium is hoping to take care of this apathy by hiring European mercenaries to form a cadre that will galvanize the few dissidents into an effective force, thus encouraging other officers and soldiers to join them in this endeavor."

Now Sergeant Major Jonas Blane had a question. "I thought mercenaries in Africa went out of business in the nineteen sixties. Who are these guys? A bunch of stumbling old codgers trying to relive the good ol' days?"

"Hardly," Munger said. "These are young, well-trained, and experienced soldiers who have served extensive time in the special operations units of their own countries. These guns-for-hire soldiered in the Brit's SAS, Germany's KSK, and the French GIGN among others. They left the military because they can make a hell of a lot more money hiring out to civilian firms. So far no Americans are involved but there are plenty of Europeans available who have performed everything from kidnappings and assassinations, to actually engaging in combat in various hot spots around the world. Don't underestimate them. As long as the money's good, they'll fight."

"What about their weapons and equipment?" Colonel Ryan asked from the back of the room.

"State-of-the-art," Munger answered almost gleefully as if he was pleased it would make the Unit's job more dangerous and difficult. "That sponsoring Consortium has some real deep pockets. Plus, they'll be getting additional matériel from Congolese Army posts as well as whatever the dissidents bring with them when they join the insurgency." He paused. "Any more questions? Okay. Then allow me to introduce Captain Edouard Tshobutu of the Congolese National Army. He represents the active loyalists who have taken a stand against the revolutionaries."

The African took Munger's place at the podium. He was a tall man, all soldier and no nonsense. "Good morning," he said, showing a friendly smile. "Alas, like our opponents in the Army, we active loyalists are not of any great numerical strength. Thus, we are in dire need of help, as are the insurgents. Before you make any judgments about me, I would like to explain that I am a graduate of the Special Warfare School at Fort Bragg, North Carolina, and have participated in several training exercises in the States as well as in Okinawa, South Korea, and Europe with American Special Forces units.

I also attended several U.S. Army training institutes over the course of my career. I am a qualified parachutist in my own country, and I took the HALO course at Yuma in Arizona. And now the present unhappy situation in the Congo has brought me to the point of organizing a resistance to the insurgency because of the indifference of the rest of the National Army."

Carlito Grey was never the most diplomatic of men. He spoke up sharply, asking, "If you're only a captain, how's come you're taking over putting down that uprising?"

Tshobutu actually grinned at the directness of the question. "I am the commanding officer of a parachute infantry battalion, but I am acting independently on my own. I am, in fact, AWOL."

Carlito wasn't finished. "What the hell do you have against the insurgency?"

"I confess I have the same disagreements with the policies of my country's present government many of them do," Tshobutu replied. "However, I resent having European mercenaries invade the borders of my homeland. There isn't a son of a bitch in the world that is going to knock me to my knees without first meeting fierce resistance on my part."

"Makes sense," Carlito commented. "Whatcha got to fight with?"

"I have one eager subaltern and a hundred and seven soldiers and noncommissioned officers from my battalion who are loyal to me," Tshobutu informed him. "They are located at an isolated base camp in the jungle. There are also about a dozen privates who have arrived fresh from recruit training, and they are eager young chaps, though without much practical experience. The weaponry I have acquired is excellent with French FA-MAS five-point-fifty-six automatic rifles and Belgian Minimi machine guns of the same caliber. For antiarmor defense we are well equipped with German Panzerfaust antitank missiles."

Lance Matoskah asked, "What about antiaircraft?"

"None," the Congolese captain replied. "But the Congolese Air Force is not exactly up to snuff. We, however, do have a French Aérospatiale SA Three-Thirty helicopter and both a pilot and mechanic to service it. Unfortunately it is not armed, but it can provide transportation." He glanced over his attentive audience. "One bit of very good news is that there will be no problem with resupply. We have well-stocked caches in several locations. These include ammunition, rations, and medical supplies. Also the five-point-fifty-six ammo is compatible with the FA-MAS and American M-Sixteens and M-Four-A-Ones." He paused. "Are there any comments or questions?"

"Not at this point," Jonas Blane replied, speaking for his team.

Captain Tshobutu returned to his chair, and Colonel Ryan called out from the back of the room, "Mr. Cartwright, will you take the floor please and introduce yourself?"

Cartwright, a thin bureaucrat with a thick, longish mane of black hair, was still a bit rattled by the open hostility expressed at the start of the proceedings. He went to the podium with a nervous half smile on his lips, clearing his throat a couple of times. "I am Booker Cartwright of the United States State Department. I am assigned to the Special Affairs Bureau that deals with, er, that is to say . . . we deal with special affairs. Like this one. The Secretary of State has asked me to proffer his desires to you. Actually, these aren't his desires, per se, but what he is talking about is State Department policy." He cleared his throat again. "Since the situation in the Democratic Republic of the Congo is rather fluid with foreigners involved while the greater bulk of the Congolese population is unconcerned, the Secretary of State thinks—that is he deems it advisable—that a sincere effort be made to bring not only the majority of people to our side, but also the dissidents by peaceful means."

"Wait a minute," Lance Matoskah said. The young Native American NCO was obviously not pleased. "Are you telling me that if some son of a bitch is shooting at me, I'll be expected to sit there and yell out something like, 'Say! Can't we just be friends'?"

"Well, no," Cartwright said. "Not in a case like that. I'm not quite sure—"

Jonas interrupted. "We'll do our best to establish a friendly rapport with the enemy, Mr. Cartwright, and win them to our cause. And when and where we meet others who are not swayed to one side or the other, we will do our best to make them want to fight the insurgents. Will that satisfy the Secretary of State?"

"Why, yes," Cartwright said. He took a breath, saying, "And that is my presentation to you." He walked rapidly form the podium, glad to get back to the sanctuary of his chair.

Colonel Tom Ryan went up to the front of the room. "Before we leave you to work out your OPLAN, I have two important announcements. We will be supplying all of you, along with Captain Tshobutu and his second-in-command, with night-vision goggles." He glanced at Staff Sergeant Bob Brown. "The second is for you, Brown. You will not be going into the OA with your bosom buddies here. Instead, you will fly to Iraq, where you will be given documents identifying you as a dismissed employee from a PMC for conduct unbecoming a human being. You will then fly from Iraq to Frankfurt, Germany. From Frankfurt you will fly to Florence, Italy. From Florence you will travel by bus to the city of Lucca and seek out the mercenaries. And, since soldiers of fortune are notoriously slack when it comes to security, we have some additional information on where to find them. We will expect you to join the mercenary force and go to the Democratic Republic of the Congo."

"Yes, sir," Bob said. "And once I am a rootin'-tootin' freebooter, just what the hell do you want me to do?"

"Well, Bob," the Colonel said a bit sardonically, "we want you to determine the capabilities and intentions of the mercenaries. Also any other valuable intelligence you might be able to learn. With that accomplished, you will head for the hinterlands over there and turn on the homing device that will be provided for you. It will actually be an AN/PRC-One-Twelve radio."

Bob didn't like the sound of that. "Won't those mercenaries be suspicious if they discover it on me?"

"Not if you tell 'em you stole it from your former employers," Ryan assured him. "Now when you switch on that beacon, Captain Tshobutu's helicopter will pick you up and fly you to the base camp to join the loyalist soldiers and your Unit buddies with all that info you'll have garnered."

"Understood, sir," Bob replied.

"It wouldn't be wise for you to show up with night-vision goggles, so Carlito will bring an extra pair for you to use when you rejoin the Unit," Colonel Ryan informed him. "Now, with that said, we will leave you gentlemen to write your OPLAN. We have a packet of maps and other documents for your reference. Also, Captain Tshobutu will be available for any questions that might arise. Now do the things you must and we'll be back in twenty-four hours for your briefback. Meanwhile I'll see to it that your gear and weapons are sent in here from the team room."

The five operators waited for the colonel and the three visitors to leave; then Sergeant Major Jonas Blane stood up. "Let's get to it."

Normally in isolation, a Special Forces team would have been given a more formal briefing by various command and staff officers along with assets or other informed personnel. The Unit dispensed with a lot of that protocol, not because they were lazy but because they were practical and wanted to rush things along. However, they pretty much followed the usual SOP after the introductory phase. Now Jonas Blane and his men would work out an OPLAN about how to conduct their mission within the twenty-four-hour period given them. They would also make a list of things needed beyond the normal TA. With that done, there would be the briefback, and if the powers-that-be accepted their OPLAN, it would become an OPORD etched in stone to be carefully followed until the situation in the OA went to hell—as it always did—and from that point on, they would play it all by ear.

21 MARCH
0900 HOURS
1500 HOURS ZULU

The team was back on the benches when Colonel Tom Ryan and Captain Edouard Tshobutu entered the Isolation Area for the briefback. Unit SOP forbade anyone who had no need-to-know about the conduct of the operation to be present, and that included CIA and State Department personnel.

Captain Tshobutu took a seat while Sergeant Major Jonas Blane got up to hand two sheets of paper to Colonel Ryan. "What the hell is this?" Ryan asked as Jonas went back to join the team.

"It's our OPLAN, sir," Jonas replied, sitting back down on the bench.

"For Chrissake, this is for a long-term mission!" Ryan shouted. "I've seen patrol orders longer than this."

"That's it, sir," Jonas said. "The first page covers the HALO insertion, linking up with the loyalist group, then getting down to business. We haven't got one single idea what we'll be doing once we are boots-on-the-ground."

"What's this second page?" the colonel inquired.

"It's the OPLAN Annex, sir."

Ryan read aloud from the page. " 'All weapons, ammo loads, commo, medical, and other gear will comply with current SOPs, the SOI, and TAs.' "

Master Sergeant Mack Gerhardt chimed in. "We could've attached them documents, sir, but you got copies of all that crap in your files."

Ryan shrugged and sighed. "Okay. It is now an OPORD."

Jonas Blane got up and turned to his men. "Okay, Big Team, let's go to war."

CHAPTER TWO

D.R. OF THE CONGO
OPERATIONAL AREA
24 MARCH
0615 HOURS LOCAL
0415 HOURS ZULU

Sergeant Major Jonas Blane plummeted downward in a faultless stable free fall position. Five other parachutists were slightly above him, and he lowered his right hand to execute a controlled turn to survey Captain Edouard Tshobutu and the four soldiers who had exited the C-130 aircraft right after him. Jonas was pleased to note that everyone was in control of his 120-mile-per-hour descent without instabilities such as flat spins or tumbling. This mission had some pretty bad potential as it was, but at least it was off to a good start.

Jonas brought his right hand back up to stop his turn, then glanced downward. The DZ was small, but ample enough for the half dozen jumpers who were to land on it. The location had been decided through a combination of a map reconnaissance and information given by Cap-

tain Tshobutu back in the Cave. It was a cleared area in
the jungle that had been used in the past as a helicopter
LZ for the Congolese officer's battalion training operations. All tree stumps and other obstacles had been removed to offer easy access to the small clearing.

Down below on the ground, Sublieutenant Pierre
Kintuba gazed up at the figures of the falling parachutists, wishing like hell he could get to a HALO school
somewhere. Kintuba was one of those thin youths
whose physiques belied their strength and agility. He
was Tshobutu's second-in-command, and the young officer was looking forward to the coming campaign that
would wipe out both the traitorous Congolese and the
European mercenaries invading his homeland.

Suddenly a half dozen ram-air parachute canopies
blossomed into life. *"Tazameni kule!"* Kintuba shouted
to alert the soldiers on the defensive perimeter formed
around the DZ. Although he spoke French, as did all
educated Congolese, he used Swahili for the soldiers'
benefit. Many had little schooling, and used the army as
an escape from home villages that offered dismal pros-
pects for a decent life.

One by one, the parachutists reached the ground,
moving into the wind while pulling the toggles to the
full-brake position just before touching down. Kintuba
had detailed a half dozen men to tend to the jumpers.
These were veteran parachutists from Captain Tshobutu's battalion who were capable of lending a hand on the
DZ when and where necessary. All had been impressed
by the display since the experienced jumpers had made
nothing but static-line jumps during their careers, and
HALO was something new to them.

Kintuba quickly spotted Tshobutu getting free of his
harness and gear, and raced up to him, stopping to ren-
der a sharp salute. *"À vos ordres, mon capitaine!"*

Tshobutu smiled at his young subordinate. "Speak
English, Pierre. You'll be working very close with these

Americans, so you must refresh your fluency in the language."

"Yes, my captain!"

"Just saying, 'Yes, sir' will suffice," Tshobutu explained. "That is how it is done in the United States Armed Forces." He was now completely out of his parachute, and allowed a soldier to help him into his rucksack. The captain looked over at the sublieutenant. "You organized this reception remarkable well, Pierre. Any attack would have been dealt with quite effectively."

"Merci, mon capitaine," Kintuba said. Then he grinned sheepishly. "I mean to say, 'Thank you, sir.' "

The rest of the Unit operators were now leaving the DZ, each with a Congolese soldier toting his expended parachute. Jonas Blane and Mack Gerhardt walked up to the two Congolese officers, and Tshobutu introduced Kintuba to the Americans. For the sake of protocol and to avoid any conflicts with Congolese officers, Blane had become a "major" while Mack was made a "captain." The other three would be "first lieutenants."

Jonas nodded to the young officer. "Has there been much activity around here, Lieutenant?"

"No, sir," Kintuba replied. "Everything has been quiet without contact with the enemy. But we have received word that a few officers and soldiers are absent from their posts at several garrisons."

"Mmm," Tshobutu mused, "that means they are joining up with the insurgents."

"Well, then," Jonas said, "we'd better get this show on the road. I'm looking forward to meeting those people."

Bob Brown, alias Ted Durant, stepped off the bus that had just arrived from Florence. He found himself on the Piazza San Martino facing a large building that carried a sign in several languages identifying it as a tourist center. Bob hefted his AWOL and kit bags and walked toward the building. A few minutes later he reemerged with a city map. It took only a few seconds to determine the location of the Hotel Rizzo off La Strada Elisa, and he was pleased to note it wasn't far.

He strolled through the area among a good number of tourists until he reached the street he was looking for, then he turned to walk down toward the Renaissance Wall. The neighborhood was noticeably more run-down than the rest of the city, and the few denizens out on the street were obviously not part of Tuscany's social elite. There was no sign on the hotel front, but he spotted the desk through the door and walked in.

The clerk, idly scanning a copy of the newspaper *La Repubblica*, glanced up at the stranger's entrance. He immediately sized up the foreigner as being like many of the visitors who had lately begun showing up in the lobby. He pointed to the stairs. *"Secondo piano."*

Bob was confused. He didn't know why the guy mentioned a piano, but he could understand *secondo*, so it seemed the clerk was sending him up to the second floor. He nodded his thanks and ascended the stairs. He went to the room identified for him back in Iraq, and knocked on the door.

"Entrez."

Bob entered the room, seeing a large muscular man sitting behind a table. A shorter individual with a shaven head sat on a bed shoved over to one side of the room. Bob sat his bags down. "I'm looking for a job."

Karl Baroudeur looked the stranger over, recognizing the soldier in him. "How do you know I have jobs available?" He spoke excellent English from being exposed to the language through commanding a large number of legionnaires from the UK. They made up close to a third of the Legion's numerical strength.

"Benny Toledo told me."

"When last did you see Benny Toledo?"

"A couple of days ago," Bob answered. "He's working for Pitman Enterprises. That's where I used to hang my hat."

"Why do you not work there now?"

Bob showed what he hoped would appear to be a grin of discomposure. "A little mix-up. I sort of shot the wrong people during a confrontation in Baghdad. I got paid off and was told to return to the States. Benny told me about you, so I decided it would be better for me to come here."

Baroudeur laughed. "You got the big troubles if you go back to America, no?"

"I got big troubles in America, yes!"

"What military service have you?" Baroudeur asked.

"U.S. Army," Bob replied. "I pulled a couple of tours with the Eighty-second Airborne in Afghanistan. I didn't adapt too well after I was sent back to Fort Bragg. I got busted down in rank a couple of times. Then I was given a less-than-honorable discharge. They called it for the 'convenience of the government.' "

This did not alarm Baroudeur. He was used to having shady individuals in his mercenary operations. "Do you have any weapons or gear?"

"Just a radio," Bob replied. "It was issued to me by Pitman. A handheld American model. I guess I forgot to turn it back in. I had it in my checked-in luggage, and it appears the x-ray examiners weren't too alarmed when they saw it."

"You might have good use for it," Baroudeur remarked. "I take it you have a valid passport."

"Yeah," Bob said. "But I'm gonna need another as soon as I can get one."

"Let me see what you have." The mercenary leader took the passport and gave it a careful inspection. "Your name is Ted Durant, eh? Well, Ted Durant, I can give you a job. If you want a different passport after it is finished, I will deduct the costs from your pay."

"How about giving me a rundown on the work?" Bob asked. "I might not be interested."

Once again Baroudeur laughed. "I think you will be interested. The pay is two thousand Euros a month with a bonus when we win."

"When we win what?"

"Our campaign," Baroudeur said. "It should take no more than three months at the longest. You will be in combat against an inferior enemy. *Kaffirs*."

"What are *Kaffirs*?"

"That is an insulting way to refer to the Negro race," Baroudeur said. "Does that disturb your American intolerance for racism?"

"I served with African-Americans," Bob replied. "They always held up their end." He instantly regretted expressing himself without thinking of the consequences.

"But they are not real Africans, are they?"

"Hell, I don't know," Bob said, wanting to change the subject. "What about that bonus?"

"The minimum will be ten thousand Euros. And there is a possibility it may go as high as twenty-five thousand."

"It sounds like somebody is gonna be making a lot of money out of this," Bob commented. "What sort of weaponry will we have?"

"Are you familiar with the Russian AKS-Seventy-Four assault rifle?"

"I've heard of it," Bob replied. Actually he had done some extensive familiarization firing of the weapon on the Fort Griffith range.

"It is five-point-forty-five millimeter," Baroudeur informed him. "The Russians wished to go down from their standard seven-point-sixty-two to closer match NATO's calibers. They are very good for how we will be employing them."

"Who are we fighting?"

"You will find out in due time. Do you want the employment?"

"Sure," Bob said. "Will there be a contract?"

"When the time is right," Baroudeur assured him. "Meanwhile, you will be put up in a hotel." He turned to Krashchenko and spoke rapidly in French, then turned back to the American. "Your roommate will be an Englishman."

"Evidently it is not important whether I speak a foreign language or not," Bob said.

"I am following the old Foreign Legion custom of placing new men with others of their own nationalities. Since you are the only American, the closest I can get for you is an Englishman."

"So you were in the Foreign Legion, huh?" Bob remarked. "I may end up there eventually."

"I would not be surprised," Baroudeur said. He scribbled something down on a sheet of paper. "You will not stay at this hotel. Here is the address where you can have a room. Show this to the desk clerk when you check in, and he will direct you where to go."

"Thanks," he replied. "Any chance of an advance?"

Baroudeur reached in his pocket and pulled out some bills. "A hundred Euros. Make them last, because we have not yet been given a definite date for departure."

Bob took the money and directions, picked up his bags, and left the room.

D.R. OF THE CONGO
COUNTERINSURGENCY BASE CAMP
1630 HOURS LOCAL
1430 HOURS ZULU

The column of Congolese soldiers was sweat-soaked and tired as they struggled upward through the tropical forest on the hillside. They were in full field gear as Jonas Blane watched them, appreciating the effort they had made during the forced march through the jungle. He had only been with Captain Tshobutu's men for some thirty-plus hours, but he was already beginning to appreciate their capabilities. Most were troopers who had served directly under Tshobutu in his parachute infantry battalion, and they were superbly conditioned. The others, including the raw recruits, would have had a hard time of it except for being encouraged by the veteran paratroopers. The new men knew this was a most important time in their careers. They would have to prove themselves in combat if they were to remain in the airborne outfit after the insurgency had been crushed.

There had been a change in protocol for Jonas that had taken place almost immediately upon his arrival. His rank of "major" had confused the Congolese, including the keen Sublieutenant Kintuba. The official language of the Congolese Army was French. In French rank structure the rank "major" was actually a senior chief warrant officer. Their word for the English "major" was *commandant*. Thus, Jonas became Commandant Blane very quickly so no officers would resent him giving them orders.

That short, word-efficient annex to the OPLAN that Jonas Blane submitted to Colonel Ryan during the brief-back actually carried a lot of information. The Unit had been in many sorts of operations, and there were always critiques at the end of each one. These skull sessions about lessons learned in the OAs resulted in SOPs that covered every possibility that could occur. Thus logistics and communications were written out in TAs and SOIs and were ready to be applied in any future missions. The men also had prepacked rucksacks in the team room with not only required items, but personal choices of the individual operators. Consequently, the Americans were equipped differently than their Congolese comrades-in-arms. They carried the vaunted M4A1 5.56-millimeter carbines with all the bells and whistles. These included Trijicon ACOG scopes, AN/PEQ pointer/illuminators, sound suppressors, and other goodies. Carlito Grey also toted an M203 grenade launcher and the 40-millimeter projectiles that went with it.

Carlito's other duties were to take care of the team commo chores with an AN PSC Shadowfire Radio for long-range situations. This was a powerful transmitter and receiver with satellite communications capabilities, allowing contact with the TOC back at Fort Griffith. Unfortunately, the satellite was in an equatorial orbit that meant it only passed over three times a day, providing a total of six hours' transmission and receiving. Carlito was happy to leave the Shadowfire at the base camp since it weighed some twenty pounds with the battery. Everyone had the LASH radio headset attached to AN PRC-126 radios for interteam commo. These were also passed out to the two Congolese officers and twenty NCOs. It was possible to speak into the throat mikes in a whisper and still be easily heard over the small net.

However, the Congolese had the same individual medical kits as the Americans. Captain Tshobutu had arranged for those and drawn them from the post quartermaster at Fort Griffith. Lance Matoskah had jumped in with a couple of trauma bags that held medical equipment that could handle illnesses and hurts that ranged from minor fevers to massive wounds.

Now the Congolese stood in formation at the end of their speed march exercise. They were sweating hard and dog tired, but proud that not one man had fallen out during the trek through the steamy vegetation. They had covered a challenging fifteen kilometers in ten hours of humping through the difficult terrain. While this wasn't up to Unit standards, the operators and the two Congolese officers were satisfied. This was an excellent start.

Jonas planned on keeping the pressure up for another forty-eight hours, then taking them out on their first mission. While waiting for the arrival of their captain and the Americans, Sublieutenant Kintuba had been running reconnaissance patrols on a daily basis. One of these excursions had discovered a clandestine storage facility belonging to the insurgents.

This would be the first objective.

Lucca, Italy
Hotel Montevista
2300 hours local
2200 hours Zulu

Bob Brown, alias Ted Durant, immediately settled in rather amiably with his new roommate. The guy was a twenty-three-year-old Englishman named Simon Cooper. Cooper was AWOL from the British Army. After a tour of duty in Afghanistan with the Parachute Regiment, he made an attempt to get out of his enlistment. The motive was money. Cooper had heard of the salaries paid by PMCs, and wanted a piece of the action.

"I figured if I was gonna get me arse shot at, I'd make it worth me while," he explained. "But the bluddy Army didn't see things the way wot I saw 'em and told me to get back to barracks and shut up. So I took a walk—know wot I mean?"

"I understand," Bob replied, though as a professional soldier, he did not admire a man who broke his word by violating his enlistment contract.

After absconding from his regiment, Cooper headed for the Continent to seek his fortune. He went through a bit of aimless knocking around and drunken binges in Paris, and eventually ran into a guy who pointed him toward Lucca and a job available there. He had done as Bob and agreed to hire on for whatever it was that Baroudeur was offering. It was a hell of a lot more than the Queen paid.

After the two roomies became acquainted, Cooper suggested that they visit a brothel that he had discovered down the street. Bob shook his head. "I'll take a rain check on that, Simon. I'm short of dough. Besides, I was banging a Red Cross worker in Baghdad, so I'm not real horny yet."

"Right," Cooper said, getting his jacket. "Well, I'm off to give me John Henry a nice treat. See you later, Ted."

Bob unpacked, putting a few things in an empty drawer in the room's one bureau, then settled down with a paperback Western. He found it hard to concentrate because of jitters about the coming operation. He had been on plenty of missions, but this one in which he would be inserted into a wild-ass mercenary organization seemed particularly ominous for some reason. He finally gave up trying to read, and got up to gaze out the window. In a way he envied Simon Cooper. The guy was getting laid, and Bob was truly horny. The alert order arrived a few days after he and his wife, Kim, had made love, and he hadn't had time for what they referred to as a premission quicky.

Cooper had been gone only a half hour when he returned to the room. Either he was a wham-bam-thank-you-ma'am type, or the bordello was close by. He broke out a bottle of cheap scotch from a suitcase under his bed. "Let's wind the day down with a nip or two, Ted."

"Best offer I've had all day," Bob remarked.

The two men shared the bottle and chatted amiably and casually as they drifted into a mellow drunk. Bob found out his new friend had not advanced much in rank during his five years in the Parachute Regiment. When he deserted he was a lance corporal, a rank that was equal to private first class in the American Army. The Englishman candidly explained his lack of promotion. "I got passed over, y'see, 'cause the sergeants didn't think I was much for leadership. I supposed I was lucky to get that one chevron, hey?"

"That's the breaks," Bob remarked.

"Yeah," Cooper said. "Me dad was disappointed. He's a car salesman and is good at it. He gets his share of the quids and then some, hey? And me mum don't have to work on account of it."

"Do you have a girl back home waiting for you, Simon?"

Cooper shook his head. "I prefer getting me jollies with the professional trollops—know wot I mean? Better'n a regular bird, yeah? I always like the directness and ease of the associations."

"I guess you have a point," Bob said.

He poured himself another scotch, glancing at Cooper, knowing the young Brit's life was dedicated to the philosophy of KISS. If he survived this latest adventure, he would probably learn a very bitter lesson. Maybe he would be able to return to the UK and turn himself in. Bob wondered if the British Army had the same regulations as the American services when it came to an AWOL status. After so much time, the absent soldier would be declared a deserter and face serious punishment. In times of war he might be executed. It would seem that Simon Cooper had irrevocably ruined his life to the extent that he would be better off if he got zapped in this Congolese adventure.

Across the room, sitting on the other bed, the Englishman had grown silent, slowly sipping the liquor.

CHAPTER THREE

D.R. OF THE CONGO
OPERATIONAL AREA
27 MARCH
0445 HOURS LOCAL
0245 HOURS ZULU

Carlito Grey was alone in the early-morning gloom as he made a silent walk through the enemy supply depot after a short period of observation from the edge of the jungle. A short time before, an insurgent sentry, caught asleep by him and the two Congolese of his security team, had been rudely but quietly awakened, then trussed up. Carlito ordered his companions to guard the guy and keep him quiet. They wanted to knife the errant soldier, but Carlito instructed that he be kept alive for interrogation. "You can cut his throat later," Carlito promised, drawing a finger across his own Adam's apple to get the message across.

Sergeant Charles "Carlito" Grey always performed his duties with a quiet efficiency. He was a wiry young man with longish black hair and a beard. As the offspring of

an Anglo father and a Hispanic mother, he could speak
both English and Spanish without the accents of one
language intruding on the other. Unfortunately his father had deserted the family when Carlito was twelve,
and the boy began playing hooky from school and hanging out on the streets with other kids. He ended up in a
gang called the Byz Lats, seemingly destined for years
in prison, or death at the hands of rival gang members.
It was a probation officer who saved him after a mis-
demeanor conviction. This ex-Army Ranger used video
tapes to show the young gangster a real man's life in
elite Army units. Carlito was hooked within five minutes. He enlisted for Special Forces and made the grade,
earning a sergeancy in his first hitch. The Unit was the
logical next step in the military career path of this gung-
ho soldier.

Now, as Carlito made his way through the midst of the
hostile garrison, his only accoutrements were the Sig
Sauer 9-millimeter pistol in his left hand and the K-Bar
knife in his right. This is what Sergeant Major Jonas
Blane would describe as "lean and mean."

The objective of his infiltration was the site's commo
shack, easily identified by the antenna attached on the
roof of the building. When he reached the corner of the
structure, he stopped and knelt down. A few seconds
of listening revealed no sounds of wakeful individuals
stumbling around, and he stood up and eased his way
to the window. A quick glance inside revealed a commo
man by the one radio set, dozing peacefully in a chair.
Carlito made his way to the door, keeping a wary eye
out for intruders; then he softly raised the latch and
gently pushed. The flimsy portal, with leather straps for
hinges, opened slowly and silently. He stepped up directly behind the man, and simultaneously covered his
mouth and slit deep into a jugular vein with his K-Bar. A
half minute of a steadily weakening struggle, with some

bubbly gasping, announced the departure of life. Then, after a slump and a shudder, the job was done.

Carlito laid the dead African out on the floor, and gave the radio a quick glance. It was an old Soviet R-108 model that had seen better days. Evidently, effective commo was not a priority in the Congolese Army. Carlito reached in the back and removed the old-fashioned vacuum tubes, sticking them in his pocket.

"Snake Doctor, this is Betty Blue. Over," Carlito said in the LASH.

"This is Snake Doctor," came back Jonas Blane's voice.

"The commo is neutralized," Carlito announced. "Give me five minutes to withdraw. Over."

"No problem. Out."

Jonas, with the main attacking force, checked the time, deciding to give Carlito an extra two minutes to return to make sure he could get back to the main group in time for the attack. He would be acting as the grenadier during the full-blown assault on the objective. Jonas held Carlito's M4A1 carbine with the M-203 grenade launcher attached. An assault vest with 40-caliber HE grenades in the pouches was also awaiting Carlito's attention.

Mack Gerhardt had a security force of a dozen men on the north side of the supply compound while Lance Matoskah had an equal number on the south to hem in the enemy. Directly across from Jonas, on the west side, Captain Edouard Tshobutu and Sublieutenant Pierre Kintuba were positioned with twenty-five soldiers ready to cut off any retreat from the pressure of the attacking force. The others would move in to join the assault one by one as the fighting went past them.

Jonas, with the main assault force of a bit more than sixty men, was well organized and ready. The Congolese were under the direct command of their noncommissioned officers in preestablished fire teams. Their task was simple: Jonas would issue the assault order over his LASH that would be picked up by the NCOs who had their own commo gear. They would then sweep forward and began laying down fire into the various buildings of the small post. Carlito would fire his grenades through windows, and after the projectiles detonated, specially chosen men would rush into the interiors to take down any enemy that still resisted.

Carlito and his two companions made their appearance three minutes early. The pair of Congolese was given extra grenade pouches in order to act as ammo bearers. Carlito quickly donned the vest and picked up the M4A1 carbine, glancing over at Jonas. "There was a guy in the commo shack."

"I can see that by the blood on your hands," Jonas remarked.

"A slight addition to whatever was already there," Carlito said. He was impatient. "Okay, boss. Let's git!"

Jonas spoke French into his LASH. *Allez! Allez! Allez!*

The skirmish lines moved out, leaving the heavy vegetation and entering the compound. A couple of beats later the first sounds of shots blasted through the still morning air. Carlito, with his grenade toters handy, cut loose with the M-203, choosing targets of opportunity as they appeared. The projectiles crashed through the screened windows, exploding and blasting off the wooden shutters. Screams immediately followed and were cut short by the fusillades of 5.56-ammo that was being fired in three-round bursts by the FA-MAS rifles and M4A1 carbines.

A couple of careless but brave insurgents charged from the doors of their small barracks, but were cut down by the cross fire. Their more prudent comrades stayed in the interiors of the buildings, firing from windows. The wood siding of the frame structures offered little protection, and shattered under the impact of the attackers' return fire. The men inside were cut down, and the defensive fire began to decrease rapidly.

Now the two security teams on the flanks began moving in to join the main attacking force. The rate and roar of the overlapping salvos raked the buildings, and the defenders could be seen running from doors on the opposite sides to escape the hail of bullets that swept through the garrison.

Captain Tshobutu and Sublieutenant Kintuba, along with their twenty-five men, now joined the fight. Tightly packed swarms of hastily aimed gunfire cut down the enemy that ran toward them in the hope of escape. Now the insurgents knew they were pinned in. Most threw their weapons aside and dove to the ground. Others sank to their knees and raised their hands in surrender.

"Snake Doctor," Tshobutu said in his LASH, "this is Checkmate. The enemy is contained. I say again. The enemy is contained. Over."

"Roger," Jonas replied. "All teams. Cease fire. *Cessez le feu.*"

The sudden silence that followed the order was almost as dramatic as the shooting itself. Dead and wounded insurgents littered the area, and the enemies on the far side were now under the control of Tshobutu and Kintuba. These were formed up by the Congolese paratroopers to be pummeled and kicked into a column formation.

Jonas and Mack Gerhardt walked up, watching the EPWs being organized in a less than gentle fashion. Captain Tshobutu saluted the senior American. "A quick victory, eh, Commandant?"

"I would agree," Jonas said. He gestured to Carlito Grey and Lance Matoskah. "Search out the supply shacks and see what kind of goodies you can find." He turned back to Tshobutu. "There are wounded enemy back in the compound."

"I will have my medical aidmen tend to them," Tshobutu said. "I have three who are well trained and experienced. And we have ample medicines and bandages to extend humane treatment to our unfortunate enemies."

Reports coming in over the LASH sets brought the good news there had been no friendly casualties. When Carlito and Lance reported back, they had more happy tidings. "There is ammo, grenades, rations, and miscellaneous items such as boots and uniforms," Lance informed Jonas.

"Yeah," Carlito said. "This evidently was going to be a major supply depot for this area."

Jonas grinned. "It already has been." He noticed a Congolese NCO was supervising the continuing round up of the EPWs. A dozen shocked men stood with their hands up under the gunsights of appointed guards. Jonas was pleased by the sight. "It looks like we're gonna have help toting the supplies back to the base camp."

"I'll have Lieutenant Kintuba organize the effort, Commandant," Tshobutu said.

"Destroy what can't be carried," Jonas instructed. "And be sure to separate any EPW officers and NCOs from the privates. We don't want any undue influence on the lower rankers before we get a chance to interrogate 'em."

"Of course, Commandant," Tshobutu replied. He left to find Sublieutenant Kintuba to get the orders carried out.

OKANDJA, GABON
PETRÓLEO ESPAÑOL-AFRICANO, S.A.
COMPANY HEADQUARTERS
1000 HOURS LOCAL
0900 HOURS ZULU

A small group of men in camouflage uniforms stood at the edge of the runway watching the approach of the

Casa 207 Azor transport. This old aircraft was originally manufactured for use by the Spanish Air Force, but was later phased out for more modern models. Several were purchased by Petróleo Español-Africano, a petroleum survey company, and put to good use hauling employees and equipment around the African continent to various work sites. Now, with wheels lowered, the airplane began its descent toward the one landing strip that served this hub of the company's operations.

The aircraft touched down, quickly slowing under pressure of brakes and the reversed engines. It taxied off the runway and over to the small building that served as a terminal for the bucolic airport. Waiting attendants wheeled the passenger ramp to the aircraft as the door was pushed open by a crewman. Almost immediately a line of twenty-three men began to disembark, going down the steps. The first man off was Vlad Krashchenko, and he signaled the others to follow him toward the terminal.

Bob Brown and Simon Cooper, wearing civilian clothing like the other passengers, walked side by side, carrying their bags. When they entered the building, they saw Karl Baroudeur waiting for them, sporting a fancy leather holster holding an unidentifiable type of pistol. He was clad in a sharply pressed camouflaged uniform with epaulets decorated by the crossed swords, a star, and lion's head of a Congolese brigadier general. He also wore the green beret of the French Foreign Legion's *2er Régiment Étrangère de Parachutistes*. A Congolese officer, also armed with a handgun, was standing beside him with similar epaulets but with one more star, indicating he was a major general. His headgear was a red beret with the Congolese Airborne Troops badge. Both men sported French-style parachutist badges pinned above their right breast pockets.

Krashchenko turned around and called the new arrivals to attention. All snapped to properly, and Baroudeur stepped forward. "I welcome you to Africa. It is here on this continent that you will take part in Operation Griffe. You will be fully briefed on this situation within a few days." He paused and squared his shoulders. "From this moment on I am General Baroudeur, and you will address me as such. Remember this and remember it well! There are no regulations in a mercenary force. All protocol and rules will be enforced by this." He patted his pistol. "Now! The gentleman beside me is General Marcel Lulombe, our commander-in-chief. Colonel Krashchenko is the chief of staff. As of now you are all assigned to Commando Nyoka. That is Swahili for "cobra," and that is what you will become. Cobras! Deadly, fast, and merciless. We are in the process of having proper sleeve insignias manufactured for your uniforms."

At this point a husky blond man stepped forward. His epaulets were decorated with two bars and a star, and he also sported the beret and jump wings of the French Foreign Legion. He turned a cold gaze on the assembled men.

Baroudeur nodded toward him. "This is Commandant Dekker, who will be your field commander. He is an old comrade of mine and Colonel Krashchenko's from the *Légion Étrangère*. I advise you not to cross him. He is demanding and not required by any laws to offer gentle counseling in the case of insubordination or inefficiency. Commandant Dekker's standards are extremely high."

Dekker stepped forward and gestured while yelling loudly in French. It was apparent he wanted everyone outside, and they complied. Bob and Simon were now buddies of a sort, and they stuck together as they walked out the opposite side of the building from where they had entered.

Once more Dekker went back to barking orders and gesturing. Not all the men spoke French, but a few did, and as they fell into two ranks, the others followed suit. Once formed up, they were faced to form a column and marched across an open space to an aircraft hangar. A long counter ran down one side and behind it were some mercenaries in uniforms. It was logical to assume they had been detailed as supply clerks from the stacks of equipment and gear behind them.

Now the newbies were formed into a single line, and began going down the counter. Items of equipment were thrown at them. Belts and harnesses with pouches, rucksacks, canteens, and other field gear. There were also uniforms, which included two camouflaged jackets (the same pattern worn by the mercenary officers), two pairs of trousers, and field hats. These items of wear were obviously used (unlike the officers' uniforms) and faded. The clerks estimated the correct sizes and passed them out accordingly. Bob tried to figure out what nationality the uniforms were, finally reaching the conclusion from the black spots on the green that the cammies were East German in origin.

Down at the end of the hangar was a large heap of boots tied together by their laces. Bob and his companions were expected to get into them and find a pair that fit. Each had two sets of socks stuffed inside that matched the size of the foot gear. It took a half hour before everyone was back outside, and Dekker had bellowed at them every minute of the time. The non-French speakers quickly concluded that *"vite"* and *"allez"* meant to hurry along.

Three trucks were waiting for them. One held all their baggage, and the other two were for them to crowd onto, struggling with their newly acquired gear. As soon as everyone was aboard, the engines were started up, and the small convoy rolled out of the airfield and onto a dirt road. This led to a crude highway of sorts, and at that point they turned eastward.

Cooper looked miserable. "I wonder where the hell they're taking us."

Bob grinned inwardly. This obviously was not what

the young Brit paratrooper had expected. A couple of other new men seemed unhappy, as well, but most of the group took everything for granted as they traveled the dusty route to their unknown destination. A tough-looking young Frenchman sitting next to Bob began to sing a short ditty:

Vive le mort! Vive la guerre!
Vive les mercenaries!

Bob knew enough of the language to understand the words: "Hooray for death! Hooray for war! Hooray for the mercenaries!"

He suddenly wished Lance Matoskah or Carlito Grey had been picked for this assignment.

CHAPTER FOUR

Sergeant Kayla Medawar finished deciphering the transmission that had come in from the OA in the Congo only minutes before, arranging the five-letter word groups into an intelligible message. The intrepid young lady could practically work the system in her sleep, and the missive had sprung out in perfect English in only a short amount of time. The satellite it had been bounced off of was in an equatorial orbit that allowed Jonas Blane three opportunities a day to broadcast from Africa: 0400 to 0600, 1200 to 1400, and 2000 to 2200 hours local. That meant 0400 to 0600, 1400 to 1600, and 2200 to 2400 at Fort Griffith.

Those five-letter groups, so carefully encoded by Carlito Grey, were now an official AAR, giving a brief but complete account of the raid on the insurgent supply depot. Kayla knew Colonel Tom Ryan would be pleased with the tactical success of the mission. She was always glad to give him good news since that was a rare commodity in an operational environment where Murphy's Law reigned supreme. The sergeant got to her feet, ripping the page from the message pad, and left the commo room for the short walk to the colonel's office.

After a knock and a gruff invitation to enter, Kayla stepped into the commander's presence. "Just in from Snake Doctor, sir."

Ryan winked at her from behind his desk. "Has he won the war already?"

"No, sir," she replied, missing the facetiousness of his remark. Sergeant Kayla Medawar was a very pragmatic, solemn young lady who reacted literally to everything that was spoken to her. "But it appears that he is experiencing an excellent beginning on his way to a mission accomplished."

"Well, let's see," the colonel said, taking the message. He quickly perused the words. "So! The sergeant major got himself some free goodies and saved the Great American Taxpayer some money. Then to top it off, he has a dozen EPWs to deal with. And it seems that there are WIAs among them. I certainly don't see a problem with that."

"Yes, sir," Kayla said. "There were also ample medical supplies to treat the wounded enemy."

"But no mention of wooing any prisoners to our cause. That goddamn Munger is gonna love this."

"I think he'll hate it," Kayla remarked, once more missing the colonel's flippancy. "He emphasized the importance in 'winning hearts and minds,' as the old cliché goes."

"No, Sergeant Medawar, he's gonna *love* it! That walking, talking sack of crap Munger will absolutely leap with joy. The CIA wants the Unit brought down hard. And I mean hard enough to be disbanded. You can bet he'll blame the lack of new adherents on the sergeant major just as fast as he can, then skip happily off to the nearest Congressional committee to tell on us."

"Don't let him in on the truth, sir."

"You know better than that," Ryan said. "The worst thing that can be done in cases like this is to try to sit on it."

"Maybe it was out of the sergeant major's ability to establish rapport quickly because of the volatility of the situation," Kayla suggested.

"Mmm," Ryan mused. "That's true. He's probably really busy at this preliminary stage of the operation."

"No doubt, sir."

"Stand fast. I'm gonna compose a message to send to the OA. I'll make it sort of ambiguous in case Munger or any of his jackass buddies manage to intercept it. When's the next transmission to Snake Doctor?"

Kayla checked her watch. "You've got another forty or so minutes, sir. If you don't make that, it can't be sent until fourteen hundred hours."

"I'll take the later schedule," Ryan said. "I'm going to have to word this carefully. I'm not going to give any specific instructions, but I want the sergeant major to know exactly what I mean."

As the Unit's commanding officer began composing the missive, Kayla knew he was no longer aware of her presence. She quietly walked to the door and left the office.

D.R. OF THE CONGO
INSURGENCY GARRISON
1400 HOURS LOCAL
1200 HOURS ZULU

Bob Brown, looking over the side of the truck he had ridden all the way from Gabon, studied the garrison as the small convoy rolled into the site. During the trip he had noticed the ease with which they crossed the international border into the Democratic Republic of the Congo. Obviously some serious bribery had been involved.

Now looking around, Bob was surprised at the sophistication of the jungle camp the revolutionary leaders had chosen as a base of operations. The barracks were typical of that part of the world with thatched roofs, floors raised a couple of feet off the ground, screened openings that ran the entire length of the buildings, and shutters to lower in case of rain. The mercenaries had their own area off to one side of the isolated garrison while the Congolese rebel troops occupied buildings in the center of the site. The entire cantonment was well policed, and a small group of local native civilians could be seen sweeping the areas between the barracks. Some were sprinkling water from cans to keep the dust down, while others swept large homemade brooms of branches back and forth across the packed earth.

As Bob and Simon Cooper stepped down from the truck, a quick glance indicated that the combined size of the mercenary and Congolese units made up what appeared to be a couple of reinforced rifle companies. Some mortars that he couldn't immediately identify could be seen neatly arranged with crew drill being conducted on them. He assumed they were looted from the armories of the Congolese National Army.

Commandant Paul Dekker appeared from around the vehicles and once again created a formation by bellowing in French. With that accomplished, he marched them over to the mercenary area where some eighty-six Europeans were already billeted. The twenty-five reinforcements who had arrived in the truck now brought General Karl Baroudeur's Commando Nyoka up to a total of 111 men and three overranked officers for a grand total of 114.

Dekker marched the twenty-five arrivals to the front of headquarters and halted them. The new men were surprised to see that Baroudeur and Krashchenko had gotten there ahead of them, meaning special transport had been provided for the senior mercenary officers. Dekker joined his two old Legion buddies, standing off to one side.

General Baroudeur stepped forward. "Welcome to the base camp of Commando Nyoka. This will be your billets when not on active campaign on Operation Griffe. I realize many of you do not speak French, so I will translate the name 'griffe.' It means 'claw' in French, and it indicates the nature of our mission. We are going to swoop down and take over the Democratic Republic of the Congo with elements of the National Army in the same manner hawks and eagles swoop down on their prey."

The mercenaries were taken aback by the enormity of the mission. Most had figured they would be involved in some aggressive police work as might be performed by a constabulary.

Baroudeur continued. "We have powerful sponsors for this enterprise, and that is all that will be said about that. Rest assured the rewards will be great when the government falls. Those of you who distinguish yourselves in combat will be offered command positions in the new Congolese National Army. However, everyone who survives will walk away with a great deal of cash. All in Euros. I shall now turn you back over to Commandant Dekker for settling in. Training and physical conditioning will begin immediately."

Bob, Simon, and the rest were assigned to barracks, where neatly arranged rows of bunks with mosquito netting ran down the two sides of the buildings. The aisle in the middle had tables and chairs, following the old European military tradition of eating in the billets rather than in a mess hall. Thus, there were no dining facilities, per se, only a single cookhouse. At this time the men noticed groups of African civilians standing unobtrusively at the rear of the barracks. The mercenaries learned they were servants hired to look after them. These natives would go to the kitchens to pick up the chow to bring back to the barracks for eating. They would also keep the living quarters clean, do laundry, run errands or any other chores required of them. Each European was to contribute one Euro a month for the services.

Commandant Dekker was in a hurry to get with the program, and he began bellowing again. Those who understood French began to shuck their civilian clothing and change into the recently issued camouflage uniforms. There was an air of relief at getting into working gear for the ex-soldiers, and they chatted happily among themselves as they changed for action. As soon as that was taken care of, they were divided into nine groups of ten men each. The eleven men left over had obviously been handpicked before, and were appointed NCOs. One was the sergeant major while the other ten were sergeants, each commanding one of the ten-man squads. There was no insignia of rank available for them, but they were quickly provided with green berets similar to what the officers sported. These wool headgear were meant to set them apart from the lower ranks, who wore boonie hats. They would also be expected to break their squads down into two five-man fire teams with one of the five picked as the team leader. These would rank as corporals, but could not be distinguished from the others who were rated volunteers.

And so Volunteer Ted Durant and Volunteer Simon Cooper found themselves members of Fire Team "A" of the Third Squad. They were assigned to side-by-side bunks, and settled in easily as experienced soldiers will. Their extra uniforms and field gear were hung on pegs mounted on the windowsills behind their sleeping area. With the billeting now neatly arranged, Commandant

Paul Dekker once again sat up his bellowing, this time yelling out only one word, "*Rassemblement!*"

All the non-French speakers imitated those who could understand the hoarse yells, and fell into formation outside the barracks. The entire mercenary contingent, minus General Baroudeur and Colonel Krashchenko, were faced to the right and marched out of the garrison at quick-time. As soon as they reached the road, Dekker again hollered and everyone broke into the dog trot of double time, so well known in all armies of the world. Everyone in the column of twos was a veteran, and as such they expected the worst.

And they were absolutely correct.

It quickly became apparent that their boots were not yet properly broken in, and the rhythmic chafing of stiff leather against heels and the soles of feet was an indication that there would be bleeding blisters before the ordeal was over. Men like Bob Brown and Simon Cooper who had only recently left their units did not suffer too much. Bob actually didn't feel any discomfort at all, though Simon began grimacing after three kilometers. Bob glanced over to the side where Dekker continually counted out a cadence in French, the extra effort not affecting his breathing one iota.

After four kilometers some of the mercenaries limped off to one side, breathing hard and groaning from the discomfort of their punished feet. A couple sat down and pulled off their boots to examine their blisters. The lucky ones were on the far side of the column from Dekker. The ones he could reach received hard clouts on the backs of their heads that knocked them over to the ground, blinking from the shock of the blows. In the Legion this was called a *stick*, and caused immediate pain and dizziness, but a well-conditioned man could quickly recover from it.

Bob had to admit Dekker was tough as nails, and participated in the run as much as the men under his command, demanding no more or no less than he personally gave to the team effort. A total of ten kilometers later, the group came back into the camp, and were slowed to quick time. A full half of the original number was still back on the road, hobbling toward the garrison on feet that stung with fresh, broken blisters. Dekker took the survivors to the barracks area and brought them to a halt. After facing them to the front, he looked at them in a baleful manner, then barked, "*Rempez les rangs!*"

The tired men broke ranks and walked unsteadily toward their billets. Bob and Simon glanced over at some of the later arrivals, struggling through the camp streets. Dekker appeared from between a couple of buildings, and began bullying them into a new formation.

"Poor blokes," Simon said with a grin. "Their day won't be over for a long time."

"Remember what they said about mercenary units," Bob reminded him. "There are no regulations."

The failures were now doing push-ups under Dekker's harsh supervision as others showed up for their share of the misery.

COUNTERINSURGENCY BASE CAMP
2020 HOURS LOCAL
1820 HOURS ZULU

Colonel Tom Ryan's latest message was decrypted and written out, then immediately passed over to Jonas Blane. Carlito Grey sat by the Shadowfire radio grinning slightly as he observed the slow burn on the sergeant major's rugged face. Jonas growled, "I got a lot on my mind right now, and I do not—I say again—*I do not* need this crap."

"Cut the good colonel some slack, boss," Carlito said.

"Part of the 'good colonel's' job is to see that operators in the field aren't loaded down with unnecessary horse puckey while a full-blown combat operation is in progress."

"I'll grant you that," Carlito said. "But you got to remember that he's the one that gets his ass dragged up in front of Congressional committees when the pressure is put on us."

Mack Gerhardt was sitting a couple of meters away, idly cleaning his fingernails with his K-Bar, and listening to the exchange. "Read between the lines, boss," he said to Jonas.

"What's to read between the lines?" Jonas asked irritably. "He's sent me a transmission inquiring about my win-their-hearts-and-minds plan."

"What he's really doing is asking for something from you to throw at Munger and that piss-ant diplomat to keep them calmed down," Mack said.

Jonas was thoughtful for a moment. "Y'know, I think you're right." He glanced at Carlito. "Compose a message, dear boy. Tell our dashing colonel that at the moment we have enemy EPWs that are wounded and receiving medical treatment from us. I am concentrating on that situation of relieving pain and healing injuries in showing kindness to helpless enemy soldiers under my care. When that is accomplished, I plan on implementing an incredibly clever program of psychological warfare to entice the Congolese insurgents to come rushing over here to kiss my ass."

"Uh-huh, boss!" Mack said with a waggling finger. "Don't be sarcastic."

Carlito laughed. "I'll change the message so the colonel can use it to his advantage."

"Well, hurry up," Jonas said, getting to his feet. "We got things to do, and that satellite is gonna be out of range in another hour-plus."

Mack turned his attention back to his fingernails as Carlito began scribbling on the message pad. Jonas hurried over to Captain Edouard Tshobutu's hut, where the officer and Sublieutenant Kintuba waited for him.

The morning was still young, yet the entire mercenary tactical contingent was lined up, sweating and panting, for a second run through Commandant Paul Dekker's obstacle course for that day. This would be the eighth time in three days. Everyone had made it, not only because of their natural youth and stamina, but also because the punishment dished out to those who failed acted as an extra incentive to achieve success. The one consoling factor in the whole affair was that they didn't have to wash or mend the uniforms dirtied and torn in the exercise. Those African orderlies in the barracks would take care of those mundane chores.

Bob Brown glanced around at the mercenaries, keeping them under observation as part of his assignment as a mole. Dekker's ways of encouragement during exhausting training bordered on brutality, but they were effective. These soldiers of fortune were now in top physical condition. Of course most of them had shown up from elite units with high standards, but some had been out of active training for anywhere from two to six months. But they had an excellent foundation of fitness to build on, and Dekker had quickly edged them back to the ultimate, thus everyone was shaping up under the ex-legionnaire's program of achieve or suffer. Another motivating factor was that Colonel Krashchenko made an announcement that those not responding properly to the training and discipline would be fined 200 Euros for each incident.

The obstacle course itself was a real ball buster, and took a muscle-cramping hour to complete. Dekker himself had taken out a crew of Congolese loggers and hacked the route out of the densest part of the forest.

The indigenous workers were strong and experienced with axes and saws, and even Dekker could find no fault with their efforts. The first thing done was to clear out a path ten meters wide, then take the fallen trees and move them back, laying them in a stacked pyramid of wood. The idea was to have the trainees climb up one side of the obstacle and down the other while dealing with rough bark and carelessly trimmed limbs that stuck out to rip the skin of the more incautious participants. A dozen men came out with serious scrapes and scratches, while one was cut so deep he required a tourniquet before he could be carried back to the garrison for medical treatment.

From the mass of logs, Dekker had the lumbermen simply cut down trees of all sizes and allow them to fall where they might. This created a hundred-meter path that required dodging, climbing, and jumping all the way to the banks of the Ekundu River that ran along the rear of the camp. That portion of the course would not have been so bad, except no one wanted to be last through the obstacles. That would earn the ignominious distinction of extra field punishment doing what the commandant called *abdominaux,* a hundred sit-ups in the stinking jungle mud. This led to a lot of bumping and shoving among the participants as they hit the logs, and even a few outright brawls broke out that became mini-riots. These altercations appeared to amuse Dekker, but it was difficult to tell if he was really entertained or not. The ex-legionnaire's version of a grin was a facial expression somewhere between a sneer and a snarl.

The final requirement of this route from hell was to jump into the river and wade waist-deep across to the other bank, where more logs were stacked. In order to leave the water, it was necessary to climb up the slippery timbers. These, of course, had been carefully stripped of all bark and protrusions, and were as wet and slimy as if they had been waxed. Once more fistfights erupted that

continued until the last man was out of the water and
standing in the soft mud in front of Commandant Paul
Dekker.

Bob Brown actually did quite well in the competi-
tion, and he was even able to slow down now and again
to help his buddy Simon Cooper. But after a couple of
trips through the course, the Unit operator noticed ap-
proving glances at him from Dekker. The last thing Bob
wanted was attention. It was best that he simply blend
into the midst of the mercenaries, unnoticed, unherald-
ed, and unknown. He eased back, doing an average job,
and Dekker soon forgot him.

Another mercenary buddied up with Bob and Simon.
This was Andre Coureur, a French Canadian who had
served in his country's Joint Task Force 2. This outfit
was a counterterrorist group organized somewhat like
the SAS. He was a short, tough individual who was descended from a long line of hunter-trapper types that
went back more than two hundred years when France
still governed Canada. Andre spoke excellent English
and also French. He came in handy translating the remarks made by the Foreign Legion Mafia. This was the
term used by non-French-speaking mercenaries when
referring to Baroudeur, Krashchenko, and Dekker. The
French Canadian's bilingual skills also aided Bob in his
intelligence gathering, when he explained tactical and
strategic terminology.

Now what he needed was to get into active ops so he
could hone this knowledge into useful info to pass on to
Jonas Blane when he returned to the team. Bob hoped
it wouldn't be too much longer.

•

MERCENARY HEADQUARTERS
4 APRIL
1440 HOURS LOCAL
1240 HOURS ZULU

Communications were somewhat lacking within the insurgent command and staff, and it wasn't until that afternoon that they received word about the raid on their supply depot on 27 March. General Karl Baroudeur, General Marcel Lulombe, and Colonel Vlad Krashchenko were seriously confused and dismayed by the incident. The main point of their consternation was not knowing who the hell had pulled it off. They knew of no counterinsurgency operations by the National Army, yet an obviously well-organized and effective attack had been carried out on the logistical site.

Baroudeur glowered at Lulombe. "I thought you said we would have no serious problems with the bulk of the Army, yet a strong force must have made that raid."

Lulombe shrugged. "I have made inquires, and my sources tell me that no unit of the Army has been out of their garrisons since February. It is my considered opinion that this was not planned or carried out by any command or staff element."

Krashchenko said nothing, preferring to let his companions deal with the problem.

"We lost a lot of valuable supplies," Baroudeur complained. "Even with the strong financial backing that we enjoy, it will take some time to replace the matériel. We must react quickly and violently to the attack. So it is important that you come up with some possibilities for us to consider. After all, this is your country."

"Well," Lulombe mused, "there is a paratroop captain by the name of Tshobutu who is missing. However, the bulk of his command remains in garrison, though a group of them deserted."

"I am confused," Baroudeur complained. "But we

must do something." He was thoughtful for a moment. "We move into an isolated area and occupy a village. Just us Europeans. I see on the map there is a convenient hamlet by the name of Mwitukijiji that would be convenient. And there is a military roadblock nearby we can neutralize. That should discourage any more mischief no matter who struck at us."

"I agree," Lulombe said. "The white mercenaries who fought here right after independence were known for their cruelty. The psychological effect will be much greater if white soldiers carried out an act of retribution."

Baroudeur looked at Krashchenko. "Issue the order!"

"*À vos ordres, mon général!*"

CHAPTER FIVE

D.R. OF THE CONGO
COMMANDO NYOKA

The mercenaries were now sharper in appearance. New French camouflage uniforms had arrived to replace the secondhand East German models first issued. Each man was given three sets with their unit insignia to be sewn on the upper right sleeves. This was a blue square bordered in white surrounding the image of a cobra with its hood extended. The snake was green with a yellow underside. The colorful patches made the men uneasy since they were more used to the subdued insignia of black and olive drab for field uniforms.

Additionally French NCO designations were available that were attached to jacket fronts by Velcro. Sergeants were distinguished by two gold diagonal stripes while corporals wore the same thing in red. Again, the bright colors were disturbing to veterans of special operations. However, the distribution of two pairs of brand-new boots called "rangers" were very welcome.

OPERATION GRIFFE
5 APRIL
0530 HOURS LOCAL
0330 HOURS ZULU

The squad of mercenaries moved in a skirmish formation through the jungle darkness. They stayed close together, keeping the men on each side of them within sight because of the foliage. The tropical forest growth was not too bad in the area, but there were enough trees that it was impossible not to lose sight of someone from time to time.

This was the left flank of the attack formation, occupied by Fire Team A of the Third Squad in which Bob Brown and Simon Cooper served as riflemen. Andre Coureur, with his AKS-74 fire selector on automatic, was between them. Over on the right, Fire Team B was similarly arranged. Their squad leader was a retired Portuguese paratrooper sergeant named José Peira. Although in his late forties, he had none of the slack-bodied qualities of an older man who had grown fond of beer and spending sedentary hours watching *futebol* on television. As a near fanatical devotee of physical fitness, he had done well in Commandant Paul Dekker's PT program, able to endure the extra pain and exertion without becoming discouraged. Boredom and a shrewish wife had driven him from the comforts of home to seek adventure in foreign lands. Peira was well-liked and respected by the other mercenaries because of his cheerful robustness and soldierly qualities. The Portuguese, like other squad leaders, was now able to leave his green beret back in the barracks when going to the field. With the new insignia showing their ranks, they could wear the lighter boonie hats. They were further distinguishable from the riflemen because of the newly issued LASH headsets each wore. When the next shipment of the commo devices arrived, each corporal would have one as well.

The first objective that morning was a road junction watched over from a sandbagged position manned by soldiers of the Congolese National Army. There were five of them, consisting of an NCO and four men who crewed a couple of Minimi 5.56-millimeter machine guns. The terminology had confused Bob at first, but when he examined one in the mercenary garrison, he immediately recognized it as the SAW used by American armed forces. The U.S. had acquired a license to manufacture the Minimis from the Belgian Government, renaming them M-249 squad automatic weapons.

When the Third Squad reached the edge of the road, they sighted the objective and went quietly to cover with their weapons trained on the position. Sergeant Peira eased up between Bob and Simon, pulling out his binoculars. He studied the target for a moment, then grinned. The Congolese soldiers' automatic weapons, supposedly to cover the crossroads, had been carelessly placed on top of the sandbags. Peira reported to the field commander Commandant Paul Dekker through the LASH, waiting for a reply. When the orders came, he quickly reacted.

"Take aim," Peira said softly in English.

Bob, Simon, and Andre did as they were told, now noting that the Congolese soldiers were all sleeping. Unknowingly, all three mercenaries had their sights trained on the unfortunate NCO. Bob regretted having to open fire on people who might eventually be on his side in the conflict, but he knew they would immediately return fire, endangering him. The Unit carried out their missions in a very perilous world replete with occasions when no quarter could be given under any circumstances. There were instances when misguided kindness and mercy shown to friendlies could result in death.

"Fire," Peira ordered.

The five bullets—Andre's was a fireburst of three—hit the NCO and knocked him completely over the sandbags. The soldiers, ill trained and young, stupidly stood up in the line of fire as the rest of the squad cut loose. It was all over in less than two seconds.

"This wasn't an assault," Bob said. "It was murder."

"*Bluddy* murder," Simon added. Andre Coureur said nothing as Peira got to his feet and signaled to the others. The squad moved forward and formed a defensive perimeter around the junction as Peira got back on the LASH to make his report.

Operation Griffe's first objective was taken. The next was a village with a tongue twister of a name: Mwituki-jiji.

0645 HOURS LOCAL
0445 HOURS ZULU

The double column of mercenaries moved silently down the narrow track of road leading to their next objective. Third Squad was on point, but because of the heavy vegetation along the sides of the route, there were no flankers out. Consequently, the soldiers of fortune maintained a close observation on both sides of the formation as well as to the front. Peira had noticed that Bob, Simon, and Andre worked well together, and he had ordered them to move the farthest forward of his fire teams on point. As they made their way, the trio's ears were tuned for sounds of any firing that might break out. If an ambush was sprung on them, the first incoming fire would hit the main body, immediately followed by killer teams to the front and rear shooting up the point and rear guard to hem the formation in for a systematic massacre. Such situations were generally over within seconds of being launched. After that, there was nothing to do but police up any available EPWs—or put bullets in their heads—and haul ass out of the area before a rescue force arrived.

Although Bob's mind was on the job at hand for the most part, he was also occupied with observing these hired guns in the field. He admired their soldiering skills, but at the same time, he was well aware that this collective expertise would make them a particularly nasty threat to the Unit and their Congolese allies. This operation was not going to be a cake walk.

Simon Cooper was in the lead, and he suddenly dashed to the vegetation and squatted down. While Andre signaled the men behind them to stop and take cover, Bob moved forward and joined the young Brit. "What's up?"

Simon pointed. "There's the village we're looking for, yeah?"

"Yeah," Bob answered. "Mwitu-whatever."

Bob worked his way ahead another fifteen meters, then stopped. Now he could clearly see the objective. Thatched mud buildings made up the community, and the populace that was visible could be seen carrying on daily routines in and around the simple buildings. One structure seemed to be a store of some kind, and a crowd of mostly women was gathered around it, examining some goods for sale. Now Bob noted the three-wheeled motorcycle parked nearby. The vehicle had a large trailer hooked to it. A man dressed in a dingy white suit and a broad-brimmed straw hat was showing his wares. This was obviously the African version of a traveling salesman.

Some slight rustling alerted Bob, and he turned to see Peira moving up to him. The American pointed, saying, "Market day."

"Any soldiers?" Peira asked.

Bob shook his head, making a "zero" of his thumb and index finger.

Peira nodded, then spoke French into his LASH to alert Dekker. After receiving instructions, he motioned Bob to follow him back to the squad. When they rejoined the small tactical unit, Peira gave the orders. "In five minutes we go forward and occupy the village. We are to move all the way through to the other side and go into the defense." He looked at his international audience of ten men. "Does everybody understand what I have said?" After affirmative gestures and noddings of heads, he settled back to check his watch.

The five minutes passed, and the Third Squad moved out. When the crowd of shoppers finally noticed them approaching, their eyes opened in alarm. These were all white soldiers, armed to the teeth. This was always bad news for the indigenous people of Africa. The salesman immediately began gathering up his goods and piling them into his rickshaw trailer. As Bob went past the man, he grabbed his arm and pulled him along.

"S'il vous plaît, monsieur!" the man begged.

Peira was confused. "Why have you grabbed that fellow?"

"He's a traveling salesman, Sergeant," Bob replied. "He moves all around this area."

Peira grinned. "Good thinking, Durant. Intelligence source. We talk to him, eh?"

When the Third Squad reached the far edge of the village, they maintained fire-team integrity as they formed a defensive perimeter in the shape of a half circle. Peira had taken charge of the salesman, who identified himself as M. Léon M'kalo. At first he protested at being taken away from his vehicle, but a stern glare from the Portuguese led him to believe that the possibility of being robbed might not be the worst thing he faced that day.

Commandant Dekker joined the squad and sat down with Peira and M'kalo for a chat. Once M'kalo understood that all that was wanted from him was information, he talked freely while smoking a cigarette given him by Peira. Bob, sitting on the perimeter glanced at the proceedings, noting that the merchant referred to

Dekker's map now and then while pointing off in all directions. Obviously, the little guy had a great deal of knowledge about what went on within the area of his sales calls.

After a half hour, Dekker and the peddler left the perimeter and went back to the center of the village. Bob felt the need to urinate, and he got to his feet to walk a ways into the jungle to take care of nature's call. It was peaceful to be alone in the denseness of the tropical forest, even when taking a piss. Although the rest of the squad was within earshot, the size and closeness of the flora gave Bob an enjoyable feeling of isolation. A lot of his training had been done on his own, picking his way to RVs on challenging cross-country land-navigation courses that covered long distances. These map exercises gave a man confidence in himself, and a certain satisfaction in the hours of being on his own.

Then the perception of remoteness was quickly shattered.

The thrashing of leaves and a female voice obviously pleading and protesting in a foreign language came from his near right. Bob brought the AKS-74 up, and cautiously moved toward the disturbance. He had to go only five meters before coming to a small clearing. Two mercenaries had a village girl struggling between them as they attempted to get her down on the ground. The front of her dress was ripped open, and their intentions toward the unfortunate nubile female were much more sexual than romantic.

Bob recognized the two men. One was a German named Hans Schleck, who had served in the KSK, and the other a nondescript Polish ruffian by the name of Josef Kowalski, a veteran of his country's counterterrorist outfit known by the acronym GROM.

"Knock it off!" Bob barked. He had lowered the muzzle of the rifle to show he meant no threat with it. There was really no sense in a gunfight.

Schleck, infuriated that his fun was interrupted, glowered at the American while speaking so rapidly in German that spittle flew from his lips. Kowalski, frowning, backed off to see what was going to happen, holding on to the girl, who now sensed help had just arrived. Schleck, placed his rifle against the trunk of a tree, and began walking around the clearing, making threatening gestures at Bob. This was an obvious challenge to settle the matter with their fists, feet, or in any manner other than firearms. Bob noted the knife on the German's belt, and was glad he had his trusty K-Bar. The German was one of those large men with a layer of fat that belied his true muscularity. That meant it was imperative to stay out of his clutches.

Bob sat his rifle down and moved opposite the other man, staying loose while balancing himself on the balls of his feet. In an instant the German charged, but Bob danced lightly out of the way and hit the guy on the side of the head with the knife-edge of his hand. This punch added some impetus to the German's assault, and he sprawled on the ground, rolling over and getting back to his feet.

This was one tough Kraut.

The pair of combatants went back to circling, each one alert for an opening. Suddenly Kowalski cursed and yelled. The girl had wrenched herself free, and crashed through the brush back toward the village. Schlek gave Bob one of the meanest looks that had ever been directed at him. Then the guy went over to the tree, grabbed his rifle, and left the clearing with his Polish friend following.

Bob picked up his rifle, and made his way back to the defensive perimeter. He fully realized what he had done was stupid. He had jeopardized his mission because a couple of misfits were going to enjoy a bit of rape with a native girl. The thing was that she had looked so small and frightened, unable to defend herself against her attackers. At least she had had the presence of mind to break free when the chance presented itself. He joined Simon Cooper and Andre Coureur at the fire team's position and settled down to wait for orders to move out once again.

"Durant!"

Bob looked up and saw Sergeant Peira gesturing to him. He got to his feet and walked over to the Portuguese. "Yes, Sergeant?"

"You've just made a couple of enemies."

"Oh, yeah?" Bob said. "You saw what happened?"

Peira nodded. "You are going to see atrocities when you are a mercenary. Get used to it."

"Yes, Sergeant."

MERCENARY HEADQUARTERS
1930 HOURS LOCAL
1730 HOURS ZULU

The head of the column of mercenaries swung off the road and entered the garrison dressed right, covered down, and in step. Commandant Paul Dekker was in his favorite place, off to one side of the column. He delivered *sticks* to men not marching properly or failing to maintain a correct position in the ranks. There were plenty who got his attention, since most of the men were from units that rarely did close-order drill or participate in march-bys in front of reviewing stands. Polishing brass insignia, spit-shining boots, and wearing impractical, fancy-dress uniforms were not part of their military careers. But Dekker had earned his spurs in the French Foreign Legion, and marching and wheeling around a drill field were an important SOP.

The entire day had been a speed march, with the only combat occurring at the road junction when the men of the Third Squad shot up the sleeping sentries, and looted their machine guns. Also, unknown to the men, the merchant Léon M'kalo had been recruited as a spy by Dekker. The little African merchant had been given some valuable Euros to travel around, visiting military installations and doing such things as counting men and making maps of the garrisons. His selling of notions and used clothing was now subordinated to this new profitable calling. He was to come to the headquarters on a weekly basis with his findings.

Now, dismissed, Bob Brown went into the barracks with his friends Simon Cooper and Andre Coureur. After turning over their gear to the servants for brushing and scrubbing, they quickly gave attention to cleaning their weapons. This was a chore they would trust no one but themselves to do properly.

With that taken care of, the three settled at one of the barracks tables to spend a quiet evening kicking back and drinking beer. The brand provided for them was Kronenbourg, which was an excellent brew, except it came in small quarter-liter bottles. However, that was offset by the fact they could drink all they wanted.

Simon was unusually quiet as the BS session started, but after a bit of time passed, he suddenly announced, "When this campaign is over, I'm gonna take me money and set up a pineapple plantation right here in the Congo."

Bob grinned. "I don't think they grow pineapples around here, Simon."

"Well, wotever they grow, I'm gonna plant it, yeah? And I'll have dozens of bluddy Wog servants too. And I'll live in a big plantation mansion with air-conditioning and lots o' loos. And I'll go to Europe on holiday and get the most beautiful and expensive tarts in the world. I'll even bring some home to keep handy, yeah? When I'm tired of any of 'em, I'll ship 'em back and get some different ones. I'll be one bluddy rich bastard—you can believe that."

Andre finished off a beer and got another. "Well, I'll settle for my own hunting lodge on a lake somewhere in northern Quebec. There's lots of money to be made from city hunters coming up north for to shoot wild game." He looked at Bob. "What about you, Ted?"

Bob Brown—alias Ted Durant—shrugged. "I don't know. Maybe I'll hire on with Simon and fetch those beautiful call girls from Europe for him."

Simon laughed. "I'll send a couple over to Canada for Andre. He can cuddle up with 'em during the cold winter nights."

Andre didn't see any humor in the remarks. "Let's face it. We're gonna be living one day at a time out here. We'd better concentrate on staying alive before we make any big plans."

"Actually," Bob said, "as of this moment, I'm more concerned about tomorrow."

Everyone was scheduled to hit Dekker's obstacle course after reveille and before mess call in the morning.

CHAPTER SIX

MELILLA, SPANISH MOROCCO

This Spanish enclave on the North African coast is an autonomous city of 64,000 people that had been a free port before Spain became a part of the modern European Union. Although Morocco claimed that city along with its sister community of Ceuta and the Spanish islands off the coast, the government of Spain completely rejected those declarations of sovereignty. The citizens of these areas wholeheartedly agreed with the mother country on the issue. Moroccan rule didn't offer a lot of advantages in the way of comfortable lifestyles or personal freedom. There was also the historical argument that Spain had possessed these cities and islands two centuries before Morocco even existed.

Melilla has always been an accommodating place for individuals and organizations that wish to conduct various activities linking European enterprises with their African counterparts. This makes the conduct of commerce more convenient between the two continents. Unfortunately, the area is also used by illegal immi-

grants who make their way north from the interior of
the Dark Continent to seek work in Europe. The worst
aspect of that tragic situation is the trafficking in human
beings, in which reckless attempts to cross the Straits
of Gibraltar and the Mediterranean Sea result in many
drownings. These tragedies generally go unnoticed until
the pathetic corpses wash up on local beaches.

Attempts to control this grievous situation were put
into effect by both the Spanish and Moroccan governments with a mutual agreement to maintain troops in
the area to cut down the smuggling of the desperate
poor of Africa.

PETRÓLEO ESPAÑOL-AFRICANO, S.A.
CORPORATE HEADQUARTERS

The corporate center of operations overlooked the
harbor that served international vessels coming in from
and going out to the Mediterranean Sea. The edifice
would not be considered imposing by any standards of
architecture, but it did have certain aesthetic qualities
that offered an ultramodern facade in comparison with
other buildings along the waterfront.

The top floor was almost-solid brick with only slits of
windows, giving it the look of a medieval castle. The west
side of what might have been a penthouse had no views
at all. This was a special area that provided private offices, a couple of conference rooms, and half a dozen apart-
ments for visitors. That part of the building was under
the protection of a staff of guards and a passive security
system. This latter methodology blocked all intrusions,
including radar, laser, and electronic.

That separate area was used by one of the most carefully guarded organizations in the Western world. The
alliance had no name, but was referred to as the Consortium by the more than two hundred men aware of

its existence. The Consortium had come into being in the waning days of World War II in Europe. The founders were individuals who had strong fascist leanings, but were not blinded by a fanatic faith in ultimate victory under Adolf Hitler, Benito Mussolini, and Francisco Franco. Most saw the handwriting on the wall with the Normandy Invasion of Europe by the Allies in June of 1944. They realistically prepared for the defeat that would strip them of their power and prestige. They could do nothing about the momentous setback, but they could set up effective safeguards to maintain complete control over the wealth they had acquired since 1933. And that is exactly what they did, in a surreptitious manner that went unnoticed by the ultimate victors in that great struggle.

In 1944 and 1945 the end came with the Allied triumphs over fascist Italy first, and then Nazi Germany. This defeat also affected the Consortium's fellow travelers in France, Spain, and Portugal. Everyone went underground to begin the rebuilding of their former power.

The start was slow since many of these individuals were wanted for various war crimes and other atrocities against humanity. Two went to their deaths stoically, declining to offer up the secrets of the Consortium in exchange for their lives. Others served lengthy jail terms, keeping the faith as their free brethren began the struggle of adding to their hidden wealth in post-war Europe. By 1960, the Consortium had evolved into an organization not unlike the orders of knighthood that existed in the Middle Ages, when powerful men took oaths to band together in order to pursue common goals and causes. It was governed by a grand master and five masters of the order. Below them were the marshals, knight-commandants, knights, and officers.

As the decades passed, the Old Guard began dying out, and was replaced piecemeal by the New Guard, i.e., their nephews, sons, and grandsons. Only exceptional young males of sixteen years of age were chosen to become candidates for membership. These elite youngsters were subjected to rigorous intellectual testing before being fully accepted in the order. With that accomplished, these male heirs were sent to a remote school high in the Swiss Alps. In this privately funded academy, they received an excellent education in the sciences, liberal arts, and commerce. Upon graduation, they were sent for advanced degrees to Europe's most prestigious universities. With their educational credentials well established, these young officers infiltrated powerful industrial organizations, political parties, the military, law enforcement, and even religious institutions to aid in the Consortium's slow and successful plodding toward its goals.

With the dawning of the twenty-first century, this knighthood of some of Europe's most powerful families was ready to make its first moves into other areas of the world to consolidate their wealth and power. This was to be accomplished without consideration of the morality or legality of the methods employed.

MAIN CONFERENCE ROOM
7 APRIL
1500 HOURS LOCAL
1400 HOURS ZULU

The four men in the room sat at a circular teakwood table, resting easily in padded leather chairs. Fifteen minutes earlier they had finished a leisurely lunch served in the next-door dining room, and now they smoked cigars and sipped cognac. The conversation among them was so soft it seemed muted, as the smoke from their expensive stogies floated around their heads.

Their presence in Melilla that afternoon was to hear a special report from the knight-commandant who had been appointed the director of Operation Griffe. This was retired French *Général de Division* Philippe Dubois, who had been the mastermind of the venture.

Jean-Paul Fubert, a member of France's banking and financial community, had been chosen as the moderator for that afternoon's activity. The other men present were a Spanish petroleum engineer named Francisco Valverde; Pietro D'Amiteri, an Italian investment banker; and the German Heinrich Müller-Koenig, who headed up an automobile manufacturing corporation. These four gentlemen ranked as marshals of the Consortium, and made up that organization's highest staff echelon.

A rap on the door caught their attention, and they turned to see Dubois being admitted to their presence by a member of the security staff. "*Bonjour,* Philippe," Fubert said with a smile. "Please come in and settle down. Needless to say, we are on pins and needles to hear your report about Operation Griffe down there in the Belgian Congo." They still referred to the Democratic Republic of the Congo by its colonial name.

The general was a tall, slim man with a closely trimmed gray beard. His hair was combed straight back, giving him more the look of a college professor than that of a retired professional soldier. He sat down without saying a word, placing a briefcase on the table before him. A glass of cognac was already poured and waiting for him. The Spaniard Valverde slid a humidor of cigars over to the general, and he took one but did not light it. He pulled a manila folder from the case and opened it, then raised his eyes to the others, who gazed at him expectantly.

"Commando Nyoka is now fully operational," Dubois announced in a matter-of-fact tone. "As of this moment we have three officers and one hundred and eleven non-commissioned officers and volunteers. They are augmented by some one hundred Congolese rebel officers and soldiers. I am not sure of the exact number, but their strength will undoubtedly grow as more disaffected members of the National Army join the revolution."

D'Amiteri leaned forward. "How many do you expect to throw in their lot with our program?"

Dubois shrugged. "The rate cannot be determined at this time. However, I estimate that with some successful and aggressive operations, the native military will collapse relatively quickly, with most joining our side. At least those with serious ambitions will do so. When successful rebellions are concluded, the hesitant and meek who did not offer their services during the struggle will reap no rewards. In fact, many face severe punishment."

"Are you optimistic about the situation?" D'Amiteri asked.

"Completely," Dubois assured him. "A few meaningful victories will convince any holdouts that it will be in their best interest to join in Operation Griffe. However, there has been one unexpected incident. On the twenty-seventh of March, Commando Nyoka's main logistical storage site was attacked by unknown persons. It was completely looted, and several members of the garrison were killed. It is presumed the others either deserted, joined the attackers, or surrendered. No Europeans of the commando were involved."

Müller-Koenig frowned. "That is strange. We were under the impression that those members of the National Army not with us were maintaining a neutral stance in regards to the campaign. Do you think some of them were the attackers?"

"There is no doubt that they are," Dubois said. "My man Baroudeur informs me that there have been some desertions from the National Army, and he thinks many of those soldiers have turned to banditry. He is convinced this is an isolated incident. I would like to emphasize that the security of the facility was not under the responsibility of Commando Nyoka. This was something set up some time before by General Lulombe."

"Is there anything that can be done to prevent additional outrages?" Müller-Koenig asked.

"An attack on an army roadblock was made under Baroudeur," Dubois informed him. "A total of five National Army soldiers were killed. And a village was occupied for a short while as a show of force to set an example. This was done by the mercenaries alone. Baroudeur rightly concluded that the sight of angry Europeans would intimidate the aborigines."

"Of course!" Fubert exclaimed.

Dubois continued. "Additionally, a spy who is able to move unnoticed throughout the operational area has been recruitd. He is an itinerant native merchant who peddles his wares among the various villages. He is being paid in Euros and is expected to prove useful to our cause."

"What about additional Europeans mercenaries being brought in?" Valverde asked.

"The original recruiters Baroudeur and Krashchenko are now in the operational area in physical command of the commando and our allies," Dubois replied. "However, another recruiting center is being set up in Marseille. I've chosen a most reliable fellow by the name of Peter Luknore to take charge of signing on more volunteers."

D'Amiteri grinned. "Is he another one of your Foreign Legion lads?"

"He did serve in the *Légion Étrangère,* but he is not exactly a lad," Dubois said. "Luknore is seventy-two years old. He was a *sergent-chef* in the First Foreign Parachute Regiment that revolted in Algeria back in sixty-one. Luknore ended up in the OAS, then eventually joined several mercenary operations in various parts of Africa for about ten years. He is now a very wealthy retired arms dealer, but he has contacts that can pull in soldiers of fortune looking for work."

"As long as the old fellow has his wits about him," Müller-Koenig remarked.

"I recommend him," Dubois stated flatly.

"That is good enough for us, Philippe," Fubert assured him, draining his glass of cognac. "What about the near future?"

"Active operations will be aggressively launched within a few days," Dubois said. "This will be led by Commando Nyoka, of course, and backed up by the Congolese cadre we now have. The first objective is to knock out the national infrastructure of the Belgian Congo, such as bridges, roads, power, water, and all that. When and where possible, television and radio stations will be occupied and operated for propaganda purposes. General Marcel Lulombe will be used as a figurehead of the revolution to give the impression that it is truly a national rebellion, and that the European mercenaries are serving out of sympathy for the plight of the poor downtrodden Congolese people."

"It sounds as if everything is on schedule," Fubert said. "What about the resupply situation?"

"I have a list," Dubois said, reaching into his briefcase once again. "Rather extensive, I fear."

"Not to worry, Philippe," Fubert said. "Our resources are practically limitless, as you know."

The retired general began passing out the logistic requests as the meeting settled down to the administrative side of the insurrection.

D.R. OF THE CONGO
OPERATIONAL AREA
9 APRIL
1600 HOURS LOCAL
1400 HOURS ZULU

The roadblock had been set up just around a sharp curve in the dirt road that cut through the tropical forest. The only soldiers visible at the log barriers were

Congolese. The four Unit operators had settled out of sight in the jungle to avoid exposing themselves. At that point in the mission, it would be disadvantageous for the Americans to be seen in the area.

The expected convoy was a regularly scheduled supply run between Camp Ukaidi and outlying garrisons, and would consist of five or six Renault TRM 2000 cargo trucks. The counterinsurgents weren't sure of the payload, but that wasn't important. The main objectives were the National Army drivers behind the wheels. They would not be too alarmed if they saw what appeared to be fellow soldiers manning the barricade. Jonas Blane had assigned Sublieutenant Pierre Kintuba and two dozen of the Congolese paratroopers to act as flank and rear security once the vehicles were stopped. Captain Edouard Tshobutu and a squad would be at the barricade, where he would address the truck drivers after they were brought to a halt.

The Congolese National Army was not big on maintaining schedules based on exact times. Instead, they assigned activities to take place on certain days rather than at particular hours. It was an environment where calendars were referred to more than clocks. Thus the convoy was scheduled for 9 April, but it could show up anytime during daylight hours. The counterinsurgents had arrived on the scene shortly before dawn, and had now been waiting all through the morning. The Congolese settled in patiently, while Jonas Blane and his operators fidgeted the hours away. They were also a bit anxious about the welfare and whereabouts of Bob Brown.

Finally, by late afternoon the deep whine of truck engines could be heard. Kintuba was the farthest from the barricade and was the first to sight the convoy as it rolled into sight. The young lieutenant used his LASH to notify the others of the impending arrival. Five minutes later he counted a quintet of vehicles go past his OP, and he kept his men concealed until the sudden squeal of brakes announced they had reached the roadblock. Then the security force moved out onto the road, hemming in the trucks on three sides.

Down at the roadblock, Captain Tshobutu walked up to the lead vehicle as the men behind him kept their FA-MAS rifles at the ready. The confused driver stepped down from his truck and saluted. Tshobutu returned the military courtesy. "*Bonjour, soldat,*" he said. "Do you have a noncommissioned officer in charge of this convoy?"

"No, *mon capitaine,*" the man answered. "We are taking supplies from Camp Ukaidi out to Camp Kabila."

"I see," Tshobutu said. "Call your comrades to come join you." The soldier did as he had been ordered, and the other drivers stepped down from the cabs. They walked up to where their buddy stood with the captain and the troopers manning the barricade. They snapped to attention until Tshobutu put them at ease, speaking in a friendly manner. "I suppose you men have heard about the threat against the government, have you not?"

They shrugged and one driver said, "We have heard rumors, *mon capitaine,* but nothing definite."

"I can truthfully tell you that there is a rebellion in the making here in our homeland," Tshobutu said. "A few bad eggs in our army want to take over the government. To make matters worse, they have European mercenaries leading them."

"Is that true?" a soldier asked.

"I fear so. Tell me, *soldats*, what do you think of that?"

"I have six years of school," the first driver said. "I was taught in history how white men were hired as soldiers to deny our independence. Is this the same thing?"

"The very same," Tshobutu told him. "Does it not anger you that these foreigners have come into our country to work their will on us?"

None of the soldiers replied.

"I am Captain Tshobutu, the commander of the Sixth Parachute Infantry Battalion. These men you see with me are under my command to fight against the mercenaries and the traitors who would put us under the heel of European rulers. We ask you to join us in this valiant struggle. Or do you wish our sovereign nation to become a colony again?"

One of the men, a simple fellow from a rural village, demonstrated the direct outspokenness of country people when he asked, "Will you shoot us if we refuse?"

"Why would you refuse?" Tshobutu asked.

The man was not defiant, but he spoke plainly. "You say there are comrades of ours with the mercenaries. Why are they doing that?"

"They have been misguided," Tshobutu explained. "In reality, the mercenaries wish to take over the government, and your comrades with them do not realize this. They do not know that if they win this campaign, Europeans will be the rulers of the Congo."

The soldiers looked at one other. Then one said, "The government is not a very good one. There is much corruption. Maybe the Europeans will be better. My grandfather is an old and wise man, *mon capitaine,* and he has said many times that things were better when we were the Belgian Congo."

Tshobutu was ready for that argument. "After the rebellion is put down, we can use peaceful means to make our government better for the people. We can insist on an election."

A driver at the back of the small crowd was from the city of Kinshasa. He was sharper than the country boys, and he wasn't going to believe anybody. "We've had elections in the past. They solved nothing. A new gang of crooks takes over and everything stays the same."

Tshobutu indicated his troopers with a wide sweep of his arm. "These soldiers will bring about a shift in the national government. We need you to come with us and fight for the changes our homeland needs. Which of you will join us?"

None of the drivers moved.

Tshobutu sighed. "All right, *soldats*. Get your personal belongings out of the trucks. I advise you to turn around and walk back to your garrison."

The men hesitated, keeping an eye on the weapons of the soldiers at the roadblock as well as the ones who surrounded the vehicles. Then one turned and walked back toward the trucks. The others followed, getting up into the cabs and grabbing haversacks that contained personal items. Within five minutes, they were all walking back in the direction they had come from.

Jonas Blane, Mack Gerhardt, Carlito Grey, and Lance Matoskah now joined Tshobutu on the road. Jonas shook his head slowly. "I don't think we're going to get anyone to join us."

"Probably not," Tshobutu agreed. "At least not until we have given the mercenaries and their Congolese friends a couple of meaningful defeats. That's the only thing that will win them to our cause."

"Yeah," Jonas said. "But it's not exactly what the United States State Department had in mind when they passed out those instructions to win people over to the counterinsurgency."

"I'm afraid they don't have a very realistic approach to the matter," Tshobutu said. He looked down the road and waved at Sublieutenant Kintuba. "Get the supplies off the trucks. As soon as that's done, set a thermite grenade on each engine block."

Kintuba shouted in Swahili and the paratroopers shouldered their weapons and got to work.

CHAPTER SEVEN

It had been a long day for both Commando Nyoka and the Congolese insurgent detachment that supported them. The entire unit had been put on an advanced status of alert for active campaigning. A total of twenty new men had arrived via the regular truck ride from Okondja, Gabon, so the numerical strength of the commando now stood at a grand total of three officers and 131 NCOs and volunteers. This influx of extra men brought about the assignment of a Belgian Minimi machine gun to each squad to increase firepower. Also transportation was now available with half a dozen SAMIL 20 military surplus trucks. These were excellent South African vehicles that could haul 4,410-pound loads up to 55 miles per hour. Qualified drivers were culled from the Congolese contingent.

Under Commandant Paul Dekker's supervision, Commando Nyoka had begun preparatory procedures

for the coming operations like many sports teams: they
got back to the basics. The first thing done right after an
early mess call was for the squad leaders to make sure
their men had all the equipment, uniforms, weaponry,
and other gear required of them to go to the field for
an extended time. Each man was ordered to stand by
his bunk with his kit laid out in a manner prescribed by
Dekker. The commando field commander had used a tri-
angle and ruler to draw out a diagram indicating where
he wanted the web gear and canteens, boots, socks, headgear, weapons, and everything else to be placed on the
bunks for the checkup.

At that point, each NCO had a list of the issued items,
and called them out, one by one. The men would pick up
the article and hold it out to show he possessed it. The
whole thing was a waste of time since the mercenaries
weren't rookies. Each had plenty of military experience
and had learned long ago to take care of not only their
issued property, but the privately owned things they had
brought with them. This was something done in basic
training centers with brand-new soldiers, but Dekker
was from the French Foreign Legion, and that outfit was
known for treating even its experienced veterans as raw
recruits on certain occasions.

With that done, the issue of live ammunition was
taken care of. The night before the native servants had
been kept up to load cartridges into thirty-round box
magazines, and these were passed out in lots of eight to
each individual. That was the maximum they could put
into French LBEs. The squad machine gunners and their
ammo bearers received 200-round belt boxes. This issue
also included French F1 fragmentation hand grenades
with safety pins that had to be twisted to be pulled out.
There were no heavy machine guns or recoilless rifles
available. These would have to be accumulated as spoils
of war.

2200 HOURS LOCAL
2000 HOURS ZULU

Now, with all equipment and ammunition issued and the cargo trucks loaded and topped off, Commando Nyoka had gone through that standard military situation of "hurry up and wait." The "hurry up" was done with, and now everyone was in the "wait" mode until first call the next morning. Most were in a contemplative mood as they downed the small bottles of Kronenbourg beer. The mercenaries faced what would probably be several weeks of combat, and now certain considerations had changed their former sangfroid attitudes. They were not in a standard national army with rules, regulations, benefits, or close ties to any civilian population. There were no arrangements to contact friends or families in case of becoming a KIA or WIA. Most of the men made private arrangements among themselves by exchanging addresses of kith and kin.

Another thing that had entered their minds, but was not openly discussed, was that serious wounds would not be treated in a field hospital. The most that could be expected would be standard field medical first aid. Also, there was no chance of evacuation to more sophisticated medical procedures if injuries were life threatening. In such cases the medics would administer overdoses of narcotics as acts of euthanasia. After all, the shrieks of agony from doomed men would be bad for morale.

It was much like that ditty that Bob Brown heard the Frenchman sing when they left Gabon for the trip to the Congo:

> *Vive le mort! Vive la guerre!*
> *Vive les mercenaries!*

At that moment, however, the Unit operator had a hell of a lot more on his mind than the potential for bad luck. He had gathered all the intelligence possible on the mercenary force. He knew their strengths, weaponry, potential leadership, morale, and other information that would prove useful in fighting against them. Now, with active operations looming the next day, it was time for him to make a break to join up with Jonas Blane and the others.

Luckily, his gear was prepared for hauling ass, and that was exactly what he had to do before morning. He didn't need everything that had been issued to him, so after lights-out, he could make an exfiltration, taking only the AKS-74 rifle, his LBE with the full load of ammo, the trusty K-Bar knife, two canteens, a compass, and the AN/PRC-112 handheld radio set he had brought with him. Luckily he had pulled his stints of guard duty on the garrison perimeter and knew which one offered the easiest way out into the tropical forest.

Simon Cooper spoke up, interrupting his thoughts. "Wot are you so quiet about, then, Ted?"

"Yeah," Andre Coureur said, handing him a bottle of beer. "Your thoughts must have carried you a thousand miles away."

Bob grinned and took the offered brew. "I'm just turning things over in my mind."

Simon chuckled. "We all are, mate. Nothing wrong with that."

Bob nodded and smiled, then turned his attention to chatting with his two friends as every nerve in his body buzzed with anxiety.

11 APRIL
0215 HOURS LOCAL
0015 HOURS ZULU

Bob Brown moved slowly down the rows of barracks toward the camp perimeter. At that particular time he would have given his left nut for a pair of night-vision goggles. The best he could do was that old trick of looking slightly off to one side of what he wanted to see and use the visual purple on the inside of his eyeballs to pick out shapes in the darkness. This was a technique taught in the U.S. armed forces before technology made it outdated. During his Boy Scout days, Bob had learned it from a scoutmaster who had been a veteran of the Cold War army. The method was not completely reliable, but if one kept one's head close to the ground when sighting upward, it was dependable in a half-assed way.

The path to the exit point he had chosen was not too difficult to follow since assigned sentries had been tramping up and down the track for the past couple of weeks. Bob had been posted at the site on at least four occasions and was familiar with the flora and layout of the terrain. When he reached a spot where there was a slight rise in the ground, he slowed up for a few paces, then sank down into a prone position. By glancing upward, he could make out a break in the trees about fifteen meters ahead. This was the spot where the sentries stationed themselves. Now Bob inched forward on hands and knees, carefully checking out places before he put his weight on them. A cracking twig would sound as loud and clear as a gunshot.

The shadowy view of a man loomed ahead. His boonie cap and the AKS-74 rifle over his shoulder showed plainly. He turned sideways, and Bob recognized an old nemesis. It was the German volunteer Hans Schleck, who had attempted to rape the village girl with his Polish buddy, Josef Kowalski. Bob damned his bad luck. This guy was tough as hell. The Unit man wished he could take off his gear, but if the situation went to hell, he wanted everything with him if he had to make a break for the deeper jungle.

Schleck yawned loudly and stretched as he stood leaning against a tree. The guards were expected to keep their ears tuned for trouble since it was impossible to see anything in the area at night. Bob eased up behind the guy, then struck down with the edge of his fist as hard as he could. The blow went true, striking the German at the base of his neck between his shoulder blades. He should have gone at least to his knees and been dazed, but all Bob had accomplished was to attract the big guy's attention.

"Aargh!" the German bellowed, turning toward the source of the attack.

Bob drove the blade of the K-Bar into Schleck's throat, slicing around to the jugular vein. Now the bellow had turned into an extremely loud bubbly howl.

"Sergent de la Garde!" a voice sounded from nearby in French.

Schleck was not through fighting in spite of the fatal wound. He brought his rifle up and squeezed off a round that erupted into a bright flash that lasted only a microsecond. But it was enough to wipe out Bob's visual purple, and he struck out blindly with his left hand, the heel smashing into Schleck's nose. The olfactory organ collapsed under the force of the blow, and the victim stumbled back to fall into a sitting position.

Now the beams of flashlights danced among the trees, and there was yelling of orders. Within seconds Commandant Dekker's voice could be heard shouting to the off-duty guards, who were now responding.

Bob leaped over Schleck, using the bouncing lights coming through the trees to guide him into the jungle. A fire burst blasted out from the rear, and the bark of a couple of nearby trees whipped into the air. Some of the pieces hit Bob's face with stinging slaps.

The chase was on.

Bob Brown was in a hell of a spot. The early dawn's faint light could be seen through the trees to the east, and he was deep into jungle environs he did not know. He had a compass, but no map. His basic plan had been to get as far away from the mercenary camp as possible, then find a good spot for the chopper to use as an LZ. At that point, he could turn on the radio's beacon to summon the aircraft. But occasional sounds that reached his ears were firm indications that he was being pursued and tracked by some of the world's best manhunters. He knew they were serious and wouldn't stop until they had him cornered. This was the morning that the big operation was to start, and the officers had obviously decided it was more important to run him to ground.

The only thing Bob knew was that the Unit was to the west somewhere, but he had no idea of how far, much less their exact location. Now, in the growing light, he was able to move much easier than in the darkness, but he had to concentrate on maintaining strict noise discipline. This meant taking opportunities to stop and settle down to listen for whatever sounds might be picked up in those unfriendly surroundings. So far the only indication of his followers had been occasional rustling of vegetation in the distance or maybe a careless curse of frustration.

Bob was behind a fallen log, peering through the brush growing on the other side. He realized he was hemmed in. The mercenaries knew his direction of travel, obviously exchanging information through the squad leaders' LASH commo systems. Every turn that he took was eventually noted and the route passed on. It had been only five minutes before that the Unit operator became very much aware of being herded into a trap like a fox at the mercy of the riders and hounds of an English country hunt.

Time to break out.

The Russian rifle, locked and loaded, was resting across the log, aimed directly at the spot where he expected the nearest team of pursuers to appear. When they came into view, he didn't recognize the man at the head of the small patrol. *Probably one of the newbies that had shown up in the past couple of days,* he said to himself. Bob shifted the stock slightly to align the sights, then put them dead on the guy's head. This was followed by a quiet breath and the gentle squeeze of the trigger. The muzzle blast and the shattering of the skull were almost simultaneous. Bob swung the barrel slightly down the column of pursuers and fired again. One guy spun around, falling out of sight while his buddy sort of leaped sideways and disappeared under the brush.

Bob got to his feet to run crouching in the direction the hunters had come from. After going twenty meters or so, he turned right and continued the same distance before going back to the original track.

0815 HOURS LOCAL
0615 HOURS ZULU

The situation had grown tighter. Slight sounds and blind instinct told Bob Brown he was losing this chess match. For one desperate moment he had seriously considered going up a tree and concealing himself in the branches. It was sort of like what Japanese snipers used to do during the Pacific campaigns of World War II. Just about all of the poor bastards were eventually blasted from their hiding places by determined U.S. Marines.

The incoming volley whacked slugs all around him, tearing chunks out of trees and sending leaves swirling like they were caught in an invisible gale. Bob dove to the ground, and scampered away on hands and knees. Another fusillade came in from the rear. After a ten-meter scurry, he found a small depression in the ground that was surrounded by thick brush. It offered more concealment than cover, but it was better than nothing. He got himself into a good spot where he could make a 360-degree response to attacks.

Bob still had the original magazine in the AKS-74 with only three rounds fired from it. Those twenty-seven cartridges left combined with the seven other magazines gave him a total of 237 rounds. He suddenly remembered the two French grenades he'd left back in the barracks. He wished he'd brought them now; then he just as suddenly realized the guys chasing him had no doubt brought theirs.

Without warning, incoming fire blasted in at him from three directions. The noise inside the trees was deafening, and he could tell the location of the attackers from where the concussion of the shots shook the brush. He aimed at the less than desirable targets, using up the remainder of the magazine as he swung the barrel back and forth to force the mercenaries to keep their heads down. A yell in some foreign language could be heard, and he knew he had hit at least one of them. He quickly exchanged the empty magazine for another, then cut loose three-round bursts of enfilading fire that swept the line of the assault.

This was not a time for subtlety, and he immediately ran to his direct rear as fast as he could go, knowing the mercenaries would have hit the dirt fast with that amount of furious firing slashing the air around them. He managed to crash through the brush for about forty meters when he came to an unexpected halt.

Bob looked down into a deep, wide gulch that had a

swift-flowing river boiling through it. He knew it was the Ekundu that ran behind the mercenary camp, and Bob realized he would never be able to get to the bottom of the gulch, then swim across to the other side before the hunter-killer teams caught up with him. For one selfish, cowardly instant, he considered turning on the homing beacon of the radio to call in the chopper, but he knew if the aircraft showed up it would be shot to pieces by heavy automatic fire from the ground. He looked left and right, seeing nothing helpful.

This was the last stand.

0855 HOURS LOCAL
0655 HOURS ZULU

The position Bob prepared wasn't the best under any circumstances except for the fact that if anyone wanted to close with him, they would have to cross a short open space where they'd be exposed for about a dozen meters. The Unit operator situated himself in a shallow hole he had scraped out of the soft earth with his feet. Then he removed his remaining half dozen magazines from the pouches and put them to his front within reach, and settled down for the inevitable.

"This definitely isn't the best day of my life," he said aloud to himself.

For a few moments he lay in the natural silence of the pristine African jungle, and his mind turned to his wife, Kim, and the kids. This was a crappy way to end it all, but he'd chosen the Army and had gone a hell of a lot farther than what was required of him. Airborne training, Ranger school, the HALO course, and then Special Forces. Add the Unit with all its attendant risks, and he'd evolved into a guy without much of a future.

The attack began with a peppering of single shots toward him. Bob could tell that they weren't sure of his exact location, but were trying to draw fire. He fought the temptation to shoot back for two reasons: he didn't really have enough ammunition to waste, and the first time he returned fire, they would know exactly where he was. A few more bursts split the air, then silence.

Then three mercenaries appeared from the distant brush, moving into the open area. They slowly approached the hidden American, their AKS-74s ready for any situation that might develop.

This was it.

Bob kicked off one shot, swung the bore, and pulled the trigger again. By the time those two targets were knocked to the ground, his third round caught the guy on the right flank. Now all hell broke loose and heavy salvos, some single shots and other bursts of automatic fire, clapped around him. Ricochets zinged off, bullets slammed into the trees behind him, and others plowed up the dirt to his direct front. Bob fired back in the general direction of the source of the incoming, smothering the blind instinct to lay down fusillades of full-auto on them.

The Unit man was down to his last magazine as the mercenaries continued pouring in the heavy firing. It would be better to get cut down in one quick instant than risk being wounded or captured. Either way meant death. He wished like hell he had a bayonet for the final charge he was going to make. It was old-fashioned, but seemed to have an illusion of glory about it.

Sudden reinforcements off to one side showed up, and he hesitated for an instant, thinking of the extra weapons that would be shooting at him. Then the firing built up fast, and Bob realized it was not coming from the mercenaries. He ducked back down until the volleys eased off and finally quit altogether. He stuck his head up and saw Jonas Blane walking across the front of his position with Mack Gerhardt. Carlito Grey and Lance Matoskah appeared with some Congolese paratroopers.

Bob stood up and yelled, "Hey! What kept you dick-heads so long?"

The others snapped their heads around and spotted him. Jonas signaled the others to check out the enemy positions, and he walked over to Bob with a scowl. "You were supposed to turn on that beacon and call in the chopper."

"The situation went to hell," Bob said. "My exfiltration got tripped up."

Mack joined them and Jonas continued to glower at Bob. "Your ass would be splattered all over the place if we hadn't stumbled across this firefight."

Bob looked to Mack for some moral support, but all he got was an impious grin.

Carlito and Lance came back with the paratroopers. Lance reported, "No casualties back there but we saw some blood on the ground. They must've hauled their dead and wounded away."

The two looked at Bob. Carlito asked, "How come you didn't call in the chopper like you was supposed to?"

Lance snickered. "Trying to get a little extra glory, huh, Bob?"

Bob stepped out of his fighting position and slung the Russian rifle over his shoulder. "I'm glad to see you guys too."

CHAPTER EIGHT

The five Americans and two Congolese officers sat in the thatched hut that Captain Edouard Tshobutu used as a combination headquarters and billets. They were seated loosely around the table that served for both eating and as the captain's desk. Bob Brown was no longer attired in his mercenary cammies. Instead he wore a Belgian camouflage uniform he had gotten from the stores taken off the truck convoy a few days before.

Jonas Blane carefully examined the jacket issued to the pseudo–soldier of fortune during his infiltration of the mercenary unit. He pointed to the insignia of the cobra sewn to the sleeve. "What's this all about?"

"The name of the outfit is Commando Nyoka," Bob explained. "It means 'cobra.' They adopted that as the unit symbol since they're supposed to be like cobras; swift and deadly."

Lance Matoskah shook his head. "I don't like that much color on my cammies. It sort of spoils the purpose, don't it?"

"Yeah," Bob agreed. "I think most of those guys will rip the insignia off eventually."

Tshobutu gazed at the garment. "It would seem we have a formidable enemy to deal with."

"They're tough," Bob said. "You can be sure of that. I haven't seen the exact strength figures, but I estimate them to be a force of around two hundred. Probably more. And they're receiving sporadic spurts of reinforcements."

"Most interesting," Jonas remarked in his usual style of understatement. Bob had already given them the rundown on weaponry, transport, logistical situation, and other physical aspects of the mercenary organization. "What about morale? You haven't said much about that."

"Their fighting spirit is fine," Bob explained. "You have to remember those guys are well trained and getting better pay as mercenaries than they received in their own countries' armies. The situation is a financial benefit to them. The downside of the job is that they are fully aware that they are not serving under established law. If some lower-ranking guy really offended an officer, there could be a summary execution. I'm talking about a pistol being drawn and fired into somebody's skull in an instant. No discussion, no repercussions, nothing."

"Well," Mack Gerhardt said, "that might bring about a mutiny."

"I don't think so," Bob said. "They wouldn't get paid if that happened. And there's to be a big-ass bonus as soon as this campaign is wrapped up. It's going to be paid in Euros."

"Jesus!" Carlito Grey exclaimed. "They're better off than we are."

"Not necessarily," Bob countered. "If they're badly wounded, there's no field hospital for 'em. The only medical personnel they have are Congolese Army medics."

Lance Matoskah looked over at Sublieutenant Kintuba. "How are those guys at treating wounds?"

"It depends on the unit," Kintuba replied. "The ones with us here are as good as can be found in any army. But some of the infantry outfits have personnel who are trained only in basic first aid."

"Uncle Sam loves us, guys," Jonas said, grinning. "We've got plenty of medicines and drugs, not to mention a well-trained medic to take care of us."

"You're too kind," Lance said. "I promise I'll do my best."

There was a rap on the doorpost and a Congolese warrant officer and sergeant stepped into the hut, rendering sharp salutes. "*Adjutant* Bhutan *et Sergent* Montka *à vos ordres, mon capitaine*."

"Good," Tshobutu said. "I believe you speak English, do you not, *Adjutant*?"

"Yes, sir," Bhutan replied. "I attended advanced helicopter training at Fort Rucker in Alabama. Sergeant Montka speaks French and Swahili."

Jonas stood up and offered his hand to both men. "I'm glad to finally meet the chopper crew. We are going to start including you in the operations."

Bhutan, a tall, slim man, smiled widely. "At last, sir! Sergeant Montka and I are at your service. I am the pilot, of course, and he is a crewman, as well as a skilled mechanic."

"The only thing that worries me is the subject of fuel," Jonas said. "I noticed there is none here."

"That is not a problem, sir," Bhutan said. "I have a chit that authorizes me to draw fuel at any army depot.

They will not know where I have come from or where I am going. As long as I present the proper paperwork when I land, they will refuel my aircraft."

"Excellent," Jonas said. "If the National Army doesn't want to throw in with us, they can at least keep our 'air force' gassed up." He turned to Bob. "How will the mercenaries react to a helicopter flying overhead now and again?"

"I don't recommend doing it directly above them," Bob said. "But there are choppers and other aircraft making appearances all the time. I think if we stay on the edges of the operational areas, we won't have any trouble."

"Then we can move fast and land in many spots as long as we're not in the near vicinity of the bad guys," Jonas surmised. He reached into his jacket pocket and pulled out a folded map of the operational area, spreading it out across the table. "Okay, Brown, here is where we pulled your ass out of the crap you'd gotten yourself into."

Bob frowned, but checked the spot. "Yeah. I figure that's close enough."

"Close enough!" Jonas said. "That's the exact location. So point out where the mercenary headquarters is located."

Bob looked at the chart. "Okay. Here's the headquarters and main garrison area. It's off the highway there and a road leads into the camp, but it's not shown on the map. I suppose it's a recent addition. The Congolese insurgent force is billeted at that site too." He put his finger down in another place. "This is the mercenary training area. See the river? That's the last leg of the obstacle course."

"Gotcha," Jonas said. "By the way, is that the same river where your mercenary buddies had backed you up to?"

"Yeah, boss, but I was in a hell of a situation not of my own making!"

"I'm not interested in any bull," Jonas snapped in a tone indicating the subject was closed. He sat back down in his chair. "The first thing we'll do is fly some recons and see what there is to be seen from the air."

"My SA-Three-Thirty is topped off and ready for flight, sir," Bhutan said.

Jonas checked his watch. "All right, then. Mack and Lance. You're going with me."

The three followed the warrant officer and sergeant out of the hut.

FORT GRIFFITH, MISSOURI
OFFICERS' CLUB
12 APRIL
1945 HOURS LOCAL
13 APRIL
0145 HOURS ZULU

CIA controller-at-large Delmar Munger had invited Booker Cartwright of the State Department to join him for drinks at the Officers' Club after a late-afternoon meeting with Colonel Tom Ryan. The two men, as government officials, were authorized temporary membership at the club as long as they were quartered on post. When they entered the building, Munger steered them toward a table at the back of the bar, where they could be off by themselves.

After ordering drinks and a shrimp appetizer from the waitress, they engaged in small talk for a few minutes. But after they were served, Munger didn't waste a second to get to the reason for his invitation. "What did you think of the colonel's briefing this afternoon?"

Cartwright took a sip of his whisky sour before answering. "It was a bit disappointing."

"Yeah," Munger said treating himself to a swallow of

his Blue Label on the rocks. "Your boss isn't gonna like the situation one goddamn bit."

"Again, I employ the adjective 'disappointing.' "

"Well, I don't know about your position, but when I send 'disappointing' news to my superiors, they get upset. Goddamned good and upset!"

"Mmm," Cartwright mused. "But the report seemed honest under the circumstances. If those men out on the operation are unable to recruit people to our side because of a genuine lethargy and lack of confidence in their national government, it's something we just have to accept. After all, it's the Congolese people's nation, and the fact they can see no particular advantage to joining either side presents a serious dilemma for us."

"Can't you see what's going on, Booker?" Munger asked, using the man's first name to spawn a spirit of togetherness. "Those bastards are lying! And it's what they've always done. They're a bunch of cowboys, and it's up to us to put a stop to their wild behavior." He paused for another slug of the fifteen-year-old Scotch. "You've not been involved with them like those of us in the CIA. There have been countless crimes—*war* crimes for Chrissake—which they've committed, and we must stop them or this country of ours is gonna pay a heavy price sometime for their atrocities."

"But why would they conduct themselves as savages?"

"Because they are cruel, vicious, arrogant megalomaniacs—that's why!" Munger said. "They get their jollies by not having to answer to anyone about what they do." He calmed down a bit. "You've got to let your superiors know what's going on, Booker. Between the Agency and the State Department, they can be brought to justice and disbanded. Then a few of those criminals can be sent to serve long jail terms." He looked around and lowered his voice to emphasize the serious aspects of what he was about to say. "We know they're stealing everything from money to weapons and collectible art on these operations. And if some poor schmuck gets wise to 'em, they take him out."

"Take him out where?"

"They *kill* the guy!" Munger snapped in angry exasperation. "Only God knows how many murders those bastards have committed to cover their asses."

Cartwright swallowed hard and blinked. "Jesus! I had no idea."

"Look now, Booker," Munger said. "I'm CIA. I know what I'm talking about."

"Well, what should I be doing?"

"When you turn in your report, just put down what Colonel Ryan told us," Munger urged him. "Say he received word from his Unit operators that there is complete apathy among the population and the people don't have faith in either side. Also mention that this is true of the National Army as well. Okay? Then say that you don't believe a word of it."

"Can you be more specific, Delmar?" Cartwright asked, now getting with the program.

"Tell him that we are concerned about the cover-up of atrocities being committed by the Unit," Munger said. "Tell him that is why nobody is coming over to support our cause in that mess in the Democratic Republic of the Congo because the population is being alienated by those criminals."

"But what about evidence?"

"Evidence?" Munger snorted. "Inform your boss that you've been alerted to the true situation by the CIA man on the case. And give him my name."

"All right," Cartwright said. "I'm convinced that's the right thing to do."

"Fine," Munger said, leaning back in his chair. "And it might be a good idea if you let me read your report before you submit it, Booker. There're certain intelligence-type buzzwords that should be used. You're probably not aware of the terminologies we employ."

"Of course."

"Well!" Munger said, satisfied. "Shall we have another drink before we order something else to eat?"

D.R. OF THE CONGO
MERCENARY HEADQUARTERS
1630 HOURS LOCAL
1430 HOURS ZULU

The merchant Léon M'kalo sat in front of Baroudeur's desk sipping from the cup of coffee just presented him by one of the native servants. Karl Baroudeur sat across from him while Vlad Krashchenko stood to one side.

M'kalo was making his first call on his new employers and was in a good mood. "All is calm and normal in the villages, *Monsieur le Général*. However, there was an incident that occurred on the road between Camp Ukaidi and Camp Kabila that I learned about in a conversation with some soldiers. A group of trucks was halted and the drivers were made to get out."

"Who halted the trucks?"

"Soldiers of the National Army," M'kalo answered.

Baroudeur turned his eyes on Krashchenko with a quizzical look. Krashchenko shrugged. "None of our native troops have been in that area."

Baroudeur looked back at M'kalo. "What reason was given for stopping the trucks?"

"A paratrooper captain talked to the men, saying that Europeans had invaded the country and that he and his men were going to fight them," M'kalo replied.

"Then what happened?" Krashchenko asked, becoming interested.

"He asked the drivers to desert the Army and come with him and his men to fight the foreigners."

"What was their reaction?" Baroudeur asked.

"The drivers refused but were allowed to leave," M'kalo said. "They had to walk fifteen kilometers back to Camp Ukaidi. After they returned, some more soldiers were sent out to the place, and they found the trucks still there. But all the supplies were gone from the back and the motors were melted."

The two Europeans knew this meant thermite grenades. Baroudeur asked, "Have there been any more such incidents?"

"No, *Monsieur le Général*."

Baroudeur nodded to Krashchenko, who took out his wallet and produced one hundred Euros. He handed the money over to the spy.

"You have done well, *monsieur*," Baroudeur said to M'kalo. "This is very important news that you bring me. Keep your eyes and ears open. Perhaps we will be able to give you a bonus. You are dismissed."

M'kalo stood and bowed, then hurried back to his three-wheeled motorcycle and trailer outside.

Krashchenko walked over to the desk. "This is some very astounding intelligence."

"Indeed," Baroudeur agreed. "These are probably the same people who attacked our supply dump."

"I am thinking things are more complicated out here than we anticipated," Krashchenko opined.

"The incident with that American fleeing to the jungle caused us to delay the beginning of active operations," Baroudeur said. "It was a fortunate decision on our part."

"We should curtail all our tactical plans until we learn more."

Baroudeur nodded his agreement. "I am going to transmit the information to General Dubois."

Mack Gerhardt was peering inside the helicopter with Jonas Blane on one side and the helicopter pilot Warrant Officer Bhutan on the other. Behind them a Congolese corporal and two privates, like Mack, were outfitted for a reconnaissance patrol with the bare essentials, i.e., weapon, combat vest, two canteens, and four ammo pouches loaded with thirty-round magazines. The only difference was that the Unit operator packed his personal K-Bar knife and an M1 compass.

"Okay," Jonas said, using the map. "Here's the LZ where the patrol is being left off. You will go from there some ten kilometers to reach the main highway. The azimuth is roughly three-two-zero degrees. Your mission is to observe the types and numbers of traffic that pass by this spot. I don't care if it's a convoy of Russian T-Ninety main battle tanks or some kid on a bicycle—you make a note of it. I want you to take Bob's radio with the homing beacon. Use it to signal the chopper for extraction."

"Right, boss," Mack said.

"And I also want to emphasize that this is a reconnaissance patrol," Jonas cautioned him. "That means you don't pick a fight. You'll only fire if you are threatened. In case you're discovered, haul ass out without starting a war. Understand?" Jonas faced Bhutan. "Pass that information on to these Congolese troops. Make sure they have no questions about the concept."

The Congolese NCO spoke up. "I am Sergeant Katungo. I attended a Catholic mission school as a boy. There I learned English." He fixed his eyes on his younger countrymen and spoke rapidly in Swahili. They expressed their comprehension. Katungo nodded to Jonas. "They know what is expected of them. But allow me to inform you that the two young privates are recruits who have finished six weeks of training. Captain Gerhardt and I will have to keep a sharp eye on them."

Jonas turned to Mack. "You got that?"

"Right, boss."

CHAPTER NINE

D.R. OF THE CONGO
OPERATIONAL AREA
14 APRIL
0645 HOURS LOCAL
0445 HOURS ZULU

Warrant Officer Bhutan worked both cyclic and collective to bring his chopper close enough to the ground to
allow his four passengers to jump off. As soon as the aircraft went into a hover, the crew chief Sergeant Montka
nodded to Mack Gerhardt. Mack pushed himself out
the door and dropped a couple of meters to the ground.
He was immediately followed by Sergeant Katungo and
the two young soldiers chosen to accompany them. The
patrol wasted no time in getting off the clearing and into
the tree line as the helicopter climbed back into the sky
and turned toward the base camp for the return flight.

Katungo ordered the rookies into a defensive posture
as Mack checked his compass. After noting the correct
direction of three-two-zero, he nodded to the sergeant
as he stepped out to follow the desired azimuth to the

highway that was their objective. Katungo spoke softly but sharply to the privates in Swahili. *"Nifuate!"* The youthful duo immediately fell into formation and followed.

The small group moved slowly toward their destination some ten kilometers away. They eased their way through the heavy brush as silently as possible. However, now and then there would be the loud crack of a dry twig as one of the privates forgot to watch where he placed his feet. This always brought an angry glare and the same guttural admonishment from Sergeant Katungo; *"Tahadhari!"*

After the unnecessary noise had been made for a third time, Mack whipped around to Katungo. "You tell them two guys to watch their step."

"It is what I do, *mon capitaine*," Katungo said in a combination of English and French. "But they still be village boys not yet soldiers."

"The next time it happens, give 'em a slap across the face."

"Oh! I think that make you mad," the Congolese sergeant said. "I now take care of it." He turned and walked back to the two youngsters. He smacked each across the face with heavy-handed blows. *"La makelele!"*

The pair, their eyes opened wide in a combination of shame and fear, stepped back instinctively. Mack rightly figured they'd been given the "word" in a way they fully understood. He renewed the trek toward the objective, happily noting that there was no more unnecessary noise.

0715 HOURS LOCAL
0515 HOURS ZULU

The highway that ran past the OP that Mack and Sergeant Katungo had set up was nothing more than a two-lane macadam road. This may have been considered a main thoroughfare in Africa, but back in the States it would have been no more than a country road linking outlying farms with a small agricultural community.

The two privates, who Mack learned were named Antoine Nagata and Lucien M'buta, had been stationed off to opposite flanks, facing rearward as security. Once more the two kids were reminded that if they spotted the enemy, they were not to fire on them. This was a reconnaissance patrol, not a combat patrol. Now, with the rear covered, the American and the Congolese NCO went back to observing the highway.

The traffic was light and not too remarkable. Pedestrians, mostly women carrying loads on their heads, passed by frequently. Less often, an overloaded truck, the shocks barely able to support the vehicle and its cargo, coughed its way past the OP. There would always be several people hanging precariously on the outside of the clunker, having paid the driver a few francs for the privilege of a ride.

Mack, with his notebook handy, dutifully noted down everything he saw taking place within sight and hearing. This included a sarcastic remark regarding a small troop of monkeys that scampered from one side of the road to the other. The Unit operator wrote down that they were either crazy apes or second lieutenants out on a map exercise.

Toward midmorning a distant engine that sounded like something between a misfiring outboard motor and a farting elephant could be heard. The sounds grew steadily louder until a weird contraption came into view. A strange little man wearing a soiled white suit with a T-shirt sat on a three-wheeled motorcycle with a trailer attached to it. This was piled with all sorts of miscellaneous goods from pots and pans to various articles of clothing. The conveyance resembled a motorized rickshaw.

Mack frowned in puzzlement. "What the hell is that all about?"

Sergeant Katungo grinned. "It is merchant who travels around to villages to make sales. Always welcome by the ladies in this area. The market town most close is fifty kilometers, so they buy much from this gentleman."

"Interesting," Mack remarked. He glanced toward the rear. "You better check out them two kids. They been awful quiet back there."

"Yes, *mon capitaine,*" Katungo replied. He quietly got to his feet and moved soundlessly off into the jungle.

A couple of minutes passed. Then Mack heard the sergeant's voice speaking in a hoarse whisper. The anger in it was not to be denied. *"Kuamka!"* This was followed by a slight thudding sound, and Mack figured somebody caught sleeping had just gotten kicked to full wakefulness.

When Katungo rejoined him, the American could see the cold anger in the man's face. The Congolese said nothing, so Mack just let it pass. Whatever needed to be done had obviously been taken care of.

MERCENARY HEADQUARTERS
0900 HOURS LOCAL
0700 HOURS ZULU

General Karl Baroudeur was extremely pleased with his spy Léon M'kalo. The man was obviously much more intelligent than he had appeared to be at first. Only two hours ago he'd come in to report to headquarters that he had heard about an army helicopter making somewhat irregular flights around the area. People of several villages said the aircraft had been landing occasionally at clearings in the jungle. This whetted M'kalo's curiosity, so he had been making an extra effort to spot it for himself. And when he did, he took notice of the number on the fuselage: 6e BPI. With that done, he had come straight to his benefactor, *le Général*, to report his findings.

Baroudeur sent one of the Congolese orderlies to fetch General Marcel Lulombe to headquarters to help interrogate the pint-sized undercover agent. When Lulombe showed up, Baroudeur had M'kalo repeat his report. The Congolese officer had immediately recognized what the aircraft identification number meant. "*Le Sixième Bataillon Parachutiste d'Infanterie*," he announced. "The Sixth Parachute Infantry Battalion."

Colonel Vlad Krashchenko, standing in his usual spot by the side of desk, spoke up quickly. "That is the unit commanded by the missing captain, *n'est pas*?"

"The same," Lulombe answered.

Now was the time to dismiss M'kalo. It wouldn't do to have a spy sitting around listening to sensitive conversations between high-ranking officers at headquarters. If he would accept pay to work for one side, he would be just as willing to turn into a double agent. Baroudeur had Krashchenko give him two hundred Euros and dismiss him. Then, with only Krashchenko and Lulombe for company, Baroudeur began musing aloud.

"I have always been curious as to why a commanding officer of an elite unit would go AWOL when a revolution breaks out," he said, "especially since he has no interest in joining the insurrection. And at the same time, one of his subalterns with a good number of men also disappeared."

Krashchenko was in an unusually reflective mood himself. "What other motives would be behind his actions? He did not rally the Army to resist us. But rather than do as others did and continue his duties, he disappears. It makes no sense."

Lulombe joined in. "And the Sixth Parachute Infantry Battalion stayed in its garrison. Yet one of its helicopters is out flying about in our operational area. And landing now and again."

"It is easy to discern," Baroudeur said. "The attack on our supply depot was done by this fellow Tshobutu. And it was he who confronted that convoy and tried to talk the drivers into fighting against us."

Lulombe added, "Then he looted the trucks and used thermite grenades to melt the motor blocks."

"Mmm," Baroudeur murmured under his breath. "If the helicopter dropped off a patrol in the area indicated by M'kalo, I would think it was to scout the highway."

"I agree," Lulombe said.

"There is another thing that has perplexed both Colonel Krashchenko and me," Baroudeur said. "And it might be an important part of this puzzle."

"What are you wondering about?" Lulombe asked.

"That American Durant," Baroudeur replied. "It is odd that he would suddenly take off running into the jungle in the middle of the night. I am now convinced he is part of whatever it is that is going on out there." He turned to face Krashchenko. "Get Commandant Dekker and have him take out twenty men to find the uninvited guests who have descended into our midst." He turned his eyes to Lulombe. "I am going to continue to refrain from commencing operations until this puzzle is solved."

"I am in complete agreement," Lulombe said.

"Thank you," Baroudeur said, thinking that Lulombe's opinion counted for absolutely nothing.

OPERATIONAL AREA
1130 HOURS LOCAL
0930 HOURS ZULU

The recon mission had turned into one of pure boredom. The sights of passing people and vehicles became like watching a never-ending, continually looping television commercial with the same tedious message repeated so many times that it made a man's hair hurt. Mack yawned widely in the pressing heat, feeling the weighty lethargy of the patrol assignment. Sergeant Katungo, on the other hand, was keen and eager, as if expecting something exciting to happen at any minute. He made a couple of more inspections of the two privates, but the physical punishment they had received was a strong stimulation for them to stay wide-awake and raring to go.

Another sound of engines eased out of the distance, and after a couple of minutes, Mack's stupor evaporated. These were definitely not rattletraps hauling loads between villages; the vehicles were well maintained and screamed "military" as they drew closer. Katungo too recognized the situation. He glanced over at Mack, and the pair exchanged nods of mutual understanding.

"I hope they ain't looking for us," Mack remarked softly.

"We have to wait to find out," Katungo responded.

A couple of minutes later two SAMIL 20 trucks appeared down the highway, traveling in the opposite direction of the rattletrap motor rickshaw. The convoy came toward them at a slow speed. As the vehicles went past, both Mack and Katungo recognized the camouflage uniforms and insignias worn by the white men in the backs. It was the same that Bob Brown had been attired in when he was rescued during his exfiltration from the enemy camp.

"Askari mgeni was mshaharai," Katungo said instinctively in Swahili. Then he repeated himself in French: *"Mercenaires."*

"Mercenaries," Mack said in English.

The two South African vehicles continued another fifty meters, then eased down to a complete stop. Shouts could be heard, followed by the sounds of tailgates dropping and men jumping off onto the ground.

"Shit!" Mack exclaimed under his breath.

"Maybe they really look for us, *hapana*?"

"Could be," Mack said. "Somebody may have seen the helicopter."

He crawled deeper back into the tree line, then walked through the jungle toward the site where the trucks had stopped. After twenty-five meters, he dropped to the ground and belly crawled up to the edge of the macadam. He counted twenty mercenaries—ten from each truck—formed up in two ranks. A short blond man spoke sternly to them in French, and each line of men split up, going to opposite sides of the highway. Mack quietly moved back into the trees, then hurried to where Sergeant Katungo waited.

"They're definitely looking for us," Mack said. "Let's get them kids and pull back. We're gonna have to hunker down."

1200 HOURS LOCAL
1000 HOURS ZULU

Mack Gerhardt had chosen a route that would take them north of the LZ used earlier that morning. His plan of action was simple enough. Every military instinct that coursed through his soldier's soul told him that somehow the enemy had become aware of their presence in the area. And the bastards must have either checked the map for potential LZs or had been told where the chopper had dropped off the patrol.

Even if he had been on a combat mission rather than reconnaissance, the Unit operator would have hesitated to attack the twenty mercenaries with only himself, Sergeant Katungo, and a couple of newbie recruits. Those two rookies hadn't been in the military long enough to have yet figured out that a firing line isn't cope.

After traveling for five kilometers, he found a natural depression in the ground that was filled with dead fall. Mack chose it as a good place for wait and see, and he set the group to clearing some of the fallen brush and tree limbs out to form a perimeter to provide cover and concealment. Nagata and M'buta worked together, and their actual experience in the jungle showed through well when they discovered a deadly mamba snake within the entangled vegetation. The bite of this serpent would kill even a full-grown healthy man, but the two kids did not panic. They had seen the poisonous reptiles innumerable times in their lives in jungle villages, and they calmly killed the angry, aggressive snake as if they were no more than swatting an annoying fly.

Mack chuckled. "I guess sending them to jungle survival training would bore the shit of 'em, huh?"

"What they must do," Katungo remarked seriously, "is have the opportunity to finish basic training."

1400 HOURS LOCAL
1200 HOURS ZULU

The patrol stayed on 100 percent alert with one man on each side of their natural fortification. There was no way to tell if or when the mercenaries might stumble across them, and if so, from what direction. Nagata and M'buta wisely stayed as quiet as possible, breathing softly and deeply as they kept all senses alert for intruders.

Mack and Katungo had the instincts of old soldiers, accepting the unknown dangers with a professional calmness. The sun had slipped a bit westward as the afternoon wore on; then a brushing sound came from the trees. It was on the side of the position where the two rookies were located. Mack started to get to his feet to see what was going on when suddenly Nagata and M'buta leaped up and rushed across the depression, jumping out on the other side. They were running like hell, and suddenly gunfire broke out with bullets cracking the air above the concealment.

Now the situation had gone completely to hell. The fleeing recruits had given away the position, and both Mack and Katungo were forced to return fire to make the surprise attack slow down. "White guys," Mack said. "From them damn trucks."

Katungo aimed his FA-MAS rifle and cut loose two quick fire bursts of three rounds.

"Make a run for it," Mack said, "in the same direction them two jackoffs went. I'll stay here and make them jokers duck their heads. Go about twenty meters, then turn and cover me. I'll be coming right after you."

Katungo immediately took off as ordered as Mack emptied one magazine in the direction of the assault. Then the American leaped from the cover and made a crouching run as the Congolese NCO covered him with a full magazine of his own. Mack reached his position and dove to the ground. Both men reloaded quickly and repeated the fire-and-maneuver tactic again, this time leapfrogging each other for a distance of a hundred meters.

"Let's hold up here," Mack said. "There may be more of 'em around."

Katungo started to reply; then a violent rustling of brush to their right rear caused both men to turn. They almost fired but hadn't quite had time when Nagata and M'buta appeared. They looked sheepish and frightened. M'buta mumbled something in Swahili.

Katungo glared at him, then turned to look at Mack. "He say they got lost."

"Lost, my ass!" Mack hissed. "The sons of bitches ran like scared jackrabbits."

"They will be punished," Katungo said.

"Well, right now we have other things to worry about," Mack said. "All we can do at this point is sit and wait to see what develops."

1600 HOURS LOCAL
1400 HOURS ZULU

The jungle had been quiet for almost a full hour. Mack whispered, "I think they pulled back."

"Why they do that?" Katungo queried. "They got more men."

Mack shook his head. "The bastards don't know that. They may think there's a hell of a lot more of us, especially if a transport helicopter was involved in our mission." He was thoughtful for a few moments. "Okay. We're gonna move to the LZ. When we get there, we'll recon the area real good. If it's all clear I'll turn on the radio beacon for an extraction." He glared over at the two recruits. "You tell them blockheads that if they as much as belch or fart or make any kind of noise, I'm gonna shoot 'em dead."

Katungo complied, and the fear was evident on the kids' faces.

"All right," Mack said. "Let's move out."

CHAPTER TEN

The first thing Mack Gerhardt faced upon his return from the recon patrol was a debriefing by Jonas Blane and Captain Edouard Tshobutu. He always hated that final phase of a mission, when he had to give an oral report after turning in any notes, maps, or other documents regarding the mission and its aftermath. This would be followed by annoying questions being thrown at him; and there were always plenty, since Mack wasn't the most eloquent or proficient of speakers and didn't get all the information over too well. However, as usual, he toughed it out, and eventually satisfied his two very efficient interrogators.

Now, with all that settled, he left the Congolese captain's hut, heading for the one he shared with the other Unit operators. As he made his way to their quarters, he glanced over at the part of the camp occupied by the Congolese paratroopers, and came to an abrupt halt.

Antoine Nagata and Lucien M'buta were on their knees in an awkward position, tightly trussed up with rope. Sergeant Katungo stood over them, his arms folded across his chest glaring at the pair. The unfortunate privates who had panicked and given their position away were obviously in great pain. Their hands were tied behind their backs, and their ankles were bound tightly together. That would not have been so bad, except a third rope drew their wrists down tightly toward their ankles, forcing them to bend backward. The unfortunate rookies moaned and grimaced in agony. Sergeant Katungo obviously felt no pity for them, and he gazed at them with cold eyes. The NCO wasn't exactly enjoying their acute discomfort, but he certainly approved of it.

Someone walked up beside Mack and he turned to see Sublieutenant Pierre Kintuba. The slim Congolese officer spoke softly. "They are being punished, Captain Gerhardt."

"Yeah," Mack said, "I guess you would call that punishment all right. I've never seen anything like it before."

"It is a holdover from colonial days," Kintuba explained. "A French military punishment used extensively in North Africa. It is called the *crapaudine*. The Belgians learned of it, and adapted the practice into their own punitive procedures, at least where native troops were concerned."

Mack noted the pain that showed on the youngster's faces. "How long are you gonna leave 'em like that? I gotta speak plain. This ain't right."

"Captain Tshobutu has sentenced them to three hours," Kintuba said. "It seems cruel, but when they are released, they will be considered completely punished. Nothing of their incorrect conduct will be noted on their records."

"Well," Mack mused, "I can tell you one thing. The next time them two kids go into combat, they'll think twice before bugging out again." He nodded to Kintuba. "See you around."

"Yes, sir, I will see you around."

Mack continued on his way to join his buddies.

Washington, D.C.
State Department Building
15 April
0930 hours local
1330 hours Zulu

The choice of the small conference room gave indication of the informality of the meeting between the two men sitting across from each other. It was an out-of-the-way little chamber, not used much and almost unknown where it was located off a back hallway. The furniture was plain, functional, and easy on the taxpayers. Both individuals had papers pulled from briefcases for reference. One was Tom Benson, deputy director of the State Department's Special Affairs Bureau. He was perusing the report from Delmar Munger regarding the operation currently in progress in the Democratic Republic of the Congo. He had already reviewed the paper sent in by his own man Booker Cartwright from Fort Griffith, Missouri.

His companion was Norman DeWitt, a senior controller-at-large from the Central Intelligence Agency. His attention was directed to details on the same subject submitted by Booker Cartwright. He finished reading the document, and looked over at Benson. "It seems our two guys are on the same wavelength."

"Yeah," Benson said. "I'm at a disadvantage here, Norman. I can't claim much knowledge of this outfit referred to as the Unit. In fact, I didn't even know which branch of the Army was going to be in on this show."

"You should know a lot about 'em now," DeWitt said. "We've had plenty of trouble with that bunch in the past, particularly when they ignore the provisions of posse comitatus."

"Wait a minute," Benson said, pointing to the reports. "Posse comitatus doesn't apply in this case."

"Of course it doesn't," DeWitt said. "I'm just using it as an example of their very disturbing attitudes. You can be assured that they've bent the hell out of posse comitatus right here in the USA every chance they got. Ignoring laws and customs is something they do blatantly, almost gleefully under the command of that uncontrollable zealot Colonel Tom Ryan. And that's exactly what they're doing in the Congo about the State Department's request to conduct an effective program to win the indigenous population over to our side through peaceful means."

"Now that does concern me," Benson said. "The Secretary has made it very plain that a friendly attitude toward us must be developed during this so-called insurrection in the Congo. The situation is fluid as we understand it, and that offers a lot of opportunities to establish a genial rapport."

"It's not going to happen," DeWitt said. "And you might inform the Secretary of that fact as quickly as possible."

"I'll pass this report from Cartwright up through channels immediately, and it will be well-known in our upper echelons within twenty-four hours." He paused a moment. "Am I to deduce that the CIA wishes to have the Unit deactivated?"

"I'm not going to tell you the entire Agency has that attitude," DeWitt admitted. "But there are enough of us that have bumped heads with Colonel Ryan that we consider him and his pirates a serious liability to the counterterrorist intelligence community."

"You sound like your faction has something specific in mind when it comes to a final disposition of those people."

"We do," DeWitt assured him. "Since the Secretary of State's instructions in this Congo affair are being ignored, we would like your department to team up with us and go after the Unit by taking them before Congress for a series of hearings. I am specifically referring to the Senate Committee on Intelligence and Special Operations."

"I'll attach an amendment with my endorsement to that effect to Cartwright's report," Benson said.

"Good. I'll stay in touch, Tom."

D.R. OF THE CONGO
OPERATION GRIFFE
1630 HOURS LOCAL
1430 HOURS ZULU

The beat-up old GM truck rattled down the highway at forty kilometers an hour. It was typical of the overused and overaged cargo carriers in that part of the world. Its original paint job had long since faded and was replaced by various colors sprayed on it from aerosol cans to keep the rust under at least a semblance of control. A large and battered old tarpaulin covered the back to keep rain and dust off cargo. The windows in the doors no longer rolled up, but that was of no consequence since the glass in them had shattered at least a decade before. The engine, however, had been lately tuned up by some mechanics who knew their trade, and it ran rather smoothly, though the lack of a muffler hindered the mechanical efficiency of the power plant.

The truck had been wandering around the various

highways and roads for a couple of days, taking short breaks in towns where the pair of Congolese drivers would enjoy some beers and conversation with the locals. They were strangers to the district and, although friendly, would not permit any riders to accompany them, even if payment was offered.

Now, in the late afternoon, the truck continued on what might appear to be aimless wandering, turning off the highway to a rutted road now and then before returning to its crisscrossing routine that seemed senseless and a waste of good gasoline.

COUNTERINSURGENCY BASE CAMP
1800 HOURS LOCAL
1600 HOURS ZULU

Captain Edouard Tshobutu's hut was the scene of a serious planning session. Besides the captain, the five Unit operators, Sublieutenant Pierre Kintuba, and Warrant Officer Georges Bhutan sat around the table in a half-circle formation. Jonas Blane stood at the front of the group with a map of the operational area behind him. He opened the meeting without ceremony. "Okay. We've all been busy, so let's hear your reports. I'll start with Bob."

Bob Brown responded in a matter-of-fact tone. "All right. I was assigned to work with the Congolese NCOs in giving their younger troops some basic skills in combat. This included squad tactics, patrolling, marksmanship, and field fortifications. I'd say things went pretty well."

Mack Gerhardt growled deep in his throat. "I just wish them two kids that went with me and Sergeant Katungo had gotten some instruction before we went on that recon. They could've got us killed. They misunderstood the concept when we explained to 'em that you weren't supposed to fight on a reconnaissance patrol. So when they seen the bad guys, they split, thinking that was the thing to do. When me and Katungo didn't go with 'em, they realized something was out of kilter."

"Christ!" Lance Matoskah exclaimed. "Did you see what happened to 'em?"

Captain Tshobutu spoke up. "I realize the punishment was cruel, and I take the responsibility for it. I ordered them into the *crapaudine* to make the right impression on them and their comrades. You must remember they are village lads raised in an environment that gives them concepts of life that do not fit into modern society, especially modern military society. If the two youngsters had been admonished verbally, it would have meant to them that what they did was not a serious breach of discipline. Now they fully realize what they did was serious and possibly unforgivable."

"At any rate," Bob said, "between what happened to those two and the training given the others, I really feel all those recruits are as ready as they're ever going to be for combat. The next step is to get them some battle experience."

"That's a big step forward," Jonas remarked. "Okay, Lance, my friend. How's by you?"

"Real good, boss," Lance Matoskah replied. "I've inventoried all our medical equipment. We're up to snuff on medicine and drugs, as well as instruments. We will be able to conduct field surgery on the seriously wounded. I know it's not as good as having a fully equipped hospital, but you do the best you can with what you've got. I've also given classes to the Congolese medics and brought them up to speed."

"How about you, Carlito?"

Carlito Grey stopped sipping the coffee in his canteen cup to speak. "Commo gear is in good shape. Every NCO is now equipped with LASH headsets, and knows how to use them. They had a tendency to gab too much, but now they realize how vital it is to speak only when absolutely necessary."

"And last but not least," Jonas said, "let's hear from our Air Force commander."

Warrant Officer Bhutan grinned. "You are making me to feel very important. Sergeant Montka and I have been running scouting missions and continue to be able to refuel at army air bases. We have also mapped out all available LZs in the operational area for future missions."

Jonas glanced at Tshobutu. "Anything to add, Captain?"

"Only that I think we are now equipped, trained, and prepared to really set this war going," Tshobutu said. "At this point—as it is said in the French language—*la victoire ou la mort*—victory or death."

"I agree," Jonas said. "And last night I finished the OPLAN for our first serious foray of this operation. I'll hold a briefing later, then a briefback tomorrow." He swung his gaze to Lance Matoskah. "What is it your Sioux ancestors used to say before a battle?"

"It will be a good day to die," Lance stated. "But I prefer to be more optimistic."

OPERATION GRIFFE
16 APRIL
1445 HOURS LOCAL
1245 HOURS ZULU

The old truck rattled along the road with the driver trying to keep his tires in the ruts while his buddy leaned out the window staring up into the sky. After a few bumpy moments went by, he suddenly yelled out in French, *"Hélicoptère!"*

"Qu'elle est le bataillon?" the driver asked.

"Le sixième parachutiste d'infanterie!"

In the back, under the tarpaulin, Commandant Paul Dekker heard the conversation. He put his face in the rear window of the cab. "Where is it?"

"Off to the right front, *mon commandant*," the driver answered.

Dekker barked orders as he pulled the tarp back. The two mercenaries with him, both armed with magazine-fed Minimi machine guns, raised their weapons. The three men were soaked in sweat from the long days spent in the sweltering confines of the truck bed with the tarpaulin covering them. It was with real relief that they caught sight of the flying chopper drawing closer.

The two expert gunners gave just enough lead as they pumped short fire bursts at the aircraft.

The incoming bullets blasted away the Plexiglas, blowing Warrant Officer Bhutan's head off in chunks that bounced off the opposite window. The helicopter began to spin crazily as it went downward. Inside the troop compartment, the centrifugal force flung Sergeant Montka away from the door to the bulkhead on the other side of the aircraft.

The SA.330 crashed through the trees to the ground, sending a ball of fire and black smoke skyward.

The two machine gunners, led by Dekker, jumped from the truck and ran into the jungle. They slashed their way through the tropical growth until they reached the scene of the fiery impact. Flames still danced in and around the fuselage, and the crewmen's charred bodies could be seen in the wreckage, twisted and curled into the obscene postures of those who are burned to the bone.

Dekker grinned viciously, announcing, *"Mission accompli!"*

CHAPTER ELEVEN

Lance Matoskah was an introspective young man with a deep spiritual side that had yet to be fully appreciated by his Unit teammates. He was a full-blooded Oglala Teton Sioux born and raised on the Wapasha Indian Reservation in North Dakota, where he lived in a manufactured home with his parents and three siblings. He attended school on the "rez" from the first through the twelfth grade, graduating with a rather good GPA, but with no desire to continue his academic education. The principal of the school was a well-meaning but misguided white man who insisted that his students use the English translations of their native names. Thus, Lance was listed as "Lance White Bear" on his scholastic records.

As Lance grew up he experienced a deep and meaningful epiphany. It was a near-religious experience of figuring out who he really was. As a result of this revelatory experience at the age of nineteen, he went back to using the Native American version of his name. It was also at this time that he became alarmed and disgusted with the way his fellow tribespeople had fallen under the influence of modern American society. Alcohol ravaged them, turning beautiful people into staggering useless beings who abused themselves and their families. When fast-food franchises appeared on the reservation, they attracted the young kids to their greasy cuisines, bringing on obesity and diabetes to a once proud and fierce race. Lance recognized that as an Oglala he was meant to be a warrior-hunter, and he swore off drinking and went back to eating the traditional foods of his people. As a result, his muscularity, strength, and even physical senses sharpened to high levels. The young man had evolved back into the Sioux tribesman nature had meant him to be.

Being a hunter was no problem since he could take a rifle and go out into the countryside to find game, such as elk, deer, and antelope to put on the table. But in order to really become a warrior, he would have to join the nation's armed forces. Lance Matoskah enlisted in the Army, and went for the elite of the elite by volunteering for the Airborne Rangers. After seven years of service, he ended up in the Unit with the rank of sergeant, cross-trained as a medic. He fit well into the environment and culture of the outfit, and was assigned to the team led by Sergeant Major Jonas Blane. As a Unit operator, Lance chose "Red Cloud" as his radio call sign. This was the name of the most famous chief of Lance's tribe during the final days of fighting the whites. Red Cloud, with eighty coups won in battle, was a courageous war chief, and later amazed the whites with his skill as an orator and statesman. This forefather served his people in trying circumstances as he struggled from a disadvantaged position against overwhelming opponents with a military force, dirty money, and dirtier politics backing them up.

Now, across a wide ocean and far from his native land, Sergeant Lance Matoskah sat in the team hut and cleaned his M4A1 carbine preparing to do that very thing for which he had been created: go to war.

19 APRIL
0515 HOURS LOCAL
0315 HOURS ZULU

The loss of the helicopter was an unexpected catastrophe that brought about big changes in Jonas Blane's tactical plans for the counterinsurgency force's first major operation. Obviously the loss of the aircraft neutralized the ability of quick transportation to isolated LZs; thus their overall mobility was drastically curtailed, as was splitting up into several elements for simultaneous and coordinated actions. A combat patrol with a couple of factions and/or missions out on its own would be in for a world of hurt if they ran into serious trouble. The primitive conditions and lack of air transport would make it impossible to provide them timely relief in case the tactical situation deteriorated.

Anybody who didn't quite understand why that would occur could look up what happened to General Custer and the 7th Cavalry Regiment when they galloped off in separate detachments to take on Lance Matoskah's ancestors that memorable June day of 1876.

The night after the helicopter disaster, Jonas sat down with Mack Gerhardt and Captain Edouard Tshobutu to work out another OPORD. They still wanted to launch a big operation to draw the enemy into a showdown in the hopes that a decisive victory would result in a quick overall success in accomplishing the mission. The skull session resulted in plans for a near Napoleonic combat formation of five columns of fifteen men each. This would leave approximately twenty-five troopers back at base camp as security and reserves as well as to keep an eye on the EPWs.

The center column would be led by Jonas and Tshobutu while the left center had Mack Gerhardt and Sergeant Samuel Katungo at its head. Bob Brown and Sublieutenant Pierre Kintuba led the right center. Out on the far left flank would be Lance Matoskah while Carlito Grey took care of the far right.

The basic plan was to head out on an azimuth of 315 degrees that would lead the force directly toward the enemy garrison. They would skirt the village of Mwitukijiji—now referred to as Mwitu-whatever by the Americans—then converge for an all-out attack on the enemy. Bob Brown had provided an excellent layout and sketch map of the area, and this helped in the planning phase.

A distance of twenty-five to fifty meters would be maintained between each column as much as possible during the approach to the objective. They would use GPS instruments to check their exact positions from time to time to stay properly aligned. Each Congolese paratrooper, including Tshobutu and Kintuba, would carry a dozen thirty-round magazines and four hand grenades. The Unit operators would do the same, but would have M-203 grenade launchers attached to their carbines. They would carry pouches containing six of the 40-millimeter projectiles. Additionally, each column had at least one trained medic with an emergency field kit and stretcher to deal with expected WIAs.

Now, with the new day's sun still not completely above the horizon, the five columns had already left the base camp, moving slowly through the jungle with a two-man point team to the front of each. These were Congolese NCOs who had demonstrated their skill in land navigation and map reading during training sessions. Communications within the columns was maintained through the LASH system. The senior men also had handheld AN/PRC-112 radios to keep in contact with one another.

0630 HOURS LOCAL
0430 HOURS ZULU

Carlito Grey on the extreme right flank, received
word from his point men that they were headed directly
toward Mwitukijiji and would enter the village if they
maintained the same course they were presently following. Carlito got on the 112, speaking as softly as possible.
"Snake Doctor, this is Betty Blue. We're about to stroll
into Mwitu-whatever. We'll have to move farther south
to avoid the place. Over."

"This is Snake Doctor," Jonas came back. "All elements, change to azimuth two-niner-zero until further
notice. Out."

The entire unit eased onto the altered route, heading in a direction that would lead them slightly north of
where their helicopter had crashed.

INSURGENCY GARRISON
DEFENSIVE PERIMETER
1045 HOURS LOCAL
0845 HOURS ZULU

A French mercenary by the name of Denis Mercier
was in an OP with two Congolese companions. He was
glad to be where he was at that particular time. If he
hadn't been tapped for security perimeter duty that
day, he would have been back in the training area going
through Commandant Peter Dekker's obstacle course.
It had been a while since they'd been forced to run that
Gauntlet of Hell, and Dekker had been positively furious at not having the opportunity to force the Europeans
into struggling in the midst of its barriers for a period of
time. While Mercier was in his barracks getting his gear
together for a day in an OP, the men around him were
preparing for a few miserable hours under Dekker's

command. One of the ex-SAS Brits, who was changing into a pair of worn-out trousers for the ordeal, groused, "The bastard is so bluddy proud of the godamn thing, you'd think it could cure cancer."

Now, safely ensconced in the cover of the observation post, Mercier felt very lucky, indeed. His Congolese companions both spoke French, and the three conversed in soft voices among themselves as they kept an eye out on their area of responsibility. This was some of the best duty in the insurgency force. The OPs were located fifty meters ahead of the garrison's MLR, and the distance kept those on duty out of the way of prying squad leaders. Additionally, the kitchens prepared rather tasty lunches for them to take out to the sites. Today's fare had been cold fried chicken, cheese, bread, and an orange. It was pleasant to be away from the discipline of the garrison, especially with those Foreign Legion bastards always stirring things up with endless and bothersome drills in everything from bayonet training to calisthenics. This was all done in accordance with the Legion's traditions of mindless harassment and a strictness that bordered on organized cruelty.

As the duty day drifted into midmorning, Mercier and his mates had settled down to a pleasant quietness, staying alert in a rather lackadaisical manner. Then one of the Congolese suddenly hissed for attention. Mercier and the other came wide-awake. The first guy pointed off to the right front, whispering, *"Patrouille!"*

Mercier grabbed the Chinese-manufactured field radio to alert headquarters.

Counterinsurgency Column

Bob Brown had pulled in one of his point men and taken his place out in front of the right center column.

The Unit operator never did like staying back in a formation or patrol, preferring to be ahead of the crowd and be the first to make contact with the enemy. Sublieutenant Pierre Kintuba had proven his excellent command capabilities, and Bob knew he could handle anything that might develop back in the column should a firefight suddenly occur.

The American's companion was Corporal Gabriel Mantuka, an excellent noncommissioned officer who had been put forward for a sergeancy just before the outbreak of the insurgency. He and Bob worked well together, moving quietly and slowly through the vegetation, using hand signals to communicate as they approached the objective.

Both heard the voices at the same time.

The first was someone not too far away saying a few brief words. The second was garbled, clearly being transmitted over a field radio. Bob spoke into his LASH to Lieutenant Kintuba. "Goalie, this is Cool Breeze. Halt the column. Out."

He crawled forward a few meters, then recognized the area from the days he had spent in the mercenary force. It was almost the exact spot where he had exfiltrated several weeks before. He picked up the 112, speaking as quietly as possible. "Snake Doctor, this is Cool Breeze. Enemy sighted to our direct front. Seems to be an Oscar Papa. Over."

"Have they spotted you, Cool Breeze? Over."

"Not sure. Out."

INSURGENCY HEADQUARTERS

The transmission from the OP set the camp in motion. The word was passed to the various units, and all other activities came to a halt while the men rushed to their billets to grab weapons and combat vests. The mercenaries struggling at the obstacle course positively laughed aloud at the look of consternation on Commandant Dekker's face as they abandoned the torment and happily ran from the training area to the garrison. Even combat was preferable to that damned Pathway of Torture.

In less that ten minutes the entire force—indigenous and mercenary—was in place, ready to deploy to the perimeter. Commandant Dekker, now girded for combat with his AKS-74 and combat vest loaded with ammo, stood to the front of the double formation.

Karl Baroudeur was about to utter the order for the men to move out to their predesignated defensive positions when gunfire broke out to the southeast.

COMBAT

Bob Brown ducked down as the incoming rounds clipped the brush around him. He spoke into the radio: "Snake Doctor, they've spotted me. We're receiving fire. Over."

"Roger," Jonas came back. He knew the right center column's exact location. "Bring your column up on line. Out."

Bob repeated the order over the LASH, and Lieutenant Kintuba moved the fifteen men forward as skirmishers. The incoming fire was light, certainly not from a heavy concentration of defenders as the young Congolese officer took the right center column into the fight.

The insurgency force moving up to the perimeter was more than a hundred strong. Each squad had a particular place to go per their unit SOP, and they reached the spots quickly, immediately jumping into the prepared fighting positions. The Congolese mortars, already set up with firing tables prepared, were situated to the rear of the MLR.

With the Ekundu River at the rear of the garrison, Commando Nyoka and the Congolese contingent had a half-circle formation to fight from, and the layout of the defenses had been arranged to provide a maximum cross fire against any attackers. However, at this particular time, no one opened fire, since the light shooting a few meters away showed that so far there had been no serious developments in the beginning phase of the battle.

The entire counterinsurgency force was now advancing steadily toward the enemy positions in a skirmish formation. The first to make contact with the enemy's MLR was the left center column under Mack Gerhardt and Sergeant Samuel Katungo. The resistance became apparent when machine gun fire, coming in regulated bursts, was directed into their midst. The column went to the ground and began laying out overlapping fusillades in an attempt to pin down the defenders. In an instant, heavy gunfire exploded all over the area.

Lance Matoskah, his natural warrior instincts honed by the proximity of battle, moved his men forward. They spotted the enemy before the bad guys saw them, and Lance's instruction to open fire was given via his LASH. There were various good fighting spots in the brush, and the Congolese paratroopers moved toward them while sending regulated swarms of 5.56 slugs into the enemy positions.

Denis Mercier and his two partners, as with all the other men at the OPs, had withdrawn and were now with their own squads on the MLR, joining their comrades in a battle that was fast growing in intensity. Commandant Dekker, back in the CP located in the center of the curved MLR, was content to let the battle adjust into whatever it was going to become. This was not the time to make a tactical commitment one way or the other.

Any rash, unwise actions could easily open up holes in the defensive perimeter for the attackers to pour through.

The squad leaders were not verbose at that time, content to let the exchanges of fire with the attackers continue, since there seemed to be no momentum to the assault. The machine gunners on the Minimis were not wasting ammunition. Instead of shooting up the jungle in their fields of fire, they swung the muzzles of the weapons to different points, sending out short, steady bursts that evolved into cones of fire.

Carlito Grey, on the extreme right flank, loaded the M203 grenade launcher mounted on his M4 carbine. He had moved to the rear of his column's skirmish line, but remained close enough to the forward positions so that his troops were in sight. He was a little nervous about a couple of the men. These were Privates Antoine Nagatu and Lucien M'buta, who had screwed up grandly during the reconnaissance patrol under Mack Gerhardt's command. If the kids suddenly panicked, he would be short two rifles. When there are only fifteen total, that is a bit more than a small loss.

"Listen up," he said in the LASH. His assistant was an English-speaking corporal by the name of Jacques Toboku. He immediately translated the words for the benefit of the Congolese members of the column. Carlito continued. "I'm going to fire two grenades into the enemy position. As soon as they both go off, I'll yell, *'Allez,'* and we'll move forward on the double. If we run into trouble, I'll yell, *'Arrièrez.'* Pull back until I call *'Arrêtez.'* " He waited as Toboku translate the instructions. Like the other Unit operators, he had picked up some words of French and used them the best he could. Even when the grammar was fouled up, the Congolese troopers could still understand him.

Carlito had always performed excellently in handling

the M203. He could usually win a few bucks out on the
range in impromptu contests in which the minimum bet
allowed was fifty dollars. Now, in combat, he made quick
work of loading two projectiles and firing them to arc
and fall into the enemy positions.

"*Allez!*"

The line jumped forward as one man, moving toward the enemy while firing bursts from their FA-MAS
bullpup rifles. The pace forward was rapid and steady,
except for two individuals. Nagatu and M'buta, shamed
by their conduct on the recon patrol and being trussed
up in the *crapaudine*, were determined to salvage their
reputations. They ran forward as fast as they could, yelling as they worked the triggers of their weapons. Bullets
cracked around the two kids, but they ignored the danger as they continued toward the enemy MLR.

The older troopers behind them caught the spirit of
the moment. The skirmish line's progress speeded up,
and they delivered a high rate of fire as they closed in
on the defensive line. The resistance to the front melted,
and the mercenaries and Congolese insurgents on the
MLR fell back under the onslaught.

Unfortunately, the maneuver opened up the flanks
of Carlito's attack, and he quickly realized that within
moments the enemy on both sides would soon be able
to pour in murderous fusillades to blow the attack to
pieces.

"*Arrièrez!* Goddamn it, *arrièrez!*" bellowed Carlito.
"*Arrièrez!*"

The assault stopped and the men began pulling back,
still delivering devastating salvos into the enemy positions. Even Nagatu and M'buta quickly obeyed the orders. Within five minutes, everyone was back in position
with the skirmish line realigned. At the same time, the
enemy group who had been pushed back came forward
to reclaim their place on the MLR.

*   *   *

A half hour after the fighting started, it ground to a standoff with each side able to thwart the overt actions of the other. Then the first setback for Jonas Blane and the counterinsurgents occurred when mortar rounds began dropping near them. The first barrage was to the front, but it would only be a matter of time before they found the range. With no ability to conduct counterfire, Jonas ordered a withdrawal.

The pullout was conducted in the fire-and-maneuver mode, with each column covering the other as contact with the enemy was slowly but steadily broken. When the moment was right, an orderly retreat continued out of the area.

The day's work was done.

CHAPTER TWELVE

FORT GRIFFITH, MISSOURI
TOC
19 APRIL
1430 HOURS LOCAL
2030 HOURS ZULU

Colonel Tom Ryan finished reading the decoded transmission, and set the missive down on his desk. Sergeant Kayla Medwar stood to his front expectantly after delivering the news. There was an hour and a half left in which an answer could be radioed back to the OA in Africa, so the colonel didn't have to rush a response. In fact, it seemed there wouldn't be much of a reason for sending one.

Ryan sighed. "Well, the words 'decisive action' don't seem to apply here."

"Too bad about the helicopter," Kayla remarked.

"Christ! It happened three days ago," Ryan said. "That really puts a crimp in the operation, but on second thought, there isn't much going on as it is. There was that raid on the enemy supply depot. That paid off rather well with some goodies picked up and EPWs taken. But from that point on, things just ground to a halt. After that was the contact made when Brown's exfiltration from the insurgents got all screwed up, then a recon patrol where two of the Congolese took off running and a half-ass firefight broke out. Now this latest operation. What a bust!"

"You must be fair about it, sir," Kayla insisted. "Snake Doctor was making a probe to check out the potential of the enemy. He really didn't want a big showdown at this point in time. He didn't have enough intelligence to risk it."

"Two of the Congolese soldiers were killed," Ryan pointed out. "And three slightly wounded. We're not dealing in thousands of men, Sergeant. This is a conflict between dozens and every casualty is a big loss. Particularly when nothing was gained by the incident."

"I'm certain there must have been KIAs and WIAs on the other side as well," Kayla said. "So things will even out in the end. The scales might even have gotten tipped in our favor."

"Yeah," Ryan said. "I'm going to have to call in Munger and that State Department wimp and bring 'em up-to-date. Naturally they'll want to know about the public relations aspect of things. I'll come up with something to keep 'em satisfied. I hope."

"Good luck on that, sir," Kayla said. "Do you want to transmit anything back to Snake Doctor?"

Ryan shook his head. "Just tell Snake Doctor that Blue Iguana says to 'carry on.'"

"Yes, sir."

Ryan watched her leave the office, then turned to the training schedule. The Second Team was slated for the Shooting House first thing in the morning. That should break up the monotony of life in Fort Griffith.

Peter Luknore, the former legionnaire rebel, OAS terrorist, and arms dealer, had arrived in style to begin the mercenary recruiting campaign for which General Philippe Dubois had hired him.

When it came to traveling, Luknore did not like to fly. This was not because of any fear of airplanes; after all he had held a *brevet militaire de parachutiste* in the Legion. It was the crowds and inconvenience of air travel that annoyed him in his old age. Also, there were probes and questions at times in airports, which included lists of names of people to detain for questioning or arrest. This concerned the old man since his original name, Legion name, and a half dozen aliases were well documented by Interpol. Thus Luknore's background was the sort that invariably attracted attention from security and police organizations. Therefore, instead of using available airlines, he had been driven down from his chalet in Switzerland to southern France in his 1995 Lincoln Towncar limousine by his chauffeur, Vincent. The old gentleman was also accompanied by his valet, Farouk, and personal secretary, Watson. The latter employee had seen to it that his boss had a reserved suite in the excellent Hotel Sofitel Vieux-Port. It cost a thousand Euros a day but Luknore would still make a profit signing up mercenaries for Dubois. He would have done it for nothing, since the work offered some amusement to break the boredom of a tedious though luxurious retirement. And he could do something good with the money, when all was said and done. There was a benevolent and gentle side to the ancient reprobate that few people knew about.

Watson rented a small office on the waterfront and hired a young girl to act as a receptionist. The place had two rooms and a half-bath of a toilet, sink, and the inevitable European necessity of a bidet to clean one's arse after bowel movements. The inner office would be for interviews, and some tasteful, comfortable furniture was purchased to make it as pleasant as possible.

The word had been sent out to the right connections regarding the employment being offered in that little storefront in Marseille. But for the present, there was nothing left to do but wait for applicants to present themselves. For those who proved satisfactory, and most of them should have no trouble with their qualifications, contracts would be offered and arrangements made to transport them to Commando Nyoka far away in the Democratic Republic of the Congo.

D.R. OF THE CONGO
OPERATIONAL AREA
20 APRIL
1100 HOURS LOCAL
0900 HOURS ZULU

The four-man reconnaissance patrol moved toward the dirt road that led up to the government checkpoint. The site had been attacked and wiped out by mercenaries a little more than two weeks earlier, and today's mission objective was to find out if it had been reestablished.

Corporal Jacques Tobuku was on point with Carlito Grey directly behind him. Bringing up the rear were the two vindicated Congolese soldiers: Privates Antoine Nagatu and Lucien M'buta. The pair had proven their courage during the attack on the insurgent camp the day before when they had recklessly risked their lives in a courageous charge straight into enemy fire. By all rights they should have been shot to pieces, but luck had been with them. When the counterinsurgents broke contact, the two were hale and hearty, rejoicing in the accolades shouted at them by the paratroopers after the return to the base camp. The fiasco of the recon patrol and the agony of the *crapaudine* were forgotten by all concerned.

"Halt," came Tobuku's voice over the LASH. "I have found where the helicopter crashed."

"Okay," Carlito said. "We're moving up."

The patrol's mission wasn't to locate the downed aircraft, but the fact they had stumbled across it required an investigation. Within minutes the two young soldiers were on security while Carlito and Tobuku looked the wreckage over. There was no doubt the crash had been fiery. Every surviving inch of the SA.330 was scorched and the paint bubbled and cracked.

At first no human remains could be found until Tobuku sighted a skull a few meters away. The two men walked over to it, then saw another along with some bones in the brush. "Wild animals dragged them over here," the Congolese corporal said.

"From the scratches on the ground, it seems there was some squabbling between the diners," Carlito observed. "Damn! It's a hell of a way for good men like Bhutan and Montka to go."

Tobuku squatted down and studied the ground, noting some tracks. "Leopards."

"If you say so," Carlito said. "I'm not up on African animals. I suppose we should bury the bones, huh? It's the least we can do."

Tobuku shook his head. "They would just be dug up. Marrow is a food. You can see that several have already been bitten in two and the interiors sucked out."

Carlito got his GPS out to make a note of the exact location for his mission AAR. With that done, he got the patrol moving again toward its objective.

MELILLA, SPANISH MOROCCO
PETRÓLEO ESPAÑOL-AFRICANO, S.A.
CORPORATE HEADQUARTERS
21 APRIL

Philippe Dubois, Major General, French Army, retired, sat in the outer room waiting to be called inside to
meet with the Marshals of the Consortium. There was a
wet bar with an offering of excellent alcoholic and non-
alcoholic drinks available for those using the facility. A
humidor with expensive cigars and a smaller box with
gold-tipped cigarettes of Turkish tobacco were also ac-
cessible. Dubois, as was typical of the man, had no desire
for refreshments. He ate when he was hungry and drank
when he was thirsty. He might take an occasional cock-
tail to be sociable, but never overdid it.

The general was a walking, talking, living anachronism,
and he made no apology about it. At the age of seventy-
five, he had seen France's colonial days fade away during his youth, and Dubois longed to return to that past
glory when only Great Britain's possessions surpassed
those of the French Republic. Of course it would be a
European Empire thanks to the Consortium, but that
was good enough for the general.

He was from a privileged family engaged in imports
and exports, but he went for a military career rather than
merchandising. He graduated from Saint-Cyr, the West
Point of France, in 1953 at the top of his class, and followed the example of generations of honor graduates by
choosing as his first posting the famous French Foreign
Legion. After the course at the Airborne Troops School
in Pau, he was shipped directly to the First Foreign Parachute Battalion in Indo-China, where a Communist revolution had raged since the end of World War II.

Sous-Lieutenant Dubois' arrival coincided with the
outbreak of the Battle of Dien Bien Phu, an ill-fated operation that was doomed to become a debacle in French

military history. With only the barest of orientations, the young officer was outfitted for combat, then put aboard a C-47 transport aircraft to parachute into combat with others who had volunteered to join the fight. The result is in the history books: the French were defeated and the survivors, which included Dubois, were marched off to the hell of Communist POW camps. He had left France in April of 1954 a hale and hearty 185 pounds, and returned in September 1954 a thin, exhausted ex-POW weighing in at 125 pounds.

The loss of French Indo-China had hit Dubois hard. He pictured the eventual demise of the old Empire, and when he returned to duty in Algeria in 1955, he volunteered for the *Paras Coloniales*—the Colonial Paratroopers—who were fighting indigenous rebels trying to win self-government. Once again Dubois, now a captain, was in for a crushing disappointment. In July 1962, Algeria was granted its independence by the French government, and the professional soldiers of the nation's Army felt betrayed and abandoned. They had fought bravely, sacrificed their lives, and were close to handing the rebels a decisive defeat. Many of the officers and NCOs decided to mount a putsch to turn the situation around, and deal a veritable death blow to President Charles de Gaulle.

When the OAS was formed to mount a counterrevolution, Captain Dubois was about to make a commitment to the organization, but he was contacted by an old family friend—a certain M. Jean-Paul Fubert, an important figure in the French banking community. Fubert urged him not to become part of a doomed terrorist group; and it was at this time that Philippe Dubois first heard of the Consortium. He was encouraged to return obediently to France and continue his army career in an honorable manner, and when the time was right, he would be called to serve not only the glory of France, but the glory of a neocolonialism movement to establish an empire for

modern Europe. After some deep reflection, the officer
saw the logic in the movement, and agreed to do as he
had been advised. He was shipped back to metropolitan
France to continue his military career. Meanwhile, he
was knighted a *chevalier* in the secret organization.

When *Général de Division* Philippe Dubois retired
from the army in the spring of 1978, he had gained the
position of Chief of Operations and Planning on the
General Staff. His peers considered the veteran officer a
master in the administration and application of strategic
and tactical matters in both conventional and unconven-
tional warfare. It was at this time that he was elevated
to the title of *chevalier-commandant* of the Consortium.

0845 HOURS LOCAL
0745 HOURS ZULU

The inner door opened and a security man stepped
into the waiting room. He said nothing to Dubois,
but his invitation to pass through the portal was clear
enough. The general stood up, grasping his briefcase, and
walked into the adjoining chamber. The marshals of the
Consortium's highest staff echelon—Jean-Paul Fubert,
Francisco Valverde, Pietro D'Amiteri, and Heinrich
Müller-Koenig—greeted their visitor with slight smiles
and nods from their seats around the teakwood table.
All had their usual cognacs and cigars as they waited
for Dubois to take the empty chair waiting for him. A
glass of the liquor with a cigar had been set down for
the general's pleasure. The others in the room were not
surprised that he ignored them.

"Good morning, gentlemen," Dubois said. "I believe
we are all aware of the purpose of my visit: an update on
Operation Griffe in the Belgian Congo." He opened the
briefcase and pulled out his customary manila folder.
After opening it, he gave a quick glance at the top page

of the papers, then began speaking. "The first item to report is that the Commando Nyoka is in excellent shape. The officers and volunteers are well trained, prepared, and equipped for the job ahead." He paused. "There was an attack on the garrison of the commando two days ago. I am happy to report that all security SOPs were in force at the time, and after a short fight, the assault was broken up and the enemy withdrew."

"Were there any casualties?" Müller-Koenig asked.

"Three native soldiers were killed and one wounded," Dubois said. "One mercenary was slightly wounded. I have been informed that he has been restored to full duty. As of this moment the commando numbers one hundred and thirty-four officers and volunteers. The strength of the native contingent remains at around a hundred."

"What about the new recruiting effort?" Fubert asked.

"An office has been set up in Marseille," Dubois said. "M. Luknore is well established and ready to receive applications. There is a small airport on the outskirts of the city that can accommodate the corporate transport aircraft. The volunteers will be flown to the company site in Gabon for trucking to the garrison in the Belgian Congo."

"How are our supply inventories?" Pietro D'Amiteri asked.

"There are no shortages at this time," Dubois reported. "In fact, we have enough surplus that even with the expected influx of new volunteers, there will be no problems about running short."

"Does that include all logistical classifications?" Müller-Koenig asked.

"Affirmative," Dubois replied. "Clothing, field gear, fuel, rations, weaponry, munitions—everything."

"And when is the 'Big Push'?" Fubert asked.

"The twenty-fifth of April," Dubois answered. "We

expect to have the commando at full strength and ready to take the initial steps in making the Belgian Congo ours."

"I have a suggestion," Jean-Paul Fubert said. "Rather than refer to the country as the Belgian Congo, I feel we should redesignate it the European Congo."

A unanimous agreement was quickly voiced, and Valverde raised his cognac. "To the European Congo and victory!"

Everyone answered the toast, and even Dubois picked up his glass.

CHAPTER THIRTEEN

Bob Brown was on the northwest bank of the Ekundu River, heavily camouflaged with black and green paint streaked across his face. He gazed into the insurgency garrison through binoculars, taking his time in observing the activities of the troops. Lance Matoskah lay beside him, taking a break after his stint of keeping the enemy area under surveillance. Back behind them, on a basic, no-frills security perimeter, Sergeant Samuel Katungo and Corporals Gabriel Mantuka and Jacques Tobuku maintained a two-on-one-off lookout that had been going on for almost four hours. At that particular moment it was Mantuka who napped while the other two stayed awake.

The surveillance mission had been a follow-up reaction of the attack on the enemy site three days earlier.

Jonas Blane had come away from the fight with two lessons learned, i.e., the counterinsurgency force of Unit operators and Congolese paratroopers was too small at that particular time to be able to take the enemy camp by storm; and any successful attack would have to come from the opposite direction. Thus, he had sent the five-man recon out to check out the feasibility of mounting an assault across the river and hitting them in the rear.

Bob Brown had reported Dekker's obstacle course with one part where the participants went into the river, going over to the other side to climb logs up to the bank. They also recrossed the waterway to get back to the garrison at that point. It was vital that Jonas and Captain Tshobutu be made aware of the potential to get from one side of the river to the other. And there was also great importance in finding out if it was possible to safely withdraw and/or break contact with the enemy if the situation deteriorated into a defeat.

When Bob and Lance had reached the river earlier that morning, they were glad to find that the obstacle course wasn't being used. The area was unoccupied as the pair eased down to the riverbank and explored it on both sides of the log barrier. Unfortunately, the fordable area was only twenty meters wide. Beyond that, the water was too deep to cross except in boats, and the banks were extremely steep on both sides. It would hardly provide a safe place to cross the waterway in an attack if the raiders had to funnel themselves down into a narrow formation at that initial point. A couple of machine guns could literally massacre them almost at leisure.

The second phase of the mission was to put the garrison under observation for a period of three to four hours to get a determination of the enemy strength. Bob had known there were more than a hundred mercenaries in the place, but he had never been sure of the number of Congo insurgents. There was not much fraternization between the Europeans and the Africans even though they were supposedly on the same side, so it was rare when he actually made contact with the Congolese during his period of infiltration.

As he perused the mercenary area, Bob caught sight of a familiar figure. It took a moment before he recognized Léon M'kalo the traveling peddler he had first seen after they knocked off the army roadblock. The little guy seemed quite at ease in the surroundings, and it was obvious this wasn't his first visit.

By now Bob and Lance had spent a leisurely three and a half hours watching the activity and working out a guestimate of how many indigenous troops were in the group. Both had taken notice of such things as how many pots of food were taken from the kitchen to the barracks; various fatigue details attending to the routine camp chores; the number of troops assigned to the nearest two billets; and various other activities.

Bob put the binoculars down and shook Lance. Lance rolled over on his stomach. "You done?"

"Yep," Bob replied. "I'm thinking there's between ninety to maybe a hundred and ten Congolese."

Lance's estimate was a little higher than Bob's. "I'm gonna say about a hundred and twenty-five Africans."

"You might be counting some of the mercenaries' servants," Bob said.

"Nope," Lance replied. "I only took notice of guys in uniforms."

"Okay," Bob said. "It's better to report too many than too few. Let's take your estimate."

"I guess that's that then," Lance said. "Shall we go?"

They left the riverbank and went down to their three Congolese comrades-in-arms. After forming up, the patrol began the trek back to their home camp.

Jonas Blane and Captain Edouard Tshobutu sat at the table in the latter's hut, sipping coffee. They had received an oral report from Bob Brown and Lance Matoskah on their reconnaissance, and now were into a discussion about the situation.

"It was most interesting about that peddler," Tshobutu said. "No doubt he is a spy. That is a situation that must be taken care of as quickly as possible."

"I'll leave that up to you," Jonas said. "It will be better for a Congolese to grab him than one of us." He paused to take a sip of coffee. "What is your estimate of the tactical situation?"

"A rear attack is definitely out," Tshobutu remarked, "unless we wanted to fire into the camp from the far bank."

"They would only return fire," Jonas pointed out. "And there are those mortars too."

"We have the exact same type."

"It would take our crews almost half an hour to get them set up and zeroed in on the objective," Jonas argued. "That was one reason we had to bug out the other day. They were already set up to saturate our positions with barrages. We would have lasted fifteen minutes. I'm sure they've got the other side of the river marked down on their range cards too."

"We also have to take into account that we are probably outnumbered at close to three to one."

"Yeah," Jonas said. "That's another great big problem. And we sure as hell can't get any reinforcements."

"Too bad none of the EPWs will join us," Tshobutu said.

"They're beginning to be a burden," Jonas complained. "Those twelve losers handle all the camp work details, but they're in the way."

"The solution to that would be a mass execution," Tshobutu said.

"We're not at that point yet," Jonas pointed out.

Tshobutu drummed his fingers on the table. "What to do? What to do?"

Jonas was thoughtful for a moment. He got to his feet and walked to the entrance of the hut, looking out over the camp scene. "Y'know something? We're reduced to only one option: hit and run. Real guerrilla-warfare stuff."

"We can't do that very well since we lost the helicopter," Tshobutu said. "You can't move very fast pushing your way through the jungle."

Jonas didn't say anything for a moment until Carlito Grey came strolling past the hut. "Hey, Carlito!"

"Yeah, boss?"

"You were in one of those LA street gangs before you joined up, weren't you?"

"Affirmative, boss. The Byz Lats."

"Did you steal any cars?"

Carlito frowned. "Hey, that was a while back. The statute of limitations has run out."

"Okay," Jonas said. "But do you still remember how to hotwire a vehicle?"

"Sure," Carlito said. "It's like learning to ride a bicycle. You never forget how."

"Do you think you might be able to steal some trucks around here?"

Carlito laughed. "Have you seen those jalopies, boss? We'd have to overhaul 'em before we could do any serious hotwiring."

"I don't mean civilian trucks. I'm talking about military ones."

"You don't have to hotwire army vehicles, boss. They have ignition switches. Just jump in and turn 'em on."

"That's right," Jonas said. "I forgot."

"Anything else, boss?"

"Nope. I'll talk to you later."

Delmar Munger and Booker Cartwright strolled slowly across the main post toward the officers' club. Munger was smiling smugly to the point of almost chuckling. "What did you think of that line of crap, Booker?"

"You mean Colonel Ryan's report?"

"That's what I'm talking about," Munger said. They had just left the colonel's office after receiving a briefing on the situation in the Congolese OA.

"Well," Cartwright said, "it seems things have almost come to a complete stop."

"He's sweetening up spoiled milk as much as he can," Munger said. "They're losing their asses over there. Getting whipped! And he once again skirted the subject of winning over the populace to our side."

"I did notice you didn't press the issue."

"Right," Munger said. "After you've been around these army assholes for as long as I have, you'll learn to read their little minds like a book. He's hoping like hell the situation won't completely deteriorate, because he knows if those Unit cowboys of his come out of Africa with their tails between their legs, the Unit will be between a rock and a hard place."

"I see," Cartwright said. "It will just make things that much worse for them."

"Now you're catching on, my friend," Munger said. "They'll have failed the mission in two very fatal ways. The insurrection over there will end up putting in a government unfriendly to the good ol' USA and part of the reason will be not only because the Unit was whipped, but also because they failed to conduct an effective program to convince the people that we were the good guys. In fact, I'll bet anything we'll have atrocities to lay on them. Oh, man! Won't the Senate Committee on Intelligence and Special Operations eat up that good news! Senator Herbert Kinkaid is the chairman, and he hates Ryan and his pirates almost as much as I do."

"Well, Delmar, it would appear things are going our way,"

"Indeed they are, Booker," Munger said. "C'mon! I'll treat us to drinks over at the officers' club."

D.R. OF THE CONGO
CAMP UKAIDI
23 APRIL
0330 HOURS LOCAL
0130 HOURS ZULU

Mack Gerhardt and Carlito Grey were on the far side of the road from the motor pool. They could see the SAMIL cargo trucks parked neatly in rows, gleaming in the illumination from the moon that was well into its descent. Behind them were Bob Brown and Lance Matoskah with a quartet of Congolese paratroopers who knew how to drive military vehicles.

Carlito noted that there was no gate in the fence around the area, and that there was only one guard standing forlornly at the entrance. "They ain't much on security, are they?"

"Nope," Mack replied. "Cap'n Tshobutu said that the knowledge of how to operate a motor vehicle is considered quite a skill out here in the boondocks. There ain't too many folks as know how to drive. So they don't have to worry about anybody trying to boost their trucks."

"They do now," Carlito said with a grin.

"No kidding," Mack commented. He turned and gestured for Lance to join him. As soon as he did, Mack whispered in his ear. "See that guard? Take him out."

Lance wordlessly handed his M-4 to Mack and pulled his K-Bar from its scabbard. He crouched and moved silently across the road, sticking to the shadows of the nearby trees. This was a natural thing for him; instinctive skills in sneaking and peeking had been passed down to him through the genes of countless generations of plains warrior ancestors.

The sentry, standing his post in the dark, was also the scion of warriors and hunters. Before he joined the Congolese National Army a few weeks back, he had lived in an isolated village where all food had to be hunted down and killed, except for what was grown or gathered by women and girls. Also quarrels with other hamlets in the area had led to bloodshed on many occasions. And, as Lance's ancestral skills had kicked in, so had the young African's. He spotted the movement of someone easing toward him. Since he was in an unknown place with no friends close by, he did what his instincts told him to do in such a case.

He hauled ass, running from his post out to the road, before turning north. Lance stopped in surprise watching the guy disappear into the night. Then he looked over at Mack and shrugged. Mack shook his head in wonderment, then led the other five men over to the entrance of the motor pool.

"Everybody pick out a truck and climb into the cab," Mack said. "As soon as you hear me start mine, then hit them switches. We'll move out of here as slow and quiet as possible. The billets seem to be over on the other side of the woods there, so maybe they won't hear us."

"I hope them trucks are gassed up," Bob remarked.

"They should be," Mack said. "Do you know of any army where they don't top off at the end of the duty day so they can roll out fast the next morning if they have to?"

"I can't recall one at the moment," Bob replied.

"Neither can I," Mack remarked. "So let's go!"

The six cargo trucks rolled into camp and came to a dusty halt beside Captain Tshobutu's hut. A swath in the trees by the road five kilometers away had been cut by a crew of the EPWs under the stern supervision of Sub-lieutenant Kintuba and Sergeant Katungo the evening before. Then the prisoners were sat down to wait under the guns of the guards. As soon as the trucks had appeared several hours later, the EPWs were ushered into the opening to close it up. All tracks and evidence of the work were quickly concealed.

The haul had been impressive and ended with a happy surprise. The last four vehicles driven by the paratroopers had each been loaded with sixty 20-liter jerry cans of fuel. That came to a grand total of 4,800 liters of gasoline or a bit more than 1,200 gallons weighing down the trucks.

"God!" Mack exclaimed with a laugh. "No goddamn wonder them four guys couldn't get any speed up. I thought they was either the worst drivers in the world or they'd picked up some trucks in need of a complete overhaul."

Jonas wasn't in a mood to celebrate. "Let's get those vehicles into the trees. The last thing we need is to have somebody—anybody—fly over and spot 'em. And have that fuel unloaded and stashed in a different area. If something sets it off, I don't want a fiery explosion here in the middle of our darling base camp."

Kintuba and Katungo set the EPWs back to work.

THE ROAD TO MWITUKIJIJI
0900 HOURS LOCAL
0700 HOURS ZULU

M. Léon M'kalo eased back on the throttle of his
three-wheeler when he saw the strange sight of a lone
soldier walking down the road. He slowly drove up to
the guy, then gave him an unabashed look of astonish-
ment. A greeting in French got no response from the
young guy except for a scowl. So M'kalo switched to
Swahili. *"Shikamoo, Askari."*

"Shikamoo, Bwana," the soldier replied.

"What are you doing out here all by yourself?" M'kalo
asked, slowing down to match the soldier's walking speed.

"I ran away from the Army," the soldier said. "Now I
am afraid to go back. They will punish me."

"It was not wise to run away," M'kalo said. "They will
find you someday and put you in prison. What made you
leave?"

"I was on guard duty and somebody tried to sneak up
on me. So I ran as fast as I could."

"Where did this happen?"

"At Camp Ukaidi at the place where the trucks are
kept," the soldier said. "I looked back once and saw
some white men with African soldiers. Then I was really
scared. A few minutes later I had to jump off the road
and hide in the trees. Then some trucks went past me. I
think those men stole them."

M'kalo wondered if they had been mercenaries and
Congolese from the force commanded by *le général* Baroudeur. Or perhaps they were the men Baroudeur was
fighting. Either way, this could be important information
worth a few Euros.

"I know a safe place for you. It is with Europeans
and Congolese soldiers. They are not the same ones you
saw last night. They will not harm you. They will protect
you."

The soldier shook his head. "I have no money to pay you to take me anywhere."

"That is all right," M'kalo assured him. "I do not need money. And the people I told you about will be interested in what happened to you. They will want to find out all about it. You can join their Army. They are very nice fellows."

The boy considered the proposition. At that moment in time, he was alone, lost, friendless, and a fugitive. Any alternative would improve his situation. "I will go."

"Get up behind me," M'kalo invited.

Within moments they sped off. The peddler took a turn at Mwitukijiji, heading for the Ekundu River and Mercenary Headquarters.

CHAPTER FOURTEEN

D.R. OF THE CONGO
MERCENARY HEADQUARTERS
23 APRIL
1030 HOURS LOCAL
0830 HOURS ZULU

The young soldier was visibly nervous as he sat in the chair located to the front of General Karl Baroudeur's desk. Colonel Vlad Krashchenko stood off to the side, as was his usual custom, casting a suspicious eye on the kid. A sketchy report of the events at the Camp Ukaidi motor pool had been given to the two top-ranking men of the mercenary force by Léon M'kalo. Now the soldier, who identified himself as Private Jean Kichangu, had Baroudeur's full attention, with M'kalo standing by to act as interpreter.

"Did you recognize any of the men who stole the trucks?" Baroudeur asked.

Jean's answer in Swahili was translated into French by M'kalo. "No, *Bwana.* They were strangers. Some were

Europeans like yourself while others were Congolese. All were soldiers and carried rifles."

"What sort of rifles?"

"I do not know, *Bwana*. I have not been long in the Army."

"Did the uniforms of the white men look like mine?"

Jean shrugged apologetically. "It was dark. Maybe so. Maybe not. I think they had spots on them like yours though."

"What about the Congolese?"

"They were soldiers like me," Jean answered. "But I do not think they were from my battalion. Their uniforms were a little different. I think. They wore red berets, so maybe they were paratroopers."

"And what did they do?" Baroudeur asked.

"One of the Europeans tried to sneak up on me, but I saw him in the shadows. So I ran away down the road. A little while later I heard trucks coming, and it scared me, so I hid in the brush. When they passed me, I could see the drivers in the lights. They were the same men."

Baroudeur exchanged a glance with Krashchenko, then looked back at Jean. "How many trucks did they steal?"

"I do not know, *Bwana*," Jean answered with an apology. "*Ninasikitika.*"

Baroudeur knew he had gotten every bit of information out of the untrained rookie that was possible at the moment. Now was the time to approach the situation from a different angle. "You left your post without permission. If you go back to the Army, they will punish you."

Krashchenko interjected, "They will shoot you as a deserter."

"I must hide," Jean said fearfully. "I did not know what to do when the man tried to sneak up on me. Now I feel lost."

"You can join our Congolese force," Baroudeur said.

"We are going to take over the nation and set up a new government. If you fight on our side you will not be shot. You will be a hero. And get a lot of money too. Would you like to fight with our soldiers?"

Jean smiled hopefully. *"Ndiyo, Bwana! Ahsante sana!"*

"Excellent," Baroudeur said. He turned his attention to M'kalo. "Take him over to the native headquarters and introduce him. They can assign him to a squad."

"Yes, *mon général*," M'kalo said enthusiastically. "I hope I did right by bringing this soldier to you. I apologize because he did not know very much."

"He knew enough," Baroudeur said. The last thing he wanted to do was discourage the spy from providing information, no matter how trivial it might be.

Krashchenko stepped forward and handed fifty Euros to the man. M'kalo took Jean by the arm and led him out of the hut. The colonel glanced over at Baroudeur. "What do you think?"

"It would appear that our enemy has gotten a few trucks," Baroudeur said. "I am not too concerned about it. They will have trouble keeping them fueled. The bastards will find it impossible to use army fuel depots so they will be spending half their time trying to figure ways to keep the tanks filled."

"Perhaps they will rob service stations," Krashchenko remarked.

Baroudeur laughed. "There are not that many around here. The first time they do it, the *gendarmerie* will be out looking for them."

"Indeed," Krashchenko agreed. "And speaking of the police, we have big doings in forty-eight hours."

"That we do," Baroudeur remarked. "I think it will be like D-Day in World War Two. Within seventy-two hours the entire nation will know the government is about to fall. The initial success should swell our ranks of native soldiers. Then we shall hunt down those miserable gnats who have been biting at our arses and be rid of them."

"I wish we knew exactly who they were," Krashchen-ko said.

"It will not matter after tomorrow."

Krashchenko checked his watch. "I believe I will go and see how Commandant Dekker is doing in getting the mercenaries prepared."

"And I will call on Lulombe, so see if he and his monkeys are getting ready."

THE CITY OF MJIKUBWA
25 APRIL
0830 HOURS LOCAL
0630 HOURS ZULU

The convoy of trucks roared into the city limits, speeding through the streets as each group of vehicles split up to hit their objectives. Two trucks of mercenaries went directly to the *gendarmerie* headquarters, coming to a squeaky halt in front of the building. They immediately unassed the truck with ten of the men surrounding the place while the other fifteen stormed into the interior. There were no formalities as the group crashed through the front door. The shocked duty sergeant was hit by a chestful of fire bursts that blasted him out of his chair to smash against the wall behind him.

Other raiders moved into the interior, knowing exactly where they were going. Four more *gendarmes* died in an office down the hall while the chief's door was kicked in. The officer, who had just leaped to his feet to respond to the shooting, was met head-on by Comman-dant Paul Dekker, who shot him point-blank in the face. While the boss cop was being taken out, another group had reached the portal that led to the cells. They tried to force an entry, but the guards behind the barrier were not about to open it. The two policemen didn't know what was going on, except that a lot of shooting and yell-

ing could be heard, and they were not about to expose
themselves to any danger.

Dekker joined the men stymied at the door, bellowing
for them to get out of the hall and back into the office.
He twisted out the pin on an F1 fragmentation grenade,
then rolled it to the doorway. The resulting explosion
knocked the door off its hinges, and Dekker charged it
to deliver a vicious kick to the badly damaged portal. It
gave way and the entry was open. He rushed into the
cell block shooting, not as much as blinking at the frantically aimed pistol shots fired at him by the guards. They
collapsed under the ex-legionnaires' salvos, sprawling to
the floor. Now a half dozen other mercenaries crowded
into the lockup area. The invaders were all European,
and the African prisoners in the cells were not quite
sure what was going on. One gave a halfhearted cheer,
then quickly shut up when scowls greeted his outburst.

Dekker didn't hesitate. These were scum: petty thieves,
thugs, and brawlers. He methodically pumped fire bursts
into each cell, killing all the inmates. With that done, the
commandant led the other mercenaries back through
the building to the trucks outside. Now their job was to
prowl the streets and shoot down any other *gendarmes*
they came across.

City hall was the target for two more squads of mercenaries assisted by a team of Congolese. This group
was led by Colonel Vlad Krashchenko, and it was not
to be a massacre as what happened at the *gendarmerie*
headquarters. They were after a particular prisoner, and
ignored the offices where bureaucrats sat at word pro-
cessors. Krashchenko raced down the hall looking for
his main objective. The sounds of shooting at the police
station had been heard by the people in the building,
and most just sat at their work stations, stunned and
confused by the deafening events.

Krashchenko found what he was looking for at a door

bearing a sign in French: MAIRE DE VILLE. He led a group of six mercenaries into the mayor's office. The man had his back to the door, looking out the window, trying to see what the hell was going on. He turned and saw the armed Europeans glaring at him. Mayor Hubert K'blutu was not a cowardly man. He glared back at the foreign intruders, demanding, "*Qu'est-ce que c'est indignation?* What is this outrage?"

"Never mind, Your Honor," Krashchenko said. "You are coming with me." He grabbed the man's arm and gave him a vicious tug.

Mayor K'blutu just as viciously jerked himself free. "I am not going anywhere with you, gangster!"

Krashchenko motioned to a couple of the mercenaries behind him. They rushed the city official, pinning his arms behind his back, then pushed him out the door and into the hallway. He fought back as best he could, kicking, twisting, and trying to ram his captors with his head. But the tough young freebooters were too much for the small, middle-aged African man.

The local television station had already been taken over and shut down by yet another assault team. While that was being taken care of, Baroudeur led the assault on the radio station with Major General Marcel Lulombe on his heels. The ratio between radios and TV sets ran at about twenty to one in favor of the former, so more people could be reached over wireless sets.

Here, as at city hall, a group of surprised and unarmed civilians was overwhelmed by speed, force, and threats. The engineer in the sound booth, with a pistol shoved against his neck, kept the station on the air as he was instructed to do. The announcer in front of the microphone, however, was pulled out of the room and sent sprawling in the hallway. A mercenary, caught up in the spirit of the situation, delivered a hard kick to the man's ribs. The unfortunate announcer, who had just been delivering a commercial for a local shoe shop, crawled away.

At that point, Lulombe sat down in front of a microphone in the broadcasting booth. After clearing his throat, he began his practiced spiel.

"People of Mjikubwa, I am *Général de Division* Marcel Lulombe of the National Revolutionary Army. Within the last half hour we have liberated the city, arrested the mayor, and neutralized the *gendarmerie* headquarters. We of the ARN are now in control of not only the metropolis, but also the province. We ask you to remain calm as we establish ourselves as the legal government. Any resistance to us will be immediately crushed without mercy."

Now Krashchenko and his men appeared, dragging Mayor K'blutu down the hall to the broadcast booth. The mayor was handed a typed-up paper by Baroudeur, who spoke to him in a firm, tone of serious warning. "You are to read this statement to your people, Your Honor."

K'blutu refused to take the paper. "I demand to know who you are."

"We are the new government," Baroudeur said.

"You are a damned European!" K'blutu snapped. "How dare you insinuate you are the new rulers of the Democratic Republic of the Congo?"

Baroudeur grabbed the smaller man by the collar of his shirt and pulled him over to the glass in the booth. "Look in there. That is General Lulombe your new president."

"I have heard of Lulombe," K'blutu said. "He is an army hooligan, unfit to have power over even a gang of miserable sneak thieves."

"You can take that up with the general," Baroudeur growled. "But you will read that paper over the radio as soon as Lulombe finishes his speech."

Now K'blutu scanned the words. "I will not read this propaganda to the citizens of Mjikubwa."

Baroudeur pulled his pistol. "If you refuse to do as I say, I will kill you."

The African spat in the European's face. "Then kill me and may God damn you for it."

A pull on the trigger, and the bullet split the mayor's forehead, blowing out the back of his skull. Baroudeur fixed his eyes on Krashchenko. "Go back to city hall and bring me the deputy mayor."

"*À vos ordres, mon général!*"

1100 HOURS LOCAL
0900 HOURS ZULU

People had now begun to appear on the streets as the firing died down. They did not rush out like someone going to a soccer match or parade; they moved slowly and cautiously, staying close to their homes and downtown buildings as more and more soldiers began to appear. The sight of the armed Europeans caused a special kind of dread, and many spectators now changed their minds about being outside. They prudently moved indoors to gaze out the windows of shops and houses at the goings-on.

A dead *gendarme* lay on a street corner, his blood draining into the gutter. The policeman had gone down fighting, and his pistol lay next to an outstretched hand. A couple of mercenaries stood close by, keeping their eyes on what went on around them, their AKS-74 rifles locked and loaded for any counterrevolutionary action. A young guttersnipe, skulking in a nearby alley, had his eye on the dead man's valuable pistol. He suddenly made a dash for it, but one of the Europeans caught the sudden movement in the corner of his eye. He spun around, quickly firing. The fire burst was one of six rounds, and all hit the skinny kid, twisting him into a heap, almost cut in two.

Now the Congolese soldiers of the insurgency began to make appearances as their initial missions were accomplished. They too kept the immediate area under surveillance, ready to respond to any act of hostility directed toward them. Most of the populace was also maintaining an alert observation of the commotion in their neighborhoods, not out of inquisitiveness, but to be ready to flee if more violence flared. All had seen corpses of the *gendarmerie* sprawled in various places, and knew that law and order was no longer an option.

When the radio broadcast of Lulombe's proclamation was made, it was recorded as was the message read by the deputy mayor. The latter gentleman had been shocked when two mercenaries dragged him from city hall down to the radio station. The sight of Mayor K'blutu's corpse with its shattered cranium was evidence enough that there was nothing to be gained by resisting the revolutionaries. He took the paper that the mayor had refused, and read a statement informing the public to remain calm and obey whatever they were told to do by the occupying force. The message the official delivered stated they were representatives of the new government, and would soon be the legitimate rulers of the Democratic Republic of the Congo.

When the news of Mayor K'blutu's death reached the populace, a wave of regret and grief swept through the city. He was a decent man who owned a clothing store, and gave liberal credit to his customers, and he was understanding to those who fell behind in their payments.

COUNTERINSURGENCY BASE CAMP
1145 HOURS LOCAL
0945 HOURS ZULU

All the officers and noncommissioned officers of the counterinsurgency force were gathered at Captain Edouard Tshobutu's headquarters hut. There were so many that most stood outside. The radio was on and they listened to the recorded messages of General Lulombe and the deputy mayor of Mjikubwa.

Tshobutu, inside at his desk, shook his head slowly. "They have made their move."

"Indeed they have," Jonas Blane agreed. He was thoughtful for a moment. "Do you think it's premature?"

Tshobutu shrugged. "They are hoping this action will bring more of the National Army to their side."

Carlito Grey, sitting nearby on the floor, asked, "How's that gonna affect us, boss?"

"It's hard to tell at this point, Carlito," Jonas replied. "If the entire Army goes for the insurgency, we'll be outnumbered, outclassed, and out of luck."

"Well!" Bob Brown said. "This sucks, doesn't it?"

"They'll be pretty busy consolidating their gains," Mack Gerhardt pointed out. "This thing just started rolling this morning."

"Yeah," Lance Matoskah said. "It'll take 'em a few days to increase their command and control in the occupied area. They'll be busy expanding too."

"Mmm," Jonas mused. "I'm thinking of an old saying: 'The mice will play while the cat's away.' "

The four other Unit operators exchanged glances among themselves. "Y'know what I think?" Mack said. "I'm thinking the boss has something definite on his mind."

"Yeah," Carlito said. "And I'll bet next month's pay call it'll be bad news for somebody."

Bob Brown smirked. "Yeah! Probably us."

CHAPTER FIFTEEN

D.R. OF THE CONGO
OPERATIONAL AREA
26 APRIL
0215 HOURS LOCAL
0015 HOURS ZULU

The truck with a couple of paratroopers acting as guards had been left five kilometers back on the road as the two teams—one for combat and the other for security—moved quietly down the bucolic thoroughfare along the edge of the jungle. All nine men had the advantage of AN/PVS-21 night-vision goggles as they walked quietly through the inky blackness of the African night. They also had their trusty LASH headsets for commo.

The attack team was made up of the five Unit operators while the four-man security detail was led by Sublieutenant Pierre Kintuba. He had brought the intrepid Sergeant Samuel Katungo and Corporals Gabriel Mantuka and Jacques Tobuku with him. Through a mutual agreement, it was decided for Captain Edouard Tshobutu to remain behind at the base camp. The night's mission was considered too dangerous to risk the lives of the two highest-ranking men in the group.

The task scheduled for those predawn hours was a quick raid on the insurgency garrison to take advantage of the situation in which the greater majority of the enemy was busy occupying Mjikubwa. Jonas Blane had come up with the idea of the night assault, putting forth two solid reasons for its inception.

The first was to show the insurgents that they had aggressive and bold enemies stacked up against them out in the hinterlands. A successful assault on their home base would rattle their confidence and lower morale.

The second reason behind the operation was to impress everyone else concerned, particularly members of the National Army who might be tempted to join the revolution after the initial success in the city of Mjikubwa. While this latter event was not a real strategic or tactical victory, it had created a marked advantage for the insurgents as far as their reputation was concerned. After all, they had taken over the media, shot up the local cops, executed the mayor, and dominated the city in a swift, merciless attack. This was all accomplished without reaction from the government in Kinshasa. It was a situation that could not be ignored by the counterinsurgents.

Bob Brown's excellent sketch map of the enemy camp was still available, and Jonas used it to work out a verbal OPORD for the night's deadly work. He needed only twenty minutes to give the teams a full briefing so that every man knew the what, where, and when of the operation.

Bob Brown was chosen as the point man for the approach and entrance into the insurgents' garrison. Now, with his teammates behind him, he reached the correct spot on the road to turn off into the jungle. Sublieutenant Kintuba and his three NCOs immediately set up on both sides of the road to provide security while the Americans moved into the jungle to pull off their assault.

The fordable part of the Ekundu River was straight ahead, some hundred-plus meters away. The going was tough, but the night-vision goggles permitted Bob to pick out the best path toward the objective. He was able to spot areas where the vegetation was the heaviest, and work around them to lessen the chances of creating unintentional noise. Jonas Blane was right behind him with Carlito Grey dogging his heels. Lance Matoskah followed them with Mack Gerhardt acting as rear security.

When they reached the riverbank, Jonas called a halt and sent Bob to reconnoiter the other side before committing the patrol to what was enemy-held territory. Bob eased over to where Commandant Paul Dekker's obstacle course ended. He carefully made his way down the logs to the water, and silently waded across the waist-deep river. After gaining the other side, he emerged and walked softly along the side of the man-made obstacles until he reached the spot where the course began. The Unit operator squatted and listened for sounds while surveying the area in the green-and-white view provided by the goggles.

"Snake Doctor, this is Cool Breeze. All clear. Come on down. Over."

"Roger, Cool Breeze."

Jonas led the patrol down the bank and into the water to follow Bob's path. It took ten minutes before they were able to join up with him. Bob pointed ahead. "It's about twenty-five meters to the garrison area. I'm sure they left security behind, so we can expect at least one sentry."

"Red Cloud," Jonah said into the LASH. "Take that K-Bar of yours and see if there's a guard to take out. And don't scare him off like you did the last one."

"Roger," Lance said. "I still don't know how that son of a bitch managed to spot me."

Lance handed his M-4 off to Carlito, then went forward to check things out. He moved with concentrated stealth, his total being focused on the job ahead. Within a minute, he came to a quick but silent stop. A sentry, with his head down, slowly paced his post. The guy wasn't asleep, but Lance could tell he was doing his security job with his head up his ass. The scion of Oglala Teton Sioux war culture went up behind the man as silent as a ghost, then simultaneously clapped a hand over the guard's nose and mouth as he drove the razor-sharp knife under the ribs and up. He turned the handle so the blade would slice and rip vital internal organs. It took less than thirty seconds for the man to die, and Lance gently lowered the corpse to the ground. He moved forward, looking around to check for any other security personnel. The immediate area was empty of activity.

"Snake Doctor, this is Red Cloud. Clear. Over."

Jonas brought the patrol forward until they spotted Lance. Carlito looked down at the dead guard as he returned Lance's carbine. "Looks like you ruined his whole day, ol' buddy."

"Bad luck comes to everybody eventually, Carlito," Lance remarked.

"Okay," Jonas said. "Everyone knows his job. Ready? All right then, execute!"

They moved forward as skirmishers with Jonas in the center. Bob was on his left and Carlito to his immediate right. Mack held the extreme left flank while Lance occupied the opposite side of the line. When they reached the headquarters hut, Jonas and Bob went in while the others continued around to the opposite side. Bob had drawn his Beretta 93R automatic pistol complete with a silencer.

A mercenary, with his right arm in a sling that showed why he hadn't gone on the raid at Mjikubwa, looked up from the magazine he was reading at the duty officer's desk. He stood up in complete surprise and confusion. *"Madre de Dios!"* he blurted in Spanish. *"Quinés son ustedes?"* Then he recognized Bob. "Durant, *que haces aquí?"*

"Lo siento—I'm sorry," Bob said. He raised the pistol and fired. The mercenary's head jerked back, and he fell to the desk, rolling off it to collapse into a heap on the floor.

Jonas wasted no time getting to the files to search for vital intelligence. He opened the drawers and began rifling through the papers. Bob looked down at the dead Spaniard with a feeling of regret. He remembered that he was a pretty cool guy who played a mean guitar Flamenco-style.

Jonas glared at Bob. "You want to give me a hand with this?"

"Right, boss," Bob replied. He walked over to the desks and began going through the drawers.

"I can't find anything," Jonas complained.

"I'm not surprised," Bob said, having the same experience with the desks. "These guys aren't much when it comes to administration. That way there's no paper trail to follow back to higher echelons."

"To hell with it," Jonas said, irritated. "C'mon! Let's finish up this job."

They went out the back of the hut and joined the other three members of the team. Once more they advanced as skirmishers, going past the empty mercenary barracks. When they reached the Congolese billets, they stopped. There were some lights on in a couple of buildings.

"Well, hell," Jonas said. "Let's do what we got to do, old pals. Prone position, pronto!"

They hit the dirt and cut loose with automatic fire, sweeping the buildings to their direct front. Then, with Jonas, Mack, and Lance firing, Bob and Carlito each threw three M-57 hand grenades as far as they could. Everyone ducked their heads as the detonations followed. Then Bob and Carlito took up firing while the other three loosed their grenades. As soon as those exploded, they began a withdrawal, firing sweeping salvos to keep anyone from getting antsy enough to want to chase them.

When they reached the headquarters hut, they all turned and sprinted back toward the river. Once more Bob was in the lead, keeping them off the obstacle course. When they reached the water, they jumped in and went over to the logs, helping each other up the slippery sides.

Ten minutes later they joined Sublieutenant Kintuba and the NCOs holding down the fort on the road. Now the entire group hurried to where the truck waited for them.

COUNTERINSURGENCY BASE CAMP
0500 HOURS LOCAL
0300 HOURS ZULU

Jonas Blane and Captain Edouard Tshobutu sat at his desk hungrily attacking a breakfast of prepared dehydrated scrambled eggs and canned bread. They washed the repast of army rations down with strong coffee. The others who had gone on the raid were eating their own meals in the billets while the rest of the camp was just waking up to begin the day.

Jonas wiped some egg off his mouth. "I hope we get the psychological effect we're after when the insurgents hear what happened to their garrison."

"You actually have two sorts of psyches to deal with here," Tshobutu said. "There's the European and the African."

"I'm pretty sure the Europeans will be shook up about

this," Jonas said. "Maybe I should also be certain about the Africans, seeing as how I'm African-American."

"You are more of the latter than the former," Tshobutu said. "I don't mean to cast aspersions on your relationship to your ancestry, but it is the truth. At any rate, I can tell you for sure that members of the National Army will be even more reluctant to join the so-called revolution when they hear about this. They may have been impressed by the occupation of Mjikubwa, but the fact the victors were struck in their own backyard while out campaigning has watered down any respect and awe originally felt for the antigovernment force."

"I haven't been here in Africa long enough to fully appreciate and realize that," Jonas said. "To tell you the truth, I wasn't real sure what the Africans' reaction might be."

"It is very difficult for outsiders to understand us," Tshobutu said. "There are many misconceptions that cause diplomacy to fail the West when dealing with African governments. Once, back in the colonial days, when our country was the Belgian Congo, King Leopold the Second of Belgium tried to do a kindness for our people and it backfired. That was in the eighteen-nineties."

"What the hell did he do?" Jonas asked.

"It all started out as something very kind and considerate," Tshobutu explained. "He charged his colonial officials with setting up orphanages here in the Congo."

"Well, that sounds like a decent thing to do."

"Certainly," Tshobutu agreed. "But what he didn't realize was that there were no orphans in the colony."

Jonas was confused. "How could that be?"

"It was our people's custom to take care of children whose parents have died," the Congolese officer explained. "Thus every orphan had someplace to live and people to watch over him."

"It sounds to me like a happy ending."

"Hardly," Tshobutu said. "Since the colonial officials

could not find children to put in His Majesty's orphanages, they went to villages and kidnapped boys for the purpose. It was not wise in those days to thwart His Royal Majesty's commands and desires, even if there was a logical reason to do so. And giving into local customs that made the king's program look ineffective was not a very good idea. Those bureaucrats had a lot to lose career-wise if there was anything negative in their records. By the way, as soon as those kids grew up, they were put in the king's native army."

"Jesus," Jonas said, shocked. He was silent for a moment. "You're going to think I'm crazy, but I've been considering an attack on Mjikubwa ever since we came back from that combat patrol."

"We're terribly outnumbered," Tshobutu protested.

"The enemy might or might not be aware of that," Jonas said. "You see, there's a Yiddish word I learned from a Jewish buddy of mine in the Eighty-second Airborne Division a few years back. It's "chutzpah." It means brazen, brash, aggressive, in-your-face, that sort of thing. A guy that acts like that is a *chutzpenik*, and he sometimes comes out a winner through bluff and outright deceit."

"You say 'sometimes.' That means there are instances when he fails and gets what you Americans call an 'ass whipping.' "

"Yeah," Jonas said.

Tshobutu guffawed. "Jonas, my friend, I think you are a *chutzpenik*!"

MJIKUBWA
27 APRIL
1000 HOURS LOCAL
0800 HOURS ZULU

When the word of the raid on the garrison reached the generals Karl Baroudeur and Marcel Lulombe, they were unable to keep the information from flowing down to their troops. The news was delivered orally by a Congolese lieutenant, who happened to announce the incident at the police station, where the insurgents had set up headquarters. The lieutenant recited the information in the presence of a couple of mercenaries and a half dozen Congolese hanging around in the building. These eight men learned that not only was the Spanish mercenary killed, but in the African billets, a corporal died and three soldiers were seriously wounded by grenade shrapnel.

The rumor quickly spread among the troops, and by late that same afternoon, the hearsay had grown all out of proportion. It was now being said that an overwhelming number of government troops had stormed the camp, killed everybody there, and looted the place before burning it down to the nubs. Now the insurgent force—European and African alike—felt cut off and out of luck. Evidently the entire National Army was looking for them, and it wouldn't take long for contact to be made, thanks to the bigmouth Lulombe's radio broadcast, which gave away their exact location.

It was early evening when the rumors spilled over to the civilian population through a couple of bartenders, who were keeping their businesses going to take advantage of the thirsty soldiery. The two heard animated discussions among their customers, who were nervously imbibing alcohol while talking about the situation. The version the barkeeps got was that the President of the Republic himself was personally leading every combat unit in the National Army toward the city to liberate it.

The populace, unable to get out of the area because of military-defense perimeters, went to their homes and locked themselves in. Windows were boarded up; mattresses were put down for cover along with furniture stacked up in the middle of rooms to hide behind.

Meanwhile, Baroudeur, Krashchenko, and Dekker

began hashing out potential situations they might run into during the coming days. The European mercenaries sensed the growing hostility of the civilians as well as a few of their Congolese comrades-in-arms, who were getting cold feet about the revolution. The white men gathered together in a defiant activity of self-defense.

CHAPTER SIXTEEN

The defensive OPs were spread thinly to make as complete a circle as possible around the city. There was no other choice for General Karl Baroudeur but to cover the entire metropolis because of the disturbing possibility that simultaneous attacks on several sides of the city would be part of the enemy's tactics.

This security force was made up of European mercenaries and Congolese noncommissioned officers, all wearing LASH headsets. They had been chosen because of their proven reliability in past phases of combat. The Europeans also were secretly charged with keeping a close eye on their Congolese counterparts as well as making sure that no lower-ranking deserters snuck out of the city. The nervous Congolese soldiers, unable to escape as the Europeans might if a counter-insurgency assault were successful, were sullen and resentful. And some of the African officers and senior

NCOs had begun to seriously suspect that General Marcel Lulombe was really not the commander of this breakaway army.

Meanwhile, Commandant Paul Dekker, indefatigable and vigilant as always, conducted constant tours of the defensive perimeter on foot. He did not make regular appearances at certain points, but varied his inspections by time and location to make sure the guards were alert and making no attempts to abandon their posts. This was another habit he had picked up in the French Foreign Legion, where unhappy legionnaires got itchy feet from time to time.

0400 HOURS LOCAL
0200 HOURS ZULU

A rumbling sound, at first very faint and distant, grew in intensity. Sergeants of the Guard made radio reports of the noise to the Officer of the Guard, who was Colonel Vlad Krashchenko. He was on duty at the *gendarme* headquarters, and quickly responded to the information by going outside to listen for himself. After only a couple of minutes, the disturbance was easy to identify as approaching trucks. Krashchenko sprinted back inside the building and went to the room where Karl Baroudeur and Marcel Lulombe had set up a combination office and living quarters. Both officers were asleep when the colonel burst through the door.

"Réveillez!" he called out. The two generals, fully clothed except for boots, responded immediately, sitting up on their bunks in answer to the rude summons. Krashchenko ignored the Congolese officer, speaking directly to Baroudeur. "Trucks are advancing toward the city, *mon général!*"

Baroudeur swung his feet over the side of the bunk and slipped into his boots. "How many are there?"

"I do not know," Krashchenko replied. "At this point they can only be heard. But they seem to be numerous."

"Organize a patrol," Baroudeur said, standing up and grabbing his pistol belt. "All European."

"I have only three men on duty here."

"Then send them out, *vite*!" Baroudeur snapped.

Krashchenko spun on his heel to attend to the order. He went to the cellblock where the trio of headquarters personnel had set up rather comfortable quarters despite the grim surroundings. The man in charge was Sergeant José Peira, who had volunteers Denis Mercier and Josef Kowalski under his command. All three were awake, standing at the cell windows, listening to the sound of the trucks.

"Get your weapons and combat vests," Krashchenko barked. "You are going to reconnoiter those motor sounds in the distance."

"*Sim, meu coronel,*" Peira responded in Portuguese, as the other two mercenaries began putting on their boots.

"You are to locate the trucks, spend a short time observing them as to number, activity, and intent, then return here as quickly as possible," Krashchenko said.

Within a couple of minutes the trio was suited up for action, and left the building. Outside, Peira listened to the sound of the vehicles for a moment, then pointed in the direction and took off with his two men following closely.

OPERATIONAL AREA
0500 HOURS LOCAL
0300 HOURS ZULU

A crossroads was located five kilometers from the city limits of Mjikubwa that offered a route into the municipality as well as access to the more populated areas of the country to the east and north. The counterinsurgency strike force of eighty men was boots-on-the-ground at the location, quickly forming up in their assigned attack echelons. Another half dozen men were busy driving the purloined Congolese Army trucks from the road junction, then making U-turns and coming back down the highway a kilometer or so to turn around again. This was part of Jonas Blane's plan to give the impression that dozens of trucks were being driven directly into the area.

Jonas, his four Unit operators and the two Congolese officers, Captain Edouard Tshobutu and Sublieutenant Pierre Kintuba, had spent a total of eighteen hours composing an OPORD for the attack on the city. Jonas and Tshobutu quickly reached a unanimous decision to name the mission Operation Chutzpah, since it required a brazen bluff to convince a stronger enemy that they were the weaker force, and have them react accordingly.

The basic idea was to break down into six combat groups of a dozen men each. These would be referred to by the group leader's name. Combat Groups Blane, Tshobutu, Gerhardt, Brown, Grey, and Matoskah would each have ten riflemen and a two-man Minimi machine gun crew. The riflemen would carry six hand grenades each in addition to an adjusted combat ammunition load of three hundred rounds. Kintuba would command a "floating reserve" of eight riflemen, available to go anywhere that enemy pressure might build up. The six truck drivers, after ceasing their noise-making driving, would stay at the crossroads and construct some hasty field fortifications for the withdrawal from the area at the end of the battle. The backs of the vehicles were stacked with extra loads of 5.56 millimeter ball ammunition in case of need.

The conduct of the attack would be a series of hit-and-run encounters at different points of enemy resistance. These would be conducted as quickly as possible, with an almost immediate withdrawal after contact was made. This would keep the bad guys on edge and unable to accurately judge just what they were up against or what their opponents' tactical plans might be. Battle Groups Blane and Tshobutu would be in the center, attacking in a direct easterly direction. Sublieutenant Kintuba and his security force would be close behind them. Brown and Gerhardt would move around to the north side of the city, while Grey and Matoskah went south.

Now Jonas Blane checked his watch. As usual, when the tension was so strong it tingled the atmosphere, he was at his calmest. He spoke quietly, saying, "Let's do it."

0530 HOURS LOCAL
0330 HOURS ZULU

Sergeant Peira and his two men passed through the guard post on the far western side of the city. He paused only long enough to set up a challenge and password with the corporal in charge. They decided on using French, coming up with "*laissez*" and "*faire*" meaning "allow" and "to do."

Peira stayed in the lead with Kowalski on his left and Mercier on his right as they entered no-man's-land. The patrol made its way down a road that was bordered by scattered cement block houses with garden plots around them. No doubt the inhabitants cultivated food to be sold on market days in Mjikubwa. The trio used the structures for cover, showing the usual indifference of the soldiery toward the welfare of civilians by tramping across the planted areas.

When the mercenaries had passed through the neighborhood, they were forced to use the road because of the dense jungle that bordered the route.

Jonas Blane and his twelve men were on the north side of the road in a spread-out column, alert and ready for trouble. Battle Group Tshobutu was on the south side in a similar formation. Corporal Jacques Tobuku was serving as point man for both elements, keeping the pace slow and cautious as they traveled toward the city. The two machine gun teams were back in the center of the formations, ready to be deployed where and when needed. Everyone was wary of possible ambushes from the jungle along the thoroughfare, and damned the inability to put out flankers.

Tobuku and the mercenary José Peira spotted each other at the exact same time. The two opened fire immediately, and Josef Kowalski and Denis Mercier joined in, squeezing out rounds from their AKS-74s as they rushed across to the other side of the road. Both were unable to see the additional troops following Tobuku, and concentrated all their fire on the Congolese paratrooper.

As Tobuku and Peira faded into the jungle still exchanging shots, the front of both counterinsurgency elements came into view, joining the fight. They turned their full attention on the two unfortunate mercenaries Kowalski and Mercier. Both died in the heavy incoming fire, and Peira now perceived he had stumbled into a sizable enemy group. He was glad he had charged into the jungle, and now took advantage of the cover to turn around and head east to get back to the city.

Jonas led a couple of men off the road in pursuit of the fleeing man, but quickly determined they would not be able to catch him in a timely manner. There was too much to do at the moment to delay the attack over one enemy evader. They abandoned the chase and rejoined the columns to continue the advance into Mjikubwa.

Peira was having a hell of a time as he crashed through the tangled vegetation. He ignored the numerous scratches he was getting from thorns and branches as well as the rips in his uniform. After going past the point where the road turned slightly, he got back on it. Now he could run like hell back toward the mercenary defense perimeter.

Combat

Mack Gerhardt and his second-in-command, Sergeant Samuel Katungo, stumbled across several paths through the jungle that led toward the city. Mack was a bit confused by the trails until Katungo explained that local people probably used them for going into the jungle to gather herbs used in their folk medicine or for wild fruits and berries. Mack got on his LASH and informed Bob Brown behind him about the handy tracks through the trees, and the two used the paths to speed up their move toward the northern limits of the municipality.

Mack went out on point and after going a hundred-plus meters slowed the pace when he became aware of the outskirts of the city. Then he spotted a mercenary OP that was no more than a couple of guys using a collapsed shanty for concealment in a run-down neighborhood. Mack figured they were unaware of the paths to their front or they would have at least moved out to position themselves in that location to increase their ability to observe things in the tropical forest. He used his LASH once more and called up the machine gun crew. The two paratroopers made an appearance within twenty seconds, and were shown their target. Meanwhile, Mack brought up the rest of his force, spreading them out as skirmishers in the cover of the trees. Then he nodded to the men lying prone behind the Minimi automatic weapon. The rapid fire slammed into the mercenaries, buffeting them violently as they crumpled under the impact of three fire bursts.

Mack led the riflemen in a charge across the short, empty distance between the trees and the houses behind the shanty. When they reached the area, they found no other enemy troops. At that point, Mack turned his men back to where they'd launched their attack, and ran into Bob Brown and his bunch.

"I'll go on ahead," Bob told him, "and find somebody to shoot at."

"I'll be right behind you," Mack said. "If you can handle the situation, I'll leapfrog you and look for some other bad guys. If not, we'll fight together. Remember you don't want to get bogged down in any one place. Shoot fast, and if you have to, break contact and haul ass. These bastards got to be made to think there's about ten million of us."

"Right," Bob said. "See you later."

Peira ran through the cement block houses and could see the OP he had come through when he'd gone beyond the perimeter on patrol. *"Laissez!"* he shouted, using the challenge for instant identification.

"Faire!" the senior man on the position answered. He noticed Peira's excited demeanor as he drew closer. "What happened?"

"Enemy contact," Peira replied. "I lost both my men."

"I am not surprised," the other mercenary said. "There has been a lot of firing. Are there many of them?"

"Yes!" Peira shouted back.

The Portuguese renewed his rush into the city, heading for the *gendarme* headquarters. When he reached it, he dashed inside and went directly to the generals' quarters. He came to a stop, saluting. "I made contact with the enemy, *mon général*," he said to Baroudeur in French. "Two-column formation. They opened fire and hit my patrol. Both killed."

Baroudeur frowned with worry. "How many were there?"

Peira shrugged. "I was unable to determine their strength, but they were advancing rapidly toward the city. I would estimate at least a hundred. Perhaps many more."

"Merde!" Baroudeur exclaimed. "Damn!"

Down on the south end of the attack, Lance Matoskah and Corporal Gabriel Mantuka had reached the mutual conclusion that there was no enemy MLR per se. They separated a distance of fifteen meters apart with the Oglala Sioux in the lead. When he reached a short, open space between the jungle and some houses, he set up the machine gun crew to provide covering fire if necessary, then split the riflemen into two five-man teams. He took the first, then rushed across the exposed area, reaching a house. After arranging the men in a defensive position, he signaled to Mantuka and his bunch to come over. With that done, the machine gunner and his ammo bearer jumped up and rushed the short distance to join them.

Lance kept the group in two teams; Mantuka took his riflemen while Lance kept the others along with the machine gun team with him. The Unit operator moved out first, ordering Mantuka to maintain the fifteen-meter distance between his team and Lance's.

Farther back Carlito Grey was having an easy time of it. He was simply following after Lance for the time being. The only concern he had was Private Lucien M'buta, one of the once disgraced young rookies. The guy was eager as hell and kept getting ahead of the others. If his buddy Antoine Nagatu had been with him, the pair would have probably cut loose and charged straight into the city, ready to take on the whole enemy force on their own. But, thankfully, the other kid was with Bob Brown's group.

General Marcel Lulombe had always resented having to kowtow to Karl Baroudeur, but as the Battle of Mjikubwa evolved, he was glad the ex-legionnaire was in charge. Lulombe had spent his entire military career on staff duties, delegating authority to younger officers, who handled all the complicated chores of administration and logistics. The general spent his time kissing ass and making contacts that would help his advancement through the National Army's officer cadre.

The only tactical training Lulombe had ever had was at the military academy, where they carried on CPXs without troops or line units being involved. In fact, they didn't even go to the field, but carried on the exercises in classrooms using maps on the walls as they wrote OPLANs and OPORDs using strategic and tactical theories that were outdated even then. Not only had Lulombe forgotten even those obsolete hypotheses, but he had no idea how to employ even a rifle squad in either the attack or defense.

Baroudeur called a skull session with Vlad Krashchenko and Paul Dekker at *gendarme* headquarters. While none had held commissioned rank or responsibility during their collective service in the French Army, they had developed certain instincts that could help them through what they considered a growing crisis there in Mjikubwa. At the end of three-quarters of an hour of discussion and arguing, they reached the conclusion that their best bet was to consolidate their forces in the center of the city and prepare for house-to-house fighting. It would be much like the remnants of the German Army in World War II making the last stand in Berlin against the Russians.

*   *   *

Lance Matoskah and his team continued moving through the residential area, noting the boarded-up windows of the houses. Mantuka informed him that there were people hiding behind the flimsy barriers, and Lance hoped like hell he wouldn't be forced to inflict collateral casualties on an innocent population.

Suddenly heavy fire swept across the group, and both members of the machine gun team were shot down in a hail of slugs. The riflemen hit the dirt and immediately returned fire while Lance crawled across to the machine gun. It had also been hit, the barrel badly bent by the strike of a 5.45 millimeter round.

Carlito Grey brought his team up and immediately posted his machine gun team in the impromptu fighting line that had formed. Then his riflemen situated themselves among those of Lance's team. The two Unit men joined in the exchange of fire that was gradually building up into a crescendo of rapid shooting. Incoming slugs whipped and cracked overhead in both semi- and full-automatic fire.

Then it stopped.

"What the hell?" Carlito exclaimed in puzzled anger.

The voice of Corporal Mantuka came over the LASH. "The enemy have withdrawn."

Jonas Blane and Captain Edouard Tshobutu had also noted that the enemy resistance had melted away. Jonas got on his AN PRC-112 handheld radio. "All stations on the net. What is your situation? Over."

Bob Brown, Mack Gerhardt, Carlito Grey, and Lance Matoskah all reported in turn, stating that the bad guys had pulled back. It was obvious to Jonas that the enemy was consolidating for either a counterattack or to set up a strong defensive position. Either was bad news for the counterinsurgency force.

"All stations on the net," Jonas radioed. "Begin pulling back to the road junction. We've shown all the chutzpah we can today. Out." Then he added, "Goalie, this is Snake Doctor. Take your team back to the road junction and set up a defensive perimeter to cover our arrival. Over."

"Roger, Snake Doctor," Sublieutenant Pierre Kintuba replied.

The four columns complied immediately, and the two dead Congolese paratroopers were gently and respectfully picked up by their comrades to be returned to the base camp for proper burial.

1000 HOURS LOCAL
0800 HOURS ZULU

Back in the center of Mjikubwa, both European mercenaries and Congolese insurgents worked frantically to set up defensive positions in stores, houses, and particularly in city hall, and the *gendarme* headquarters, the two most solidly constructed buildings in the community. Civilians cringing in shops and homes were cruelly turned out with threats and punches. They fled to the eastern side of the city, hoping to find refuge with friends and family.

There was a marked desperation in the actions of the insurgents, since losing this battle could well mean summary executions for any survivors.

CHAPTER SEVENTEEN

D.R. OF THE CONGO
MJIKUBWA
30 APRIL
2200 HOURS LOCAL
2000 HOURS ZULU

A grand total of thirty-six hours had passed since the insurgency force had been standing to in readiness for the expected attack of a superior government strike force. The worst time for both the apprehensive mercenaries and the Congolese was in the middle of the night. As darkness fell over the city, everyone had concluded that the National Army would launch its big assault at anytime.

By dawn on 30 April everyone in both Commando Nyoka and the Congolese contingent was tired, irritated, and apprehensive. The hours of darkness had crawled by with false alarms and sleeplessness as small occurrences of civilian nocturnal activity caused alarms to be sounded by nervous sentries. Commandant Paul Dekker finally issued an order, to mercenaries and Congolese alike, that any sightings of civilians on the street were to be dealt with by firing directly at them without questions or warnings. And these were to be carried out with nothing less than full deadly force.

These orders resulted in three noncombatants being shot down at 2200 hours by a European and a Congolese who were sharing an OP in an abandoned soft drink stand. None of the trio of citizens survived the salvos fired at them, and it was later determined that they were a butcher and a couple of his employees. They were going to the shop where they worked to check the status of some live pigs that arrived two days before. If the animals were still in their pen, they would have to be fed. The incident put an end to any more residents leaving their homes or their places of hiding.

All in all, in the fighting the day before, Commando Nyoka had suffered five KIAs and seven men slightly wounded. Those killed included Josef Kowalski and Denis Mercier of Sergeant Peira's patrol; the two men caught in machine gun fire on the north side of town; and one who had been hit by rifle fire on the south city limits. The seven wounded were at various other locations when they were hit by scattered rifle fire. None had sustained serious injuries and they had been put on light duty. The Congolese lost only two men killed with no wounded.

Now, in the *gendarme* headquarters, Karl Baroudeur, Vlad Krashchenko, and Paul Dekker were holding a council of war. By then they were completely ignoring Marcel Lulombe, who had withdrawn to a corner office. He was not complaining about the cold-shoulder treatment. The results of the fighting had shaken him up badly. At first he was convinced an overwhelming number of Government troops was about to smash into the city; then, when only small skirmishing occurred in the morning, he grew confused; and finally, after a disturbing but long, quiet night, he had reached a point of confusion and indecision on his part. As far as he was concerned, those arrogant *fichu* Europeans had made a series of misjudgments, and he wasn't going to get involved in their stupidity. He concentrated on working on a plan of escape to use if and when the National Army retook the city.

Meanwhile, the senior officers of Commando Nyoka were being quite candid among themselves. And the first thing all admitted out loud that morning was that they had been badly fooled by the enemy. A prolonged discussion brought them to the conclusion that it was a force weaker than their own who had fooled them into thinking they were a much larger group through audacity and bluffing. Baroudeur openly declared, "The bastards outsmarted us. They came on like Napoleon's Imperial Guard, then faded away when it was convenient for them. In reality they were nothing more than weak rabble."

Dekker agreed. "If we had launched an immediate counterattack, there would have been one of two results. They would have either withdrawn in haste or we would have smashed them into defeat."

Krashchenko was his usual surly self. "We must withdraw from the city. What has happened here may encourage the government in Kinshasa to get serious about putting down the insurrection. In a case like that, we will be facing some stronger opposition. We will be better off back at our home garrison for the time being."

Dekker was in accord with the suggestion. "And there may be officers and soldiers of the National Army who have grown bold enough to choose sides, and decided not to join ours. That captain's parachute battalion may also be itching to join their old commander."

Baroudeur leaned back in his chair and sighed. "*C'est pas la peine*—there is no use. We must return to our garrison."

Dekker got to his feet. "I shall put out the word to the squad leaders."

"Tell them we are going back to regroup for an aggressive payback," Baroudeur said. He sighed regretfully. "I am not looking forward to reporting this to General Dubois."

COUNTERINSURGENCY BASE CAMP
1 MAY
1000 HOURS LOCAL
0800 HOURS ZULU

The funeral for the two dead Congolese paratroopers was a solemn one. Coffins had been made from the wood of ammunition boxes by a former carpenter who used a military tool kit kept at headquarters. After construction, the interiors were lined with surplus ponchos to keep moisture out after burial. This was important, since the two men would be disinterred for proper entombment at the battalion garrison when the insurrection had been brought to a successful conclusion—hopefully, that would be the case.

The entire camp population was formed up for the somber ceremony, including the twelve EPWs, who showed their respect by falling in properly in two ranks. Both dead men were Catholics, but since there were no chaplains of any faith available, Captain Tshobutu read the services in French from the Congolese National Army's official prayer book. This was followed by two short eulogies delivered by the men's best friends. They were remembered as good comrades, brave soldiers, and true patriots of the Democratic Republic of the Congo. With that taken care of, an honor guard fired a salute, then Taps was sounded by a paratrooper who had been a member of the battalion's drum-and-bugle corps.

Then it was back to soldiering.

Once more the powers-that-be gathered in the headquarters hut. Jonas Blane and Captain Tshobutu had already gotten together the day before as soon as they all returned from Operation Chutzpah. They settled down to what became an intense three-hour discussion combined with a thorough map reconnaissance. Now the pair was ready to address the four Unit operators, Sublieutenant Pierre Kintuba, and all the Congolese noncommissioned officers. It was decided to let Tshobutu be the main speaker since he could deliver the briefing in fluent French. Jonas would take care of his team after the event.

The captain, like all the others, was beginning to look a little worse for wear. There were no laundry facilities other than an occasional dumping of clothing in a nearby creek, and no iron available to put creases in uniforms. His epaulets were a bit askance on his shoulders, but the jump wings over his right breast pocket shined bright. His boots had waterproof dubbing rather than polish on them and his field hat's brim had been torn at the side of the crown. He grinned as he looked at his audience, who were just as grubby as he was. In the case of Mack Gerhardt, he looked like a tramp who had wandered into a farmyard looking for handout, except for his M4A1 carbine and combat vest.

"We all did a fine job in the attack on Mjikubwa," Tshobutu began. "You were brave and aggressive, convincing a stronger enemy that we outnumbered them. I want you to emphasize that to your men. Tell them the name of Operation Chutzpah means *audacieux* in French and *jasiri* in Swahili.

"This was a great accomplishment, no doubt, but it is something that cannot be done again. It is certain the enemy has already figured out why we did not continue advancing into the city's interior, and they are undoubtedly both ashamed and very angry. Commandant Blane and I have decided that our aggressive activities will be slowed temporarily, and we will take on a more subtle but vigorous strategy. We have the trucks available to us with plenty of fuel, so we are going to take advantage of this ability to take small combat teams out and drop them off in locations where quick raids can be made. Extractions and exfiltrations, of course, will be made at locations different from where the missions began. The best thing we can do at this point is keep the enemy guessing.

"I will not try to fool you. Our estimates are that we are outnumbered some two hundred plus to our one hundred plus. Two to one. What I ask you to do, as leaders, is keep the faith. Continue the fight until our own strength is built up so that we may deal with the traitors and foreigners in a final, fatal *coup de main*. And that may take some time. Are you with me?"

The paratrooper NCOs, grimly confident after the attack on the city, cheered for several minutes before the more senior men were able to regain control of the informal formation. Sergeant Samuel Katungo stepped forward to form them up and march them back to their bivouac area.

The five Unit operators and Captain Tshobutu and Sublieutenant Kintuba were left alone. Jonas turned to the captain. "I had almost forgotten about that traveling merchant that Bob sighted in the enemy garrison. It would be a good idea to pick him up to be brought in for a prolonged conversation."

"I agree," Tshobutu said.

Mack Gerhardt spoke up. "I could take care of it with Corporal Mantuka and a couple of paratroopers. And a truck."

"See to it," Jonas said.

He started to say more but there was a knock on the doorpost. They all turned to see Corporal Jacques Tobuku. He had not been present at the gathering because of duty as corporal of the guard over the EPWs. He stepped inside and saluted. "I have all twelve prisoners outside. They called me over to them and said they wish to join our detachment."

Jonas and Tshobutu stepped outside with the others following. All twelve of the EPWs were standing at attention under the rifles of two guards. The senior ranking prisoner stepped forward and spoke some words in French.

Tshobutu looked at Jonas. "It is true. He and his comrades wish to enroll in our ranks to serve against the insurgency."

"Ask them why," Jonas said.

Tshobutu exchanged some cordial words with the spokesman, then turned back to the American. "They have observed us and have seen that we are a group of excellent soldiers. Also the wounded have recovered fully now, and they are grateful for the kindness we showed them with medical attention."

Jonas was not too sure. "Can we trust them?"

"This is another part of African culture not understood by the West," Tshobutu replied. "An offer this important is made with sincerity and truth. This is not a time for guile or duplicity." He shrugged. "I cannot say that is true regarding our politicians, but our soldiers and common people may be completely trusted in a case like this."

Mack Gerhardt showed a typical lopsided grin. "Looks like we got another squad, boys."

THE SWISS ALPS
ORGANISATION EUROPÉEN DE SATELLITE CARTANT
MISSION CONTROL CENTER
2 MAY
0300 HOURS LOCAL
0200 HOURS ZULU

Dr. Charles Berger was the director general of OESC—the French acronym for the European Organization for Satellite Mapping—and he was also a *chevalier* in the Consortium. The only people in the Mission Control Center were a security watchman, the doctor, and two visitors. Dr. Berger was sitting in front of a large computer with a view of the eastern hemisphere on the cathode ray tube. Behind him stood General Philippe Dubois and Jean-Paul Fubert, carefully watching his manipulation of the work station. Dr. Berger used the pull-down menu to select "Africa." It appeared on the tube with the entirety of the continent in plain view. After a couple of more left clicks on the mouse, it was narrowed down to central Africa. One more click and the Democratic Republic of the Congo filled the screen.

Dr. Berger asked, "What part of the country are you interested in?"

"South central," Dubois replied.

Berger moved the arrow to the right spot and once more used the mouse. The image expanded, growing larger with each new picture. Within a minute it appeared that the terrain was less the five thousand meters below. The image was then moved around until Dubois exclaimed, "There it is!" The orderly appearance of thatched buildings, roads, vehicles, and even some individuals was easily discerned. "That is the garrison where Commando Nyoka and the Congolese detachment are billeted."

Fubert looked closely. "*Mon Dieu!* It is a miracle."

Berger shrugged. "Only science, *mon cher* Jean-Paul. Is this what you look for?"

"No," Dubois interjected. "The camp we seek is believed to be southeast of there."

"Eh, *bien,*" Berger said. He worked the image in the correct direction, moving slowly as a scene that consisted mostly of tree tops slid by. "Ah! There is a village."

Dubois nodded. "In his reports, Baroudeur has identified it as Mwitukijiji."

Fubert laughed. "How can you remember such a name?"

Dubois showed an uncustomary smile. "After service in Indo-China and North Africa, it was a habit easy to acquire." He continued to watch the screen, then spoke sharply. *"Arrêtez!* Look!"

At first the two civilians could see nothing unusual beyond a cleared area in the jungle, but after a moment the experienced Berger nodded. "Yes. There are tracks of a sort. Perhaps they are from motor vehicles. Also, I see footpaths. If one was on the ground there, they would be invisible."

"Por Dieu!" Dubois exclaimed. "Those bastards know how to camouflage."

"Not for satellite views, *mon général,*" Berger said. "I will switch on the infrared." He pushed a function key; then the image changed to light and dark. "See the light spots? Warmth. Those are either animals or human beings."

Now Dubois actually laughed aloud. "They are human beings, *docteur!* And now we know the exact location of the counterinsurgents' base camp." He studied the image beamed down from space. "I estimate there could not be more than a hundred people in the area."

"Just a moment," Berger said. "I will call up the coordinates of the location." He moved the arrow over the campsite and pressed another function key. "Ah! That location is seven degrees, fifteen minutes, twenty seconds south latitude and twenty-three degrees, forty minutes, ten seconds east longitude." He turned and looked at Dubois with a wide grin. "Is that close enough for you?"

"*Le plus satisfaisant*—most satisfactory," Dubois responded.

D.R. OF THE CONGO
OPERATIONAL AREA
1045 HOURS LOCAL
0845 HOURS ZULU

Léon M'kalo moved along on his sputtering motorcycle, hauling a trailerload of used clothing, kitchen utensils, old tools, and other previously owned products to sell in the villages in his area of business. He was in a good mood. The Euros he had earned from the European general had now mounted up to close to a thousand. He already had a plot of land and a house, but now he could afford to expand the dwelling and give his wife an easier life with an automatic washer, a larger refrigerator, and some new furniture. As for himself, he planned on expanding his business by purchasing a secondhand truck. He had found one that could be converted into a store on wheels so he could sell his wares over a counter on the back of the vehicle.

M'kalo came around a curve in the road, and slowed down when he spotted an army roadblock ahead. There was the usual portable barrier and a truck. Two loitering soldiers looked up at him as he drew closer. When he came to a stop, they approached him and gave him a friendly nod.

The peddler showed a smile. "Hello, *chef*," he said to the one who wore two stripes of a corporal on his epaulets.

"Hello, *m'sieur*," Corporal Gabriel Mantuka said. "May I see your identification, please?" The soldier beside him was Private Antoine Nagatu.

M'kalo reached into his inside jacket pocket and produced his national ID card. He noticed another soldier appear from behind the truck. The kid, who was Private Lucien M'buta, sauntered up in a lackadaisical manner.

Mantuka yawned widely while he looked at the card. M'kalo waited patiently for the procedure to be taken care of. This was a usual practice when he was wheeling around the countryside. The Congolese National Army loved to put up roadblocks. Nothing much was accomplished, but it gave the appearance of efficiency and devotion to duty.

The two privates suddenly grabbed the peddler and hustled him toward the truck. Now M'kalo was alarmed. "What are you doing?"

A European appeared from the truck cab and walked up to the peddler. He gave him a quick but close look, then jerked his thumb toward the rear of the truck. The soldiers took M'kalo around and lifted him up into the back, then clambered aboard.

Mack Gerhardt returned to the cab and started the engine while Mantuka climbed aboard the three-wheeled motorcycle to follow after the truck.

CHAPTER EIGHTEEN

The two trucks, with twelve men on the first and thirteen on the second, rolled into the garrison off the dirt road and came to a halt at the headquarters building. The European detachment was involved in PM on their weapons and equipment in the billets, but all came out to see the new arrivals. Most hoped to catch sight of an old acquaintance or comrade among the reinforcements.

Commandant Paul Dekker made his presence known by walking up to the vehicles and yelling for the men to get off. They were dressed in civilian clothing with newly issued uniforms in duffel bags. The group looked rather seedy, and some were obviously out of shape. Even the most casual observer could easily tell that a few of these new men had been experiencing recent hard times. These were the freelance soldiers recruited in Marseille by Peter Luknore, and it was obvious they were veterans from the way they quickly formed up in two ranks, setting their rucksacks on the ground while slinging their rifles over their right shoulders.

One of them had a manila folder, and he handed it to Dekker. The commandant pulled out a roster, then began calling out the names listed on it to make sure none of the levy had strayed or become lost.

The vocal responses were purely international as each man responded in his native language. *"Hier!" "Présent!" "Presente!"* and "Here!" were among the shouts. And finally someone replied with a vigorous *"Z'dyes!"*

The last response caught Colonel Vlad Krashchenko's immediate attention. He turned to Karl Baroudeur. "It appears that Luknore has snared a Russian in his hiring net."

"I am surprised that you still remember how to speak the language," Baroudeur said. "How long has it been since you were in Mother Russia?"

"Almost thirty years," Krashchenko replied. He walked over to the man who had answered in *Ruski*. He was a tall, tough-looking guy with his shirtsleeves rolled up to his elbows. His forearms were covered with cheap tattoos that looked almost homemade. Krashchenko exchanged a few words with him, then walked back to Baroudeur. "He is a Russian all right. His name is Sergei Malonov and he deserted from his army unit during a clandestine mission to Serbia."

"What sort of unit did he serve in?"

"The full designation is *Spetsialnoye Nazranie*," Krashchenko said. "It is better known shortened to *Spetsnaz*. It boils down to special-purpose troops—a title that would be special operations in other countries."

"What was he doing in Serbia?" Baroudeur asked.

"It was a clandestine mission to train a new Serbian *Spetsnaz* battalion," Krashchenko said. "Malonov deserted because of striking his commanding officer. It seems the captain had pilfered a substantial amount of money from the men's savings accounts. Malonov did not even wait to be arrested for it. The fellow was still lying unconscious on the ground when our new soldier left him and made his way across the border to Albania. After reaching a seaport on the Adriatic Sea, he stowed away aboard a freighter. Then he was in Italy and finally France. I did not get the details of how he was recruited by our old *copain* Luknore."

"The fact that he and his twenty-four companions have joined us is good enough for me," Baroudeur said. "We must get them changed into their uniforms as quickly as possible."

"I can imagine that Dekker is impatient to run them through his obstacle course," Krashchenko remarked.

"Tell him to take it easy," Baroudeur said seriously. "These fellows are not in very good physical condition at this moment in time, and I do not want any of them hurt. The numerical strength of the Europeans has now risen to more than one hundred and fifty men. With our Congolese we can now field a grand total of two hundred forty-nine."

"When will the *général* arrive?" Krashchenko asked.

"Tomorrow," Baroudeur said. "He must have some important task to perform with us to risk a trip to the Congo."

ALEXANDRIA, VIRGINIA
CIA SAFEHOUSE
2100 HOURS LOCAL
1600 HOURS ZULU

Norman DeWitt, a CIA senior controller-at-large, was ensconced in a rather comfortably fitted-out sitting room of the large house with Delmar Munger. The furniture in the room was plush easy chairs and a couple of settees. The two men sat across from each other as De-Witt scanned a hard copy of a transmission containing the latest report from the Congo sent to Colonel Tom Ryan at Fort Griffith, Missouri.

Munger waited patiently for his superior to peruse the message. He had been picked up by an agency driver at Ronald Reagan National Airport an hour earlier, and was brought directly to Alexandria for this meeting. Since this was a document produced at the TOC at Fort Griffith, Munger wanted it into the hands of his boss ASAP.

DeWitt completed the read, then looked up. "So Sergeant Major Blane claims the twelve EPWs that he had captured finally decided to join up with him and his cohorts. How much credence do you put in that assertion?"

"Is there anything less than 'none'?" Munger remarked.

"Then you think it's an outright lie?"

"Certainly," Munger said. "It's impossible to put a positive spin on this situation. The only thing I can say regarding the incident of the prisoners is that perhaps Blane had the poor bastards shot, and now is going to claim that he made an eloquent pitch to them about the righteousness of his cause, and they rushed to him in gratitude, trusting to his kind words."

"You could be right about that, Delmar," DeWitt said. "Blane is African-American, and they might think he was completely trustworthy."

"Of course," Munger said. "And, now that they are buried in a mass grave somewhere, he will claim they were all killed in action fighting evil and despotism in deepest, darkest Africa under his sterling leadership."

"Now that makes sense to me," DeWitt said. "What do you think is the truth behind this attack on that city of"—he looked at the report—"My-ee-koo-bwah or however it's pronounced?"

"I think he and the other operators drove their Congolese sidekicks ahead of them into the place, then immediately shot the chief of police and mayor when they overwhelmed the local authorities," Munger said. "Then those freedom-loving American soldiers looted the town treasury and a couple of banks, then hightailed it back to their jungle lair. You'll notice that he placed the blame squarely on the insurgents."

"Do you think we can prove that?"

Munger laughed. "We're gonna drag those bastards up before Senator Kenneth Allen's Committee on Intelligence and Special Operations. Who do you think the Senator is going to believe: the Central Intelligence Agency or a ragtag bunch of bandits who refuse to reveal their chain-of-command and administrative echelons?"

"Another thing in our favor is bringing in the State Department on our side," DeWitt reminded him. "That will give us an extra boost with the good senator."

Munger's laughter dissolved into a wide grin. He reached into his jacket pocket and pulled out some sheets of paper. "This is the copy of the report that Booker Cartwright sent to Tom Benson, the deputy director of the Special Affairs Bureau at the State Department. It agrees with what I've just told you. And here is the very same thing in a report I've written for you." He reached down to his briefcase and retrieved the document.

DeWitt took the statement. "This is going to be like feeding those bastards to the lions. I'll be glad when that Congo operation is over and they get back Stateside."

"Just remember that the longer they're over there, the more rope there'll be to hang 'em with."

Léon M'kalo was brought into the hut by two para-trooper guards. A camp lantern, turned down low, glowed weakly on a table to his direct front. Behind it sat Jonas Blane, Captain Edouard Tshobutu, and someone who looked vaguely familiar to M'kalo: the irrepressible Bob Brown. The prisoner was forced down into a chair facing the trio, whose faces bore expressions that were neither friendly nor unfriendly.

"Bonsoir, M. M'kalo," Tshobutu said politely. *"Parlez-vous anglais?"*

M'kalo shook his head. "I speak only French and Swahili."

"In that case," Tshobutu said, "I will act as translator so that my two friends will understand my questions and your answers to them. We hope that is convenient for you."

"Are they from Britain?" M'kalo asked.

"I am sorry, M. M'kalo," Tshobutu said. "But circumstances dictate that only I ask the questions. Do you understand?"

"Perfectly, *monsieur le capitaine,*" M'kalo said. His initial nervousness began to subside a bit. His experience with police and other authorities usually began with a fair-to-middling beating that left him sore and bruised. This capture or arrest—he wasn't sure which it was—and the subsequent confinement in a small clearing under the guns of soldiers had made him fear for his life, but nobody had punched or kicked him. However, he would have felt better if he knew who these people were or what they wanted from him.

"We have brought you here to clear up some confusion," Tshobutu said. "We hope that you will be able to help us. If you can, we will be most appreciative." He smiled. "Would you like a cigarette? Perhaps a cup of coffee?"

Now M'kalo relaxed. "Why, yes, *merci beaucoup*. That would be nice. And I am hungry too, if I may make so bold, *monsieur le capitaine*."

"I'm afraid you'll have to wait a bit for food," Tshobutu said. "Please forgive me, but it is the lateness of the hour."

"*Je comprends, monsieur le capitaine,*" M'kalo said. "It is no big thing."

Within a couple of minutes a cup of hot coffee and a pack of cigarettes were placed in front of the prisoner. He first lit up, then treated himself to a quick gulp from the cup. At that point he smiled at Tshobutu. "I am ready."

"Fine," Tshobutu said. "We are confused as to why you were present in the insurgent's camp a little more than a week ago. On the twenty-second of April, to be exact. We would be most grateful if you would clarify that incident. It would put us at ease as to your activities. We would not normally bother you, but this is most important to us."

A flit of nervousness flashed through M'kalo. "Uh, *bien*, I cannot recall being there at that time." He took a quick sip of coffee. "In fact, I have not ever been there."

"Mmm," Tshobutu said, nodding his head toward Bob Brown. "This is most confusing because my friend says he saw you there on that date."

"I am sure he is mistaken."

"I do not think so, M. M'kalo. He has seen you before and recognized you. It was at Mwitukijiji on the day when the insurgents killed the soldiers at the roadblock. He says he even grabbed you by the arm and took you to his sergeant."

M'kalo knew there was nothing to be gained by denying it. "Yes. That is true." And he now recognized Bob. "They wanted to ask me questions. But I had no answers for them. I am but a simple seller of secondhand goods and not well educated. When your friend saw me there a short time ago, I had visited only to see if I could sell something or perhaps purchase items for resale. It was all quite innocent, please believe me, *monsieur le capitaine*."

Now Tshobutu threw in a bluff developed by reaching a logical conclusion. "We believe that when you were taken to them on that day in Mwitukijiji, they asked you to spy for them."

M'kalo was not a stupid man. He had developed a definite shrewdness from a lifetime of dealing with government and military officials on everything from sales permits to internal passports. This included bribery and even blackmail at one time when he came across a tax collector having sex with another man behind a village hut. The peddler had not paid once for tax stamps since the incident. Now he smiled. "Yes! I remember now. They asked me to tell them about anything unusual I might see during my sales trips. Of course I told them I would be happy to do so." He shrugged. "But I saw nothing to report. And even if I did, I would not know what was important and what was not. I am not a sophisticated man."

"But my friend said you were talking to officers at headquarters on that day," Tshobutu said.

"I talk to them all the time when I pass by," M'kalo said. "And, as I told you, I wished to conduct business. I fear if I tried to ignore them, they would be angry with me."

"What are their names?"

"Let me think," M'kalo said. He figured they already knew the names since the white man who recognized him was part of their organization. After all, he had been right there when the village was occupied. "There is a general by the name of Baroudeur. And he has a friend who is called Krash—er, I am not sure. He is a European with a strange name. Also there is a Congolese General Lulombe."

Tshobutu fell into a calculated period of silence, looking pointedly at the prisoner. M'kalo was now totally confused. He could not figure out why the white man who had grabbed his arm at the village was here at this camp. Perhaps he had divided loyalties, or this was Congolese politics and intrigue as usual in that everybody was on the same side, but there was a struggle for dominance among the top dogs. Politicians pulled dirty tricks on one another all the time.

Suddenly M'kalo felt confident. Of course! If this white man had seen him at the camp, and he undoubtedly had, then he was part of that group. That led him to the conclusion that Baroudeur and this captain who now questioned him were out to knock each other off for the supreme leadership of their combined forces. If he were smart, he could work one against the other in such a manner that no matter who came out on top, he would profit from it.

Now Tshobutu continued the interrogation. "When did you tell them about the helicopter?"

"I am not sure," M'kalo said. He smiled in what he hoped was a meek manner. "I actually did it more to make conversation than anything else."

"Do you meet with them regularly?"

"No, *monsieur le capitaine*. Only when I just happened to be in the area. But I am now pleased to meet with you regularly if you require me to do so. You would find me a valuable friend, I assure you."

"Excuse us, please," Tshobutu said. He nodded to the paratrooper guard, who tapped the prisoner on the shoulder as a signal to stand up. Then he led him out of the hut.

Jonas Blane shrugged. "He really isn't much of a spy,

but he's dangerous. If we turned him loose he would hightail it straight over to the insurgents."

Tshobutu was in agreement. "The man was obviously being paid. He cannot be blamed for taking advantage of the situation. Life is not easy for him. I believe he has reached a conclusion that this European Baroudeur and I are struggling for supremacy. It is a common thing here in the Congo." The captain paused. "However, I cannot forgive him for being responsible for the deaths of Warrant Officer Bhutan and Sergeant Montka. They were in my battalion and under my direct command."

"I feel the same way," Bob said. "He shouldn't be freed. Even if he didn't actually shoot down the chopper, he sure as hell set up the circumstances for it to happen."

"Let me handle it," Tshobutu said. He called out to the guard to bring M'kalo back into the hut.

"I hope I have been helpful, *monsieur le capitaine*," M'kalo said, sitting down. "And I also hope you realize how much you can depend on me in your service."

"Indeed I do, *monsieur*," Tshobutu said. "You will be free to go in the morning. Meanwhile, let me take you to our billets to spend the rest of the night. We have comfortable bunks with mosquito netting." He nodded to the paratrooper. "I believe we are having ham and bread for breakfast."

"That sounds most delicious, *monsieur le capitaine*."

The paratrooper quietly set down his rifle while pulling the garrote from his waistband. He deftly stepped up behind his victim, and slipped it over the spy's neck and tightened it. M'kalo struggled violently, twisting out of the chair and falling to the floor kicking. But his killer calmly maintained the pressure until the final throes.

"Y'know," Jonas said, "I was thinking we could perhaps have turned him into a double agent."

Bob looked down at the corpse. "It's a little too late for that now, boss."

"It would not have worked out," Tshobutu said. "In Africa a double agent soon becomes a triple agent." He was thoughtful for a moment. "Or would that be a quadruple agent? I am never sure."

MERCENARY HEADQUARTERS
4 MAY

Philippe Dubois, retired general and *chevalier-commandant* of the Consortium, had arrived at the garrison in a convoy of three Mercedes sedans. His entourage included three drivers, six bodyguards, an interpreter, and a male secretary from the Consortium offices in Melilla, Spanish Morocco. While everyone was dressed casually in slacks and short-sleeve open-collar shirts, the retired general was wearing a pith helmet, khaki shirt with epaulets, olive drab denim trousers, and canvas boots with rubber soles. While the garb was not exactly a proper uniform, the retired general looked quite soldierly.

The first thing Dubois did was angrily order Baroudeur to return General Marcel Lulombe to the staff to continue the facade that he was the commanding officer. Baroudeur locked his heels and complied as Dubois testily explained how important it was to the big picture of the insurrection that it appear that it was a national endeavor and that the Europeans involved were in sympathy with the revolution, not actually directing and supplying the effort.

After Lulombe had been sent for and showed up, Baroudeur apologized for slighting him, saying that in all the confusion he had been distracted. Lulombe, encouraged by the French general's presence, accepted the apology, and his ego was restored to its natural inflated state, but not enough to deny to himself that it was the Europeans who were really in charge.

Dubois was ready to get down to the business of his visit.

1800 HOURS LOCAL
1600 HOURS ZULU

A large map of the operational area was attached to the headquarters hut wall on top of the old one. It bore all the latest markings on its acetate cover that Dubois had personally written down. Additionally, an enlarged satellite photograph of the same territory was spread out on Baroudeur's table and tacked down on each corner. By now Commandant Paul Dekker was present. He, Baroudeur, Krashchenko, and Lulombe were gathered around the table, waiting for Dubois to begin whatever it was he had come to do.

Dubois put the tip of a finger on a location shown in the photo. "That is the image of your enemy's base camp." He moved the finger to another spot. "And this is where we are at this very moment. It is this garrison."

"So they are on the other side of Mwitukijiji from us," Baroudeur remarked. "And out in the middle of nowhere."

"You see this?" Dubois said. "It is no more than a track that leads from the Mwitukijiji road down to a place, where it is possible to enter the jungle for access to the enemy site. The trucks you reported stolen from Camp Ukaidi were driven along that route and hidden here."

"The tracks are plain," Dekker said in amazement.

"If you were on the ground, you would not be able to see them," Dubois said, "which is why we must get air support for you sometime in the near future. If not CAS, at least for reconnaissance and aerial photography. It is hoped that aviators for hire will be available soon." He snapped his fingers, and the secretary stepped forward with the general's briefcase. Dubois took it and pulled out five sets of papers. He gave one to each of the other four men, keeping one for himself. "These are the *ordres opérationals* for the attack on the enemy's base camp. Please open them."

The mercenary officers and General Lulombe complied, quickly scanning the first page that contained an abbreviated list of dates, times, who, where, when, and how of the plans.

"By the way," Dubois said. "I have brought enough night-vision goggles for your key leaders. They will be invaluable in this operation since it begins during darkness."

"Merci bien, mon général!" Baroudeur exclaimed.

"So let us get down to how the attack will be organized," the general said. "At zero-one-hundred hours day after tomorrow, you will move your mortars from this garrison to the location shown on the photograph. Here is where you will set up the weapons. You reported that you have a section, did you not?"

"Yes, *mon général*," Baroudeur said. "We have four Spanish Model L sixty-millimeter models. And plenty of HE shells."

"There is a competent *chef de mortiers* among the new men who lately arrived," Dubois said. "He is a Russian by the name of Malonov. He was especially recruited by Luknore."

"I have already met him," Krashchenko said. "He seems an excellent soldier."

"That he is," Dubois said. "And since we know the exact coordinates, locations, ranges, and azimuths of the impact area, he can set up the elevations, traverses, and charges of the mortars in advance. Thus, there will be no need to fire for effect. He can organize the section, put out the aiming stakes, and sight in within ten minutes at the most. The barrage will commence at zero-four-forty-five hours and end exactly at zero-five-hundred hours.

Therefore, a careful synchronization of watches is most important."

Now Lulombe spoke up. "There are skilled mortarmen among the Congolese soldiers." He glared at Baroudeur, revealing the smothered resentment that smoldered within him. "No other Europeans will be necessary for that part of the operation."

Surprisingly, Commandant Paul Dekker backed him up. "That is true, *mon général.* I have personally put the Africans through crew drill on the weapons. They are experienced and capable."

"Très excellent," Dubois said, having more faith in Dekker's assessment than Lulombe's. "However, Malonov speaks only Russian. Thus Colonel Krashchenko will have to accompany him on the operation to translate firing orders for the Congolese gunners."

"Sûrement, mon général!" Krashchenko responded positively.

Dubois paused a moment for a final glance at the satellite photograph. "Now turn to the *ordres opérationals,* and we will discuss the execution of the coming attack." He waited until everyone was ready before continuing. "The first thing I would like to point out are the twenty-five new men recently recruited by Luknore in Marseille. I have already mentioned Sergei Malonov. He is the only one trained in special operations, but he is similar to the other military arrivals in that his military career is tainted with misbehavior and, in some cases, outright insubordination. Although these men left their national forces under clouds, they have been checked out as competent, experienced soldiers and noncommissioned officers. Some had dishonorable releases from service and were sentenced to terms in military prisons. Be that as it may, they are still well trained."

"Sauf votre respect, mon général," Baroudeur said, "they might fit well into the Foreign Legion after proper indoctrination and harsh discipline, but can they be trust-

ed in an uncultured situation as we have here? We are, as you know, outside the law of any nation. If they desert there will be no conflict with police organizations."

"That has been taken into consideration," Dubois said. "They will remain together and be at the vanguard of the frontal attack that will take place at zero-five-hundred hours immediately after the mortar barrage ceases. Your entire Congolese detachment will be directly behind them. Their mission is simple: charge straight ahead."

Paul Dekker was not pleased with the quality of the new men. "What if they hesitate or withdraw without orders?"

"Then the Congolese will be free to shoot them down like dogs," Dubois stated.

Lulombe spoke up loudly. "You may depend on my soldiers to do their duty, *mon général*!"

"What about the rest of the Europeans?" Dekker asked.

"They will be distributed as follows," Dubois said. "You have a total of 149 men remaining. Divide them into four echelons. The first will be made up of the twenty-four new men and the Congolese riflemen for a total of one hundred eleven men under the command of General Baroudeur. The second and third will consist of thirty men each led by Sergeant Peira and Corporal Coureur. They are the flank attacks and will hit the north and south sides of the enemy base camp. The fourth echelon under Commandant Dekker will number a total of sixty-five men. They will be positioned on the track leading from the Mwitukijiji road that runs along the east side of the enemy base camp. Their mission will be twofold: first, contain the enemy if they attempt to withdraw in that direction from the mortar barrage; and second, to strike into the enemy at the correct time."

"What are those times, *mon général*?" Dekker asked.

"Turn to the last page of the *ordres opérationals*," Dubois replied.

0100 hours—Entire force moves out to assigned assault positions.
0445 hours—Mortar barrage starts, and front, flank, and rear areas contained.
0500 hours—Mortar barrage stops, and front, flank, and rear attacks are launched.

"It is not a complicated plan," Dubois admitted. "But we are conducting the operation in a limited area with a small amount of men. There is not time for complicated maneuvering or a complex series of commitments of troops. Bombard them, then smash and destroy them. You have a decided advantage in numerical strength. Any questions? No? Good! You have forty-eight hours to prepare your men."

Baroudeur called the group to attention and all rendered snappy hand salutes, simultaneously stating, *"À vos ordres, mon général!"*

CHAPTER NINETEEN

It had taken extra time to lay in the mortar team designated *Section de Mortiers* by General Dubois. Only Colonel Vlad Krashchenko and Volunteer Sergei Malonov had night-vision goggles, and they had to work together on each of the four weapons. This was the process of sighting through the gunner's scope on the aiming stakes to be certain that every tube was laid in on the same azimuth. This assured that barrages would travel in the same exact direction when all the crews fired at once. Without it, even at the same elevation and charges, the falling shells would be scattered helter-skelter on and around the impact area. The process of laying the section automatically included the adjustment of the elevation knobs while the traverse angles were set at zero degrees. With a small target area and only four weapons, there was no reason to shift the lateral strike of the rounds.

The two Russians finished the job by preparing the shells with the proper charges. The Spanish ECIA Model L Mortar could actually fire thirty rounds a minute, but if that rate of fire was going to be followed from 0445 hours to 0500 hours, they would need a grand total of 1,800 of the 60-millimeter shells. Since they had 610, it was decided they would fire ten times a minute with Malonov using the second hand on his watch to time each salvo. That meant they would be sending more than a total of 600, leaving ten extras in case of misfires. Krashchenko and Malonov worked together in the dark to pull the extra charges off the shells.

The ECIA 60-millimeter Model L mortars were manufactured in Spain by Esperanza and Company, a firm that has been in the arms-making business since the 1920s. The Model L weighed twelve kilograms and had a range of 3,800 meters, and was made up of the usual parts, i.e., baseplate, tripod, and tube. The projectile used was the Model AE bomb, weighing 2.05 kilograms with an aluminum tail fin. A smoke shell was also available, as was a practice shell for training purposes. This ammunition could be either drop- or trigger-fired.

Now, with everything ready to go exactly at 0445 hours, the *Section de Mortiers* sat back, stayed quiet, and waited.

GROUP DE FRAPPE BAROUDEUR

After General Philippe Dubois organized his attack, he designated the separate units as *groups de frappe* (strike group), naming each one after its leader. *Group de Frappe* Baroudeur was located twenty-five meters ahead of the mortar positions, and Karl Baroudeur had his men forming up at the same time that the mortars were being prepared. This group consisted of the twenty-four new mercenaries and the entire Congolese detachment for a total of 111 men. The Africans were situated to the direct rear of the European group as General Dubois had ordered. They would all charge straight ahead into the counterinsurgents' base camp at the 0500 zero hour as soon as the mortar barrage lifted.

GROUP DE FRAPPE PEIRA
0300 HOURS LOCAL
0100 HOURS ZULU

Sergeant José Peira led his thirty men slowly along the south bank of the Ekundu River eastward toward the North Mwitukijiji Road that led directly to the village. Although the going was slow since Peira was the only one with night-vision capability, there were no undue delays since the terrain along the waterway was relatively open and flat. With two hours to reach the assault position, there was no need to be concerned with speed.

GROUP DE FRAPPE COUREUR
0315 HOURS LOCAL
0115 HOURS ZULU

Andre Coureur, the French-Canadian pal of "Ted Durant" and the young Brit Simon Cooper, had conducted himself well in the Battle of Mjikubwa when his rifle team stood fast under heavy fire. He had even managed a short counterattack before being forced back, and Commandant Paul Dekker had seen to it that he was made a permanent corporal.

Now, in charge of his own strike group, he led his

men toward the south side of the counterinsurgency
base camp, and was having an easy time of it. He'd gone
south along the Ekundu River to the West Mwitukijiji
Road, straight to the village. *Group de Frappe* Coureur
turned onto the South Road, traveling steadily until they
reached the proper coordinates to go into the jungle. At
that point they moved to a position just south of the enemy's bivouac. They would be at their assault position
within forty-five minutes.

Group de Frappe Dekker
0400 hours local
0200 hours Zulu

Commandant Paul Dekker was ferociously happy. He
was pleased to have the most dangerous assignment of
the attack on the enemy camp. His sixty-five mercenaries were close to 44 percent of the total NCO and volunteers of Commando Nyoka. The commandant was so
anxious to get the operation in gear that he had actually
left the mercenary garrison with his strike group a little
before midnight, much earlier than necessary. They traveled through the jungle with each mercenary hanging
on to the belt loop of the combat vest of the man to
his direct front. They were in a single-column formation,
which stretched them out in a line that varied from sixty-
five to seventy meters depending on the terrain. Dekker,
with his NVGs, moved slowly picking out the places of
least resistance in the jungle growth. When some diffi-
culty arose, he would whisper a warning that would be
passed back down the single row of men following him.
Most of the time the words of caution were "*Attention à
les branches*—watch out for the branches."
    He took them south to the West Mwitukijiji Road,
where they were now able to step out much faster.
The strike group went through the village to the East

Mwitukijiji Road until it met the Ukaidi junction, moving so quietly that they created no disturbance among the population. A couple of dogs yapped, but not long enough to awaken anyone. A south turn was made at the crossroads, then an abrupt pivot to the east and back into the jungle.

When they reached the combined defensive/assault position, the *group de frappe* was surprised to find fighting positions already prepared by the counterinsurgents. Now Dekker knew he was in a most advantageous place. Obviously the enemy would head to that exact spot when the mortar barrage started. The commandant figured that at about a quarter of an hour after that, he and his men would be laying a deadly cross fire on the retreating counterinsurgents. And he had four machine gun teams with him to add to his killing power.

SECTION DE MORTIERS
0445 HOURS LOCAL
0245 HOURS ZULU

There was just enough growing daylight to allow the mortar crews to be able to set the shells in the tops of the tubes with each assistant gunner gingerly holding on to the projectiles, ready to drop them on command. They waited for the order to begin the barrage, and when it came they responded quickly to Colonel Vlad Krashchenko's shout of *"Feu!"* The bright orange flashes momentarily blasted away the gloom of the predawn hour, illuminating men, weapons, and the jungle around the clearing.

At that point Sergei Malonov watched the second hand of his watch, nodding his head every six seconds. Each time, Krashchenko repeated the command to fire, and another barrage of four shells was sent arcing toward the counterinsurgency base camp.

COUNTERINSURGENCY BASE CAMP

The first four rounds hit almost simultaneously, the detonations echoing off into the early-morning sky as shrapnel whipped and whizzed through the air. By the time the second group struck, the entire camp was up.

It was Captain Edouard Tshobutu's SOP that all men sleep with their battle rattle near them. This included combat vests with six thirty-round magazines, a full magazine inserted into their FA-MAS rifles, and four bandoleers of four magazines, each giving the men individual totals of 690 rounds. This was one hell of a heavy load, but the location and circumstances of the base camp could well force a requirement for instant evacuation. The men also toted two full canteens, a pair of F1 hand grenades, and individual medical aid kits. Officers, NCOs, radio operators and medics also carried specialty items. And now, loaded down, everyone headed to their subunit's emergency rally point.

Jonas Blane and his four operators rushed toward the headquarters hut, then hit the ground as a third group of shells clobbered into the dirt, exploding and hurling shards of metal around. The shrapnel hissed like angry steel hornets as it sliced through the air. Captain Tshobutu was the man in charge, and he was busy moving the paratroopers eastward out of the bivouac area. The Americans joined him, going with the whole group as they plunged into the heavy jungle between the camp and Ukaidi road.

After pushing through the vegetation for fifty meters, they came to a halt. Mack Gerhardt retraced his steps about ten meters and peered back at the explosions that continued erupting regularly, four at a time. He went back to where Jonas and Tshobutu stood. "It ain't a creeping barrage, boss," Mack reported. "We're okay here."

"We need to get on the other side of the road,"

Tshobutu said. "There will obviously be an attack coming after the mortar fire. We have some fighting positions prepared for just a contingency."

"Were you keeping that a secret?" Jonas asked, surprised by the news.

"I have been keeping several secrets, my friend," Tshobutu said candidly. "And you may discover them before this day is over." He turned back to his men and ordered a point team to lead the way.

The incoming shells continued falling onto the now empty bivouac zone as the counterinsurgents headed for the fighting positions. But when the point team reached the road they came under heavy rifle and machine gun fire. All three men were cut down.

Bob Brown spat. "The bastards closed the back door."

Tshobutu grabbed Jonas' arm. "Listen, my friend. I will fight this battle. I suggest that you and your men work as a squad." He gave Jonas a hard look. "You are under my command." It was a short statement, delivered in a calm tone of voice, but the intent of the few words was loud and clear, i.e., don't mess with me.

Jonas grinned and winked, using a French phrase he had picked up. "*À vos ordres, mon capitaine!*"

Tshobutu smiled back. "Go south and see if we can make a flanking maneuver and get around the enemy. I shall send Sublieutenant Kintuba north."

Jonas turned to his team. "Let's go!"

COMBAT

Andre Coureur had his men arranged as skirmishers behind a slight embankment. A two-man machine gun team was located in the middle of the line. His orders, like the other groups, was to hold fast at the assault position until the barrage halted at 0500 hours or the enemy made contact with him.

"Enemigos adelantes!" a Spanish mercenary called out.

Five men could be seen sprinting across the road to their direct front. Andre shouted the order to open fire, and the machine gun and twenty-eight AKS assault rifles blasted bullets at the interlopers.

"Damn it!" Jonas Blane yelled.

He and the rest of the operators swung their M4 carbines toward the source of shooting, providing their own covering fire. They slipped into the safety of the jungle, and Jonas led them directly back toward the rest of the counterinsurgency force. They arrived at the same time that Sublieutenant Kintuba was reporting in with his men. Jonas said, "We're pinned in on the south."

"Yes," Tshobutu said. "Kintuba reports the same to the north."

Suddenly it was apparent that the mortaring had ceased. At that exact moment Sergeant Samuel Katungo's voice came over the LASH from where he was commanding a rifle team on the west. "The barrage is lifted and an enemy attack has now reached the base camp and is moving through it fast."

"We are surrounded," Kintuba said. He looked at his commanding officer expectantly.

Tshobutu nodded affirmatively. *"Condition Rouge."*

"Tout de suite, mon capitaine," the young lieutenant said, reaching inside his jacket. He brought out a French military model handheld radio, putting it up to his ear. He pressed the transmit button. *"Condition Rouge! Condition Rouge! Condition Rouge!"*

"Condition Red?" Jonas said. "What's that all about?"

"Another of my secrets," Tshobutu said. "We are going to set up a tight perimeter at this exact spot. Take your men to the east side and situate yourselves."

As Jonas and the Unit men hurried off to their assigned fighting position, the captain quickly organized the rest of his men through the LASH. His first order was to pull in tighter to form a circle of defense; then he set about organizing his force before the enemy launched what would be heavy, aggressive attacks.

Tshobutu now had a total of 107 paratroopers after losing the three killed on the Ukaidi Road. He decided each side of the perimeter would have twenty-three riflemen and a two-man machine gun crew. That would leave seven men to stay with him in the interior. They would be a sort of reserve to be sent to places where extra help was needed.

Sublieutenant Pierre Kintuba was given command of the north side while Sergeant Samuel Katungo commanded the west. Over on the east side Jonas Blane was in charge with the Unit operators aided in the leadership by Corporal Tobuku. Corporal Mantuka was given the honors on the south side.

Commandant Paul Dekker was fuming. Somehow his men were misaligned in the midst of the heavy vegetation, so he was unable to order them to attack at the exact moment the mortar barrage ceased. It took ten minutes to get everyone back in contact with one another, and he accomplished the task with curses and the liberal administration of *sticks* to the back of the head Legion style. One ex-SAS Brit turned around violently when struck and started to bring his rifle up, but he quickly saw that the bore of Dekker's weapon was aimed at his chest. The Englishman growled a curse, then turned around to get down to business.

"En avant!" Dekker yelled.

His sixty-five men surged forward from the concealment of the brush and rushed westward across Ukaidi Road.

The paratroopers on the Minimi machine gun didn't need orders to open fire when the enemy skirmishers came into view. Their weapon spit bullets as the rest of the east-side group joined in from the jungle just off the road. Jonas Blane squeezed out fire bursts, moving the barrel of the M4 back and forth. Lance Matoskah and Carlito Grey were on his left with Mack Gerhardt and Bob Brown on the right. All five men swept and mingled their salvos, setting up a deadly cross fire that the enemy line ran straight into. A half dozen fell, but the others came on.

Incoming insurgent firing whipped through the trees, dropping a trio of paratroopers. But the mercenaries were at a distinct disadvantage being in the open on the road, and four more of them dropped. Suddenly, as one man, the survivors began backing up, exchanging fire as they withdrew to the concealment they had only recently left.

Paul Dekker, bellowing in rage, was the last to get off the road as he slowly pulled out of the battle. Slugs cracked the air around him as he disappeared into the brush.

Baroudeur was behind the three bunches of skirmishers under his command, keeping them aligned by shouting orders. Their assignment on the west side of the base camp had begun at the exact moment the mortars ceased firing. The newly hired mercenaries to the front led the way into the bivouac area with the Congolese following directly behind them. The going was easy for a bit; then they began taking both semi- and full-automatic fire from their direct front. The Europeans immediately took cover within the huts and structures, but the Congolese were caught up in the ferocity of the moment. They rushed completely through the camp and came under the direct fire of Sergeant Samuel Katungo's machine gun crew and twenty-three riflemen.

It was slaughter pure and simple.

A dozen Congolese crumpled under the volleys. Then one of those things that always go wrong in war occurred when the mercenaries tried to fire through their African comrades. They hit more than they missed, and by the time the Congolese managed to get out of harm's way by pulling back into the bivouac, half their number were sprawled to the front.

Baroudeur, not sure what the hell had happened, assumed the worst. He ordered everyone—European and African alike—to take cover and trade shots with the enemy.

The fighting around the perimeter settled down to attacks by the insurgent groups that were driven back by Tshobutu's paratroopers and the Americans. Although it appeared the good guys were winning, each attack thinned their ranks. Things were deteriorating to a battle of attrition, and that was one situation where the counterinsurgents would eventually be defeated or massacred. After an hour of heavy fighting, Captain Tshobutu's original 112 men were down to seventy-five.

Baroudeur's *group de frappe,* with a total loss of six mercenaries and fifty-five Congolese, now totaled seventy-three. He got a head count over the LASH from the other three groups. Peira had twenty-six men, Coureur twenty-four, and Dekker fifty-five among them. That was a total of 105. The three strike groups had lost twenty men. With his eighteen surviving mercenaries from the new levy, fifty-five Congolese plus the eight mortarmen who had joined him, the insurgents' strength now stood at 186. Vlad Krashchenko and Sergei Malonov showed up later and that added two more to his strength total. Krashchenko would stay with Baroudeur while the Russian was sent to join the other new mercenaries.

Now the fighting was lighter as the two sides settled down to sniping or exchanging fire between small teams. Baroudeur and Krashchenko pulled back from the line to take in some rations and relax during the semi-lull in the action.

Krashchenko took a spoonful of pasta and meatballs. "It is too bad that General Dubois has gone back to Europe."

"It was not wise for him to remain in the Congo with all this going on," Baroudeur said. "It is imperative that he keeps his distance."

"Nevertheless, I think we could use him in a situation like this," Krashchenko said. "We must face facts, Karl. You are a former warrant officer and I was a chief corporal. This situation we are in today calls for more advanced tactical training than you or I ever received in the Legion."

"I suppose you are right," Baroudeur conceded. "But I think the general made a mistake in trying these tactics in a jungle."

"Surely he knows jungle fighting," Krashchenko said. "He served in Indo-China, did he not?"

"Not in the jungle," Baroudeur said. "He arrived there and went straight to Dien Bien Phu. He was captured, then repatriated and went to the colonial paras in Algeria."

Krashchenko shrugged. "We will have the enemy worn down by noon tomorrow anyway. We still outnumber them in spite of our losses."

"I suppose Lulombe will want to come out and see the final victory," Baroudeur said. "It will make him feel the hero."

"Useless bastard!"

7 MAY
0800 HOURS LOCAL
0600 HOURS ZULU

The unexpected arrival of a large combat unit of the Congolese National Army caught the insurgents by surprise. Four hundred paratroopers, cocky and wear-

ing their red berets, charged into the operational area,
attacking Commando Nyoka's separated force. They
knew the exact location of each group, and all their as-
saults were on the flanks. They literally rolled up the enemy lines of resistance while inflicting heavy casualties.
The fighting began at 0600 and was over in two hours.

Jonas Blane and his team stared in open-eyed wonder
at the arrivals when they gathered at the defensive perimeter. When Tshobutu went out to greet them, he was
saluted and cheered. Jonas joined him, and was introduced to the captain's second-in-command of the Sixth
Parachute Infantry Battalion. His name was Lieutenant Robert Nobundo, and he and Tshobutu embraced
warmly.

Nobundo laughed, speaking in English as a courtesy to
Jonas. "I could not believe it when the communications
sergeant ran into headquarters to tell me that Condition
Red had been declared. I knew you would be in this location since you mentioned no other coordinates."

"I got to tell you," Jonas said, "that I am completely
confused by all this."

"It was one of my secrets," Tshobutu said. "I am not
really AWOL as I told you. My battalion was trusted by
the national government and assigned a counterinsurgency mission. However, because of the political situation and certain elements in the Army, it was best to keep
it secret. I took a few men with me to begin what was to
appear as an unauthorized antirevolutionary force. The
bulk of my command stayed in garrison to give the impression that all was normal. However, we arranged for
a contingency in case the situation deteriorated. It was
to be activated with the code words 'Condition Red.' "

"Jesus," Jonah said. "So that's what that was all about."
Then he frowned. "What about when you tried to recruit the drivers from the convoy we stopped?"

Tshobutu shrugged. "A few extra soldiers, if surreptitiously recruited, would come in handy if needed quickly."

"I see," Jonas said. "And that was why the chopper could easily refuel, huh?"

"Of course," Tshobutu replied. "It was flown back to the battalion garrison." He couldn't help but grin at the expression of surprise on Jonas' face. "I also passed the word through my battalion about the sneak attack on the insurgency garrison."

"I get it," Jonas said. "That way the rest of the National Army heard about it as well as the insurgents in Mjikubwa."

"And they thought loyalist troops were coming after them," Tshobutu explained.

Lieutenant Nobundo was still fired up from the fighting. "Are we now able to commit the entire battalion to fight the insurgents? They are on the run. Victory is within our grasp."

Tshobutu shook his head. "I am afraid we are not authorized as of this moment, Robert. It still is not the right time. However, I will need some replacements for the brave men who died in this last battle—detail enough to bring our strength up to a hundred."

"That should be enough to keep things even," Nobundo said. "We counted over a hundred and twenty dead enemy." He laughed again, and glanced at Jonas. "What is it you Americans say? We tore them new assholes?"

"That's it," Jonas said with a chuckle.

"I am ever the optimist," Tshobutu said. "Perhaps something will happen, and we can get rid of the traitors and invaders without calling any attention to it. The President does not want this insurgency to become known to the people."

"I thought he didn't trust the Army or that the military didn't care much one way or the other about the outcome of the rebellion," Jonas said.

"No," Tshobutu said. "The President did not want

the public to know about any unrest in the hinterlands. Thus, there could be no movement of entire units or any other overt actions. I had to leave the bulk of my battalion back in their garrison, but I was allowed to recruit individual soldiers or perhaps a few to join my counter-insurgency mission."

"I agree with Lieutenant Nobundo," Jonas said. "This is the perfect time for an all-out attack on the enemy."

"Sorry, my friend," Tshobutu said. "But orders are orders. The President of the Republic is most insistent that all his orders are explicitly obeyed."

Nobundo frowned in frustration, then looked once more at Jonas. "Are your politicians like ours?"

"All politicians are dickheads," Jonas said.

CHAPTER TWENTY

D.R. OF THE CONGO
MERCENARY HEADQUARTERS
21 MAY
0900 HOURS LOCAL
0700 HOURS ZULU

Impasse.

The French word for "stalemate" had not been spoken aloud among the four men in Commando Nyoka's headquarters that morning, but it was certainly on their collective minds. *Le Général de Brigade* Karl Baroudeur, *le Général de Division* Marcel Lulombe, *le Colonel* Vlad Krashchenko, and *le Commandant* Paul Dekker all sat in silence around the table, paying no attention to the pot of hot coffee and the *feuilleté* sweets served them by the headquarters servants. The tactical map on the nearby wall gave evidence of the standoff that had evolved two weeks after the big attack on the counterinsurgency base camp. There were no battle lines, deep penetrations, or occupied areas indicated. The main camps and garrisons of the antagonists were shown in two circles drawn on the acetate covering a map of the Democratic Republic of the Congo.

The sudden surprise attack that had overwhelmed them left the entire force badly shaken. And now the nervousness had been replaced by confusion. Why wasn't the victory followed up with an all-out effort by the enemy? It was decided that an unidentified weakness had held them back. It was quite possible that another desperate ruse had been instigated by the antirevolutionaries with some unexpected reinforcements. That gave Baroudeur hope. Perhaps there was a way to smash the counterinsurgency. But how?

It was Krashchenko, usually taciturn and introverted, who broke the stillness in the room. "We should have had a triumphant victory march into the city of Kinshasa by now." And with that profound statement, he picked up his cup of coffee and drained it. After shoving one of the pastries into his mouth, he leaned back in his chair as a sign that he had nothing more to say.

Paul Dekker was now stirred up enough to suggest, "The only answer to this tactical situation is an aggressive campaign of *attaque et détruire*—attack and destroy. One does not gain victories by sitting around on one's arse. A dynamic fighting spirit is what is called for here. We must begin vigorous campaigning."

Baroudeur gave him a cold look. "That is what we have been doing all along. And the enemy has been doing the same thing. Unfortunately, we have both been doing it equally well." He snorted. "Or equally badly."

Dekker shrugged. "*C'est la guerre.*"

"The answer is reinforcements," Lulombe said. "Unfortunately, we are not receiving any. It would seem that Luknore's recruiting efforts in Marseille have ground to a halt. Therefore, this campaign is going to be based on simple attrition. The side with the most men will be the ultimate victor."

"I have informed General Dubois of our dwindling

numbers, and he is working on it," Baroudeur said. "At least they sent us enough money to pay our mercenaries bonuses to remain here until the end of their contracts."

"They are being spoiled," Dekker complained. "And promoting all the sergeants to lieutenants and half the volunteers to corporals was unwarranted. Hard discipline would have kept those fellows from deserting. Put the fear of punishment in them. That is my philosophy."

"You are an excellent field commander, Commandant Dekker," Baroudeur said. "But you still think you are in the Legion. If we did not offer some sort of monetary incentive, the men would leave *en masse*. There are no national laws or police for them to fear. No government in the world would consider them deserters. They would simply be unemployed mercenaries."

Dekker the old legionnaire patted his pistol in its holster. "This would stop them, *par Dieu*!"

"There are a little less than a hundred men in the Commando," Baroudeur said. "I do not think the four of us would be able to outshoot that many. We might get a few, but in the end we would be shot down. Our corpses would end up being thrown into the jungle to rot and be eaten by wild beasts."

Dekker, seeing the facts of the matter, became sullen and quieted down.

Baroudeur walked over to his desk and returned with a bottle of cognac. He tossed the coffee in his cup out through the screened window, and filled it with the liquor. After downing the entire drink in a couple of swallows, he took a deep breath. "At this point we are all in agreement. It is the first side that scores a decisive victory who will win this war of ours. It would have to be a surprise attack so unexpected and violent that the enemy is massacred or completely routed."

Now Krashchenko once again expressed himself. "It would not necessarily have to be an attack, *mon général*.

It could also be an ambush. A ruse of some sort used as a snare, eh?"

"Excellent thought," Baroudeur said, complimenting his old comrade. "But what would lure them into a trap? And where could it be sprung? And how many of the bastards would appear on the battlefield? It is impossible to keep track of their numerical strength."

Further conversation was interrupted by a shout from the entrance to the camp. *"Officier de la Garde! À la Première Poste!"*

Krashchenko got out of his chair and walked to the front door to see what was going on. He spotted a small military vehicle of a type he knew well. It was a French Army Auverland Type A3 scout car. It had come to the front of the gate leading out to the highway. A mercenary guard, his AKS-74 trained on it stood motionless, while the officer of the guard spoke to two men sitting inside. This was newly promoted Lieutenant José Peira. After a few moments, he left the vehicle and trotted over to the headquarters building. He stepped inside and nodded to General Lulombe. "There are two Congolese officers who wish to speak to you, sir."

Lulombe was confused. "Are they part of Operation Griffe?"

"No, *mon général*, they are from the Congolese National Army."

Baroudeur was interested. "Bring them in here, Lieutenant Peira. But keep a close eye on them."

Peira saluted and went back to the gate. A couple of minutes later he returned with a captain and lieutenant. When they stepped inside the command center, Lulombe cried out in happy surprise, "Laurence! Andre!" He exchanged manly embraces with both, then turned to the mercenary officers. "Gentlemen! Allow me to present two old friends of mine. I attended the military academy with them. Captain Laurence Nikobu and Lieutenant Andre K'buno." He turned back to the visitors. "So what can I do for you, *mes amis*?"

Nikobu looked at Lulombe's epaulets in surprise. "You are a major general, Marcel?"

"I shall soon be the highest-ranking officer in the National Army," Lulombe said. "This means I'll be the commander-in-chief."

"We have been following the revolution with great interest," Nikobu said. "Like many other officers, we were biding our time to see how things might develop."

K'buno interjected, speaking plainly, "Despite some obvious setbacks you have suffered, we wish to join the insurrection. And we believe we can swing the situation back in your favor."

"Ha!" Lulombe exclaimed. "The tide is turning!"

Nikobu glanced over at the Europeans, then lowered his voice. "We bring a platoon of *infanterie blindée* — armored infantry."

"That is great news!" Lulombe said. "But you may speak freely in front of my comrades." He introduced the three mercenary officers.

Baroudeur stepped forward. "What is the makeup of your platoon, Captain?"

"We have four Cobra IFVs, *mon général*," Nikobu replied.

"And thirty-six infantry soldiers," K'buro added. "Each vehicle also has a driver and two machine gunners. That is a total of forty-eight men. Fifty, if you count Captain Nikobu and me."

Now Baroudeur was very interested. "What sort of armament do these vehicles carry?"

"Each has two machine guns," the lieutenant replied.

"Nothing heavier?" Baroudeur asked, disappointed. "Such as a cannon?"

"No, sir," Nikobu answered. "But the two automatic weapons provide adequate support for the riflemen."

Dekker got to his feet and walked over. "You say a platoon? What about the rest of the company?"

"There is another platoon," Nikobu answered. "But they are not interested in joining the insurgency."

"Would they resist your coming to us?" Baroudeur asked.

"No, *mon général,*" Nikobu said. "They could not care less what we do. And I am the company commander. Only one officer would be left in the garrison, and he is a very junior lieutenant."

Krashchenko now joined the conversation. "How soon can you arrange to have the IFVs and men transferred here?"

Nikobu grinned. "They are in a convoy formation out on the highway."

"Then bring them in," Baroudeur ordered. He turned to Dekker. "See that they are given an area to bivouac. I am going to the communications hut. General Dubois must be informed of this new development."

As Baroudeur went out the door, the young Lieutenant K'buno turned to Lulombe. "Can we be generals too, Marcel?"

Lulombe's laughter boomed through the room. "Of course! I can promise you for sure that when we march into the capital to take over the nation, both you and Laurence will be at least brigadier generals."

OKONDJA, GABON
PETRÓLEO ESPAÑOL-AFRICANO, S.A.
COMPANY HEADQUARTERS
22 MAY
1400 HOURS LOCAL
1200 HOURS ZULU

The Casa 207 Azor transport sat on the runway in
front of the small terminal building. It had landed on
the airfield fifteen minutes earlier, bringing in retired
French Army general Philippe Dubois from Melilla on
the Mediterranean coast. Now he and Karl Baroudeur
sat in the small company office located in the storage
warehouse. The local company manager had politely
withdrawn, and the Consortium officer and the mercenary commander were alone.

Dubois, who had brought no luggage other than a
briefcase with him, was in a hurry to get the session going. Baroudeur had arrived the night before via a Mercedes limousine purloined during the raid on Mjikubwa.
His Congolese driver and two mercenary bodyguards
waited for him outside.

Dubois had taken over the manager's desk and Baroudeur sat on the opposite side. The Frenchman un-
snapped his briefcase and pulled out a manila folder. He
handed it to the mercenary commander. "This is the *or-
dre opérational* you are to put into effect two days from
now. Will there be a problem with that?"

"None at all," Baroudeur assured him. "I keep Commando Nyoka on full alert at all times. The only thing
we will have to do is issue ammunition and rations. That
takes less than a half hour."

"Excellent," Dubois said. "You will have a chance to
study the plans more thoroughly later, but I will give you
a quick rundown in case you have any questions." He
paused and lit a cigarette. "You will begin this mission
by sending a small detachment to occupy the village of

Mwitukijiji. No more than ten men. It is important that they be native troops. And let two of your least desirable mercenaries act as their commanders as they may suffer heavy casualties in the early stages of the operation. And make no effort to conceal when they leave and arrive, understand?"

"Yes, *mon général*," Baroudeur said. "You want things made very apparent, *n'est pas*?"

"Right," Dubois said. "We want word of the occupation to get back to the enemy. The idea is for them to attack the place to drive your men out."

"They should have no trouble doing that," Baroudeur said. "There will be only two mercenaries and eight Congolese."

"Oh, yes, they will," Dubois said with a smile, "because you will have more than those ten men there. You must surreptitiously have the entire force—mercenaries and Congolese—be in the near vicinity of the village. And that, of course, will include those four Cobra IFVs. And I must say acquiring them was extremely fortunate for our cause. They will be the most important part of our plan."

"I believe I understand what is to happen," Baroudeur said. "As soon as the enemy attacks and enters the village, we will counterattack with the IFVs leading the assault."

"Exactly! From that point on, I will leave the operation up to you. You may be able to work out an envelopment maneuver or perhaps simply smash into them and blast the bastards to hell. Our satellite reconnaissance indicates they number a hundred or so. Thus a quick success will not be difficult."

"What is to happen after our victory?" Baroudeur asked.

"It is imperative that you move fast to avoid the counterinsurgents' reaction force," Dubois said. "I am speaking of the Sixth Parachute Infantry Battalion. If they are able to interfere again, things will be more difficult than ever."

"I understand completely," Baroudeur said.

"Gather up any prisoners you may capture and follow the final annex of the operations order," Dubois said. "You must do your best to capture that Captain Tshobutu alive. He will make an excellent hostage, and his execution will break the morale of his men."

"That is something I will certainly concentrate on," Baroudeur said.

"After you destroy the enemy at Mwitukijiji, you will proceed to Camp Ukaidi," Dubois continued. "When you arrive there, make a public show of your victory and prisoners. General Lulombe will speak to the troops about the revolution."

Lulombe grinned with delight. "They will flock to our colors, *mon général*!"

"That is why you were chosen to be the next president of the Democratic Republic of the Congo," Dubois said. "And we have a speech already prepared for you." He turned to Baroudeur. "Next you go to Camp Kabila and do the same thing. Make another appeal to the troops stationed there. This is the last step before you march into the capital, led by your armored infantry platoon."

"Should we keep the mercenaries in the background?" Baroudeur asked.

"Not at all," Dubois said. "They will show that there is strong international support behind the insurrection."

"I understand fully," Baroudeur said.

"There will be a time of possibly three or four months in which Lulombe and his chosen officers can actually run the government. Then we Europeans will arrive on the scene and take control of everything. That will be done quickly and violently." Now his attention was switched to Lulombe. "You will continue holding office as a figurehead for us."

"I will comply," Lulombe promised.

"Understood," Baroudeur said, picking up the manila folder holding the operations order.

Dubois stood up and offered his hand. "Good luck, General Baroudeur. We know we can depend on you." He offered his hand to Lulombe. "And we also have faith in your abilities, General."

"I will cooperate fully."

INSURGENCY GARRISON
23 MAY
1930 HOURS LOCAL
1730 HOURS ZULU

It had been one hell of a busy day for both the mercenaries and their Congolese allies. The servants had been pulled from their domestic duties to attend to their usual extracurricular activity of loading cartridges into thirty-round magazines for the FA-MAS and AKS-74 rifles. Additionally, a group was culled to take care of the ammo belts for the eight machine guns carried on the Cobra IFVs.

The soldiery concentrated on drawing rations and preparing their personal equipment for the final battle of Operation Griffe. The drivers of the SAMIL trucks topped off their vehicles, checked the oil and tire pressure, and performed other necessary PM for the transportation job ahead. They were expecting to put a hell of a lot of kilometers on the odometers in the next week or so.

The four IFVs were parked in a row next to the command center, looking ominous with their armored bodies, tracks, and machine guns. These were excellent vehicles developed in Belgium in the mid-1980s. The Cobras, capable of carrying nine infantrymen, each had steel bodies and sported two machine guns: a roof-mounted Browning M2 12.7-millimeter heavy machine gun and a 7.62-millimeter general purpose machine gun.

The power plant was a six-cylinder turbo diesel that provided a maximum speed of 75 kilometers an hour, and could go 600 kilometers on a load of fuel. In addition they were fully amphibious and could get up to 10 kilometers an hour in water. This power was provided by water jets located on the rear.

Amidst all this activity, Baroudeur, Krashchenko, Dekker, and the mercenary officers carefully went over General Dubois' operations plan that was to be implemented beginning early the next morning.

CHAPTER TWENTY-ONE

The three-man reconnaissance patrol could hear the voices of people as they crept quietly through the thick jungle growth toward the village. Bob Brown, Lance Matoskah, and the Congolese NCO Samuel Katungo were assigned the mission that came about from intelligence brought in by some of the Congolese paratroopers. They had chanced upon some local women digging roots out in the countryside the day before, and stopped to pass the time of day. During some casual joking and flirting, the conversation turned to the strangers who had arrived in the village that day. The women said that eight soldiers of the National Army and two European soldiers had shown up, and had situated themselves in the little rural community. It appeared they might be staying for a while.

When the paratroopers returned to the counterinsurgency base camp, they immediately went to Captain Tshobutu's headquarters and reported what they had heard. This resulted in a quick conference between the five Unit operators, Tshobutu, Sublieutenant Pierre Kintuba, and Sergeant Samuel Katungo, who had been appointed acting sergeant major. Bob Brown knew the village, having been there briefly as an occupier during his infiltration of Commando Nyoka. Jonas Blane quickly decided that the information should be checked out; thus Bob, Lance, and Katungo were selected to conduct a reconnaissance.

Now the patrol had neared the edge of the tree line, and Bob found a good spot to set up a simple OP. He took out his binoculars while Lance and Katungo acted as security on both flanks. Bob had a good view of the village square, remembering what it had been like on the day the National Army roadblock had been shot up. M'kalo the peddler had been displaying his wares for the local ladies. It seemed like a hundred years ago after all that had happened since then.

A few minutes passed and Bob saw a couple of Congolese soldiers strolling among the huts and emerging into the square. A few moments later, two white men appeared and Bob recognized the cammie uniforms with the cobra insignia. One of the men was a complete stranger, but he recognized the other as a Frenchman who was billeted in the same barracks he shared with Simon Cooper and Andre Coureur. Then a group of more Congolese military appeared. Bob counted six. That tallied with the report turned in by Tshobutu's paratroopers.

Bob was confused. Why the hell would Baroudeur or Krashchenko or whoever dispatch ten guys to this isolated place? They evidently didn't have anything to do, except stand around and drink brew. Bob whispered into his LASH, "We're gonna camp here for an hour or two and see if something develops. So far all those guys are doing is just hanging out. I haven't seen any vehicles, so they may get picked up for a trip back to their garrison."

Lance had an idea. "Maybe they're AWOL or got girlfriends living here."

"I do not think so," Katungo said. "Local girls do not like soldiers too much. And it would be shameful for them to take any as lovers. Their fathers and brothers would beat them, and they could not get husbands."

Bob studied the scene again in his binoculars. "This is really mind-boggling. They're not on guard duty or minding a roadblock or anything at all."

Lance opined, "Well, there must be some reason or other that the sons of bitches are there."

1045 HOURS LOCAL
0845 HOURS ZULU

Bob put his binoculars back in the case on his pistol belt. "Well, crapola! Let's get on back. There's nothing going on. Jonas is gonna have to make a decision about what to do about this." The three moved back into the jungle, turning toward the base camp. "Katungo, take the point," Bob said. "Lance, you're Tail-End-Charlie."

They moved out, walking slowly and carefully through the thick vegetation. They remained within sight of one another because of the foliage, staying alert for more careless villagers who might be tramping around the immediate area. That could create a very awkward and tragic situation. The insurgents would learn they had been discovered if anyone who came across the patrol was allowed to return to the settlement. The only way to prevent that was unthinkable but would have to be done.

The patrol hadn't gone much more than fifty meters

when Katungo suddenly dropped into a crouching position. Bob and Lance did the same. "I hear talking," the Congolese said over the LASH.

"Any movement?" Bob asked.

"Very little," Katungo reported.

Bob turned and gestured to Lance, then led the way up to where Katungo had dropped down behind some brush. When the two operators reached the spot, they could hear a bit of movement and a voice that was definitely feminine. Then another. And a third.

Katungo rose up slightly, then looked back and grinned. "Three young girls from the village. It looks like they pick wild fruit."

"Let's talk to them," Bob said. "They won't know we've reconned their hometown."

Katungo stood up and walked in the direction of the noise. *"Hamjambo,"* he said.

"Hujambo," came back simultaneous greetings.

Now Bob and Lance walked up and saw a trio of skinny teenage girls with baskets of fruit they had picked. Two wore tank tops and skirts, the third one had shorts on. She pointed to Bob with a big smile and spoke in Swahili.

Katungo turned to Bob. "She is saying she knows you. She is saying you saved her from bad men."

Bob stepped forward and recognized her. She was the one that Schleck and Kowalski were getting ready to rape. "Tell her that I'm glad she is well."

This started a short but animated conversation between Katungo and the girl. Then the other two joined in, and it became apparent that the Congolese sergeant was interrogating them in a gentle, friendly fashion. When he finished, he looked at the two Americans with a serious expression on his face.

"They told me about the ten men in the village," he explained. "I acted surprised of course. Then they said there are more of the 'bad' soldiers farther away. They say they have steel cars with guns on them."

"Did they give you the location?" Bob asked.

"In a way," Katungo said. "There is an old field that was once used for farming two kilometers on the other side of the village. It is there where the others are."

"We got to check that out," Bob said.

"Yes," Katungo said. "I told the girls to be silent about us. I said they must not tell that we are out here. They will do so. I trust them. You are a hero to them because you saved Johari from being ravished. I told them we will drive the bad men away. The girls will not tell even their families of us being here."

Now Bob knew the name of the girl he had aided during the attempted rape. He gave her a nod and a smile, then issued an order. "Let's have a look at that old farm or whatever it is."

As the patrol moved out, Johari called out, *"Ahsanteni sana. Kwa heri, askari."*

Katungo translated for Bob. "The girl say, 'Many thanks. Goodbye, soldier.' "

1200 HOURS LOCAL
1000 HOURS ZULU

It had taken a long time to locate the area revealed by the village girls. The instructions were vague, and Bob used his compass to decide what azimuth they should move toward the opposite side of the village. The girls were a bit off in their directions, but eventually, the patrol drew near the highway, and Bob swung a tad more to the west. If there were vehicles involved with this unknown force, they would not be able to go too far off the roads into the tropical forest.

Bob had taken the point, and he almost stumbled out of the jungle onto the site they were looking for. He had caught sight of a mercenary through the trees just in time to keep from being seen. Noise discipline was be-

ing strictly observed by the insurgents, which accounted
for his being unaware of their presence. He went to the
ground, signaling Lance and Katungo to hold up where
they were. Then he crawled slowly and very carefully
forward until he found good concealment that offered
a view of the old field.

Bob's eyes opened wide when he was able to take in
the entire picture. He estimated there was a combined
force of maybe a hundred and fifty mercenaries and
Congolese insurgents camped in the immediate area.
He recognized four vehicles parked under a spread
of camouflage netting as infantry fighting vehicles. He
waved back at Katungo to come forward. The sergeant
took three full minutes of wary crawling to join him. Bob
pointed to the vehicles and whispered in his LASH, "Do
you recognize that type of IFV?"

"Belgian Cobras," Katungo whispered back. "Standard in the National Army. They carry nine infantrymen,
have two machine guns. Good for attack."

"You ain't kidding," Bob replied in a worried tone.
Then he spotted Commandant Dekker emerge from behind the vehicles. The mercenaries quickly formed up,
and Karl Baroudeur and Vlad Krashchenko came onto
the scene. They began speaking to the Europeans, and
Bob figured it was a briefing of sorts. "Those jerks are
up to something big."

He nodded to the Congolese sergeant and they pulled
back to join Lance Matoskah in the rear.

COUNTERINSURGENCY BASE CAMP
1600 HOURS LOCAL
1400 HOURS ZULU

Bob Brown, with Lance Matoskah and Samuel Katungo standing behind him, had given a thorough oral
report of the reconnaissance to the assembled group

in the headquarters hut. Now, after digesting the intel-ligence, Jonas Blane and Captain Edouard Tshobutu sat in silence, each man mulling over the disturbing news that had been presented. Mack Gerhardt and Carlito Grey stood off to one side, waiting for the reaction of their leader.

Finally Jonas spoke up. "I think I know what those sons of bitches are doing. They put ten men in the village to be easily discovered."

Mack smirked. "I'll bet those guys were real winners. They'll be the first ones blown away if the place is at-tacked."

"Exactly," Jonas said. "This is designed to draw a raid on the place. Those expendable bastards in the village get wiped out, and we waltz into the place big, fat, dumb, and happy, thinking we scored a victory."

"Indeed," Tshobutu agreed. "Then they unleash the IFVs on us, followed up by the infantrymen, mercenar-ies, and insurgents in a mass assault."

"I figure the sons of bitches will form into three groups for the attack against us," Jonas continued. "One for head-on contact, and two to sweep around the flanks and pin us in." He started thinking again, and everyone continued to give him their full attention. After a min-ute he fixed his eyes on Tshobutu. "What about Condi-tion Red?"

Tshobutu shook his head. "It would take time to have another one so soon."

"What's the status of our antitank weapons?"

"Not bad," the Congolese captain replied. "We have sev-eral Panzerfaust-Three antitank missiles in our arsenal."

"I'm not familiar with 'em," Jonas said.

"They are of German manufacture," Tshobutu ex-plained. "It is a disposable launcher tube with a rocket that carries a shaped charge warhead. It is a caliber of one hundred and ten millimeters, which is a bit more than four and a quarter inches."

"Sounds like a handy gadget," Jonas remarked. "What's the range?"

"Five hundred meters for a stationary target. Three hundred for one that is moving. By the way, it can penetrate seven hundred millimeters of armor."

"Inches again, please," Jonas requested.

"Approximately twenty-seven and a half," Tshobutu replied.

"Do you have any personnel who know how to use 'em?" Jonas inquired.

"Of course."

"Okay," Jonas said. "If this works out, we won't need Condition Red. So here's the basic plan as of this moment. We'll refine it later. We mount what will appear to be a reckless charge against the village. We'll make a lot of noise during our approach for two reasons. The first is to give the impression we are cocky and arrogant, and the second to give the villagers a chance to haul ass out of the place and get out of harm's way."

Mack grimaced. "That initial contact group is going to sustain heavy casualties."

"Yes," Jonas agreed. "No doubt about that."

"I volunteer to lead it," Mack said.

"You're the man," Jonas said with a grin and a wink. "Now while that is going on we want four antiarmor teams to be established along the road leading into the village. Each will have a couple of those panzer-whata-ya-call-'ems." He looked over at Mack. "The instant those IFVs come on the scene with the riflemen, you break contact and haul ass straight down the road."

"I get it," Mack said. "We'll get 'em to chase us into an armor ambush."

"Yeah," Jonas said. "And you better get your asses through that area as fast as you can or you gonna be wearing antitank missiles for hats."

"Will do," Mack assured him.

"When the IFVs are knocked out, the rest of our

brave army will join the fray, and we'll engage the enemy foot soldiers in what is commonly referred to as 'mortal combat.' "

Carlito Grey grinned. "Then we win the war and go home."

"You bet," Jonas said. Then he added, "If we, indeed, win the war."

Bob Brown asked, "And if we lose?"

"Nothing to worry about," Jonas said. "Copies of our wills are in Colonel Ryan's files."

"Now there's a cheerful thought," Bob remarked.

CHAPTER TWENTY-TWO

D.R. OF THE CONGO
OPERATIONAL AREA
26 MAY
0445 HOURS LOCAL
0245 HOURS ZULU

The entire counterinsurgency force was now in position to launch the attack on the village of Mwitukijiji. It had taken most of the night to get the job done in the almost complete darkness of the jungle. Only the five Unit operators, Captain Edouard Tshobutu, and Sublieutenant Pierre Kintuba had night-vision goggles, which meant they had to physically lead the Congolese paratroopers into the proper assault positions. It took most of the night, and noise discipline was something of a problem, so the youngest soldiers were stationed in the rear, where they would be with Jonas Blane, backing up Mack Gerhardt and his team.

Now Mack and his fifteen-man attack force traveled by foot up the road leading to the village. This group was in the most precarious position of the operation since it was their job to lead the four IFVs into the ambush site. Jonas was right behind him with the fifteen recruits.

The thirty men out on the left flank of the trap were led by Bob Brown and Captain Tshobutu. Another thirty, with Carlito Grey and Sublieutenant Kintuba, were securely located on the right. Each of these groups had two teams for the Panzerfausts, spaced along their line of fire at ten-meter intervals. And farther back, to act as both the support and security team for the armor ambush, were Lance Matoskah and Sergeant Samuel Katungo with the remaining twenty men. There wouldn't be much for them to do in the action until the first of the infantry fighting vehicles was right up on top of them.

Dawn had begun to lighten the eastern horizon, and all the leaders gazed at their synchronized watches, waiting for the exact time to begin this risky assault that would decide the final outcome of the campaign.

0500 HOURS LOCAL
0300 HOURS ZULU

Jonas Blane's voice came over the LASH commo system, crisp and low. "Execute! Execute! Execute!"

Mack ordered his line of skirmishers to move toward the village. After going fifty meters, they began firing high to avoid hitting civilians. They also yelled and whistled as loudly as they could to announce their presence. Behind them, Jonas' backup team was also wildly bellowing to add to the din. The reasons behind what seemed useless and risky noise were to scare the hell out of the villagers so that they would flee, and to make the mercenaries and Congolese insurgents think a strong frontal attack was rolling their way.

The two mercenaries and their eight Congolese comrades, who had been sleeping beside a storage hut when the shooting started, frantically kicked themselves free of their envelope rolls of ponchos and blankets. They grabbed their weapons and rushed to a hastily prepared fighting position at the edge of the hamlet.

As the sounds of firing and bellowing built up, the panic-stricken villagers fled their huts in disarray. These were people who knew the terror of surprise raids in their lifetimes. Several times in the past they had fled bandits, renegade soldiers, and other armed groups with violent agendas who came out of nowhere to murder, rape and pillage. There was only one thing to do in the shock and confusion of such a moment: run and hide as fast as possible. Due to their previous experiences, they knew the shortest ways to the safest places in the jungle.

The insurgents ignored the people fleeing the village, and got behind their sandbag emplacements for the fight. They immediately began firing at the shadowy figures that appeared in the roadway.

Mack's men now left the road and sought concealment and cover in the jungle alongside it. As soon as they were positioned, they renewed their fusillades. The swarms of 5.56-millimeter slugs pounded the sandbags of the emplacement, sending dust and dirt flying with each impact. Within sixty seconds, Jonas' group was close enough that they could add more gunfire to the effort.

The French mercenary in charge of the village defense decided enough was enough. Two of the Congolese had already been hit, and were sprawled behind the barricade. And the rate of incoming rounds was quickly increasing.

"Retirez! Allez! Allez!"

They left the cover of the sandbags, scampering rearward, hoping to reach the rest of the commando. But their luck was bad and they were slow. Before they were able to go fifteen meters, another Congolese insurgent and both mercenaries were knocked rolling to the ground, their bodies torn up by the hail of metal being poured at them. The five living Congolese disappeared into the village as they fled for their lives.

The insurgent bivouac had been on fifty percent alert, and the moment the firing broke out, Commandant Paul Dekker was on his feet getting everyone out of their envelope rolls. The trio of drivers, eight machine gunners, and thirty-six riflemen assigned to the IFVs rushed for the vehicles, where Captain Laurence Nikobu and his second-in-command, Lieutenant Andre K'buno, already waited for them.

The surviving Congolese soldiers who had been assigned to the village burst onto the scene. They had no idea what they were supposed to do, and they hesitated for a few moments, observing the activity going on to their direct front. After a quick consultation among themselves, they rushed to join their squads.

Dekker quickly assembled the force into prearranged attack positions. The armored infantry riflemen were formed up directly behind their vehicles to follow them into the battle. The IFVs would provide cover as they advanced toward the enemy with their total of eight machine guns blazing.

The mercenaries, organized into four sections of twenty men each, were to trail after them. The mass of almost fifty Congolese would bring up the rear.

Brigadier General Karl Baroudeur and Colonel Vlad Krashchenko stood off to the side, letting their old Foreign Legion buddy Dekker get the ball rolling. Baroudeur had issued his orders the night before, and he was positive that the commandant could get the operation under way in an expedient and timely manner.

It turned out his confidence had been put in the right man. Only ten minutes had passed since the firing started, and Dekker had everything organized well enough to order the IFVs to move out. The ground force immediately followed. The ex-legionnaire's battle ardor was so great that as he watched the small army advance to engage the enemy, he instinctively shouted out his old outfit's battle cry.

"*À moi, la Légion!*"

Mack Gerhardt and his men entered Mwitukijiji, and he brought them to a halt after penetrating the village for some fifteen meters. After a quick survey of the scene, Mack went on his LASH, saying, "This is Dirt Diver. All civilians are out of the area. Over."

"Roger, out," Jonas Blane answered. He showed up a couple of minutes later with the recruits, and he held them at the edge of the hamlet. The kids knew what they were to do. It was a simple task of waiting until the counterattack closed in on them with the armored vehicles to the front, then turning and running like hell down the road into the ambush area. They understood completely that they were to fool the enemy into chasing after them into a trap. Gerhardt's veterans had a slightly more difficult assignment. They would fire a few defiant rounds at the enemy before hauling ass, but for the same purpose.

Back at the ambush site, Captain Tshobutu was in charge of the killer teams concealed on both sides of the road. During the initial assault on the village, he had gone to the support and security team where Lance Matoskah, Sergeant Katungo, and their twenty troopers had the responsibility of hemming in that side of the battle. Normally they would be expected to provide covering fire for the withdrawal of the killer teams, but this was an unusual situation in which the ambush was set up especially for stopping a counterattack. Thus, their job was to wait for the lead vehicle to be destroyed, then leave their positions to perform an aggressive assault that would carry them as far down the road as possible toward the village. They were to keep going until meeting the main body of the enemy.

The captain checked in with Matoskah, who was standing behind the firing line. "How does it look, Lieutenant?"

Lance always grinned when he was referred to as an officer. "Well, sir, we're all down and dirty. Bring the bastards on."

"If for some reason not all of the IFVs are destroyed, you will have to attack any survivors with hand grenades. That could end up being the most dangerous part of this morning's work."

"Right, sir," Lance said. "Don't worry. Everybody's briefed and ready."

Now satisfied, Tshobutu walked down the two lines of the killer teams. The panzerfaust crew closest to the village would wait for the fourth vehicle to appear before firing. Fifteen meters down the road was the second antiarmor weapon that would be responsible for number three. The other two crews, in their turn, would take out vehicles one and two. Each had an extra missile in case of a miss, but it would have to be fired hastily to maintain control of the situation.

Mack's men had no cover, but they did have huts for concealment. They now waited out of sight for the first sign of the enemy. It didn't take long. The lead IFV, with both machine guns spitting rapid-fire bursts, broke out of the jungle and sped toward the village.

"Fire and run!" Mack yelled.

His men complied, their uneven volleys bouncing and pinging off the steel hulls of the vehicle. With that formality taken care of, they left their cover, running as fast as possible toward the opposite side of the village.

A couple of the men were raked with the automatic incoming, and collapsed under the violent impact of the 7.62- and 12.7-millimeter slugs.

Jonas and his youngsters were already tearing down the road when Mack's men emerged from the huts, running after them. Within seconds the first IFV, still firing, appeared. Then the second showed up, quickly followed by the third and fourth. A wide gap between them and the riflemen following had developed in the headlong rush of the attack.

The men under Jonas and Mack's command continued dashing down the road between the two killer teams. Up at the front end closest to the village, Bob Brown stood with the first panzerfaust crew. He counted aloud as the enemy vehicles rolled past. "One! Two! Three! Fire, goddamn it, fire!"

The Congolese paratrooper wasn't required to aim carefully. As soon as the IFV was in front of him, he pulled the trigger. It took only a bit of an instant for the rocket to slam into the side of the vehicle, and only a millisecond for it to burn its way through the armor and explode. The gunner on the heavy machine gun in the turret shot straight up into the air some twenty feet, then fell back bouncing off the steel hull. Smoke and fire came out of the viewing ports.

The first IFV, farther up and close to where Lance Matoskah and Sergeant Samuel Katungo waited with their support and security team, was the second hit. In this case the machine gunners in the turret sighted the panzerfaust crew before they could fire, and knew what was happening. The pair scrambled up and out of the vehicle, jumping off just as the missile slammed into it. They hit the road, rolled, and leaped to their feet in time to be hit by furious automatic fire from the paratroopers in the cover at the sides of the road. Neither heard the final explosion that blasted the turret up to tumble off the chassis.

The second and third IFVs suffered the same fate as their brothers, with the 110-millimeter warheads simultaneously burning through the steel of their sides then exploding. The dynamics of the detonations turned the men inside into chopped charred hunks of meat that bounced around the interior.

Now Lance and Katungo rushed forward with their men closely following. The killer team commanded by Bob Brown and Captain Tshobutu joined in as did the one led by Carlito Grey and Lieutenant Kintuba. At the same instant, Jonas Blane and Mack Gerhardt, along with their combined force of twenty-five survivors, re-entered the fray. As the entire counterinsurgency group entered the village they spread out.

The first enemy group to collapse under the heavy fire of the counterattack was the armored infantry riflemen. They were bunched close together as tactics dictated, and they went down like bowling pins. The mercenaries behind them hesitated, then quickly sought cover to return fire.

Now the Unit operators and their comrades continued to spread out, maintaining team integrity. The killer team on the left flank moved to the north, curling around the insurgents. The one on the right went in an opposite direction in the same maneuver. The two groups on the road under Jonas and Mack charged straight ahead. Deadly cross fires raked the enemy with enfilading volleys that swept their battle formations from one end to the other.

The Congolese insurgents in the rear perceived the attack beginning to rapidly break up. They could see the battle was lost, and they broke ranks and turned tail. The instant their support was gone, Commander Paul Dekker instantly surmised that the tactical situation had deteriorated for him and his mercenaries. He spoke into his LASH to get the squad leaders to pull their men back and consolidate. The ex-legionnaire also instructed one squad to head into the jungle and find the local people hiding in the trees. "Force them back to the village into a position between us and the enemy!"

The squad leader chosen for the job led his men into the trees. They found the entire population crouched and terrified in a small clearing. The mercenaries began kicking them and striking out with rifle butts to get them moving back into the village. Men, women, and children were rushed along until they began to move into the huts. At that point the squad leader ordered his men to break away and return to the main group of mercenaries.

Dekker could now see he had some human shields between him and the advancing enemy. He gave a quick order to fire through them at the counterattackers. The bullets struck the mass of the civilians, inflicting heavy casualties.

"Cease fire to the front!" Jonas Blane yelled into his LASH. "Both flanks keep maneuvering."

The leaders on the north and south sides of the formation obeyed, continuing to work their way into an enveloping formation while not firing. Jonas, Mack, and their bunch in the center squatted down to avoid the bullets flying at them through the crowd of screaming and dying villagers.

Karl Baroudeur, with Vlad Krashchenko and Marcel Lulombe close behind him, ran like hell across the open ground, where Commando Nyoka had bivouacked the night before. They reached the road on the other side, where the Mercedes limousine was parked. When they reached the big car, Baroudeur suddenly pulled his pistol and swung around. He shot Lulombe straight in the face, then put two more slugs into his chest.

He and Krashchenko got into the vehicle and took off down the road in the direction of their garrison.

*   *   *

Now the counterinsurgency flanking units closed around the surviving mercenaries. Jonas and Mack with their teams worked their way through the stunned civilians and were able to resume firing. They poured furious salvos into the surviving enemy. Commandant Paul Dekker ordered his men into a tight circle. He screamed out in French, "This is in the traditional grandeur of the *Légion Étrangère*! A last stand. We shall die in the glory of battle!"

A pragmatic German mercenary turned his AKS-74 rifle on the man and shot him dead. "*Dummkopf!*" he said, spitting.

"They're surrendering on this side," Carlito Grey announced over the LASH.

"Yeah," Bob Brown came in. "Over here too."

Jonas Blane wasn't celebrating. "I want all medics in the village to start giving aid to the wounded civilians. Do it immediately if not sooner!"

The entire counterinsurgency group now moved in, forcing the mercenaries into a tight group with their hands raised. Then the enemy was pulled out, one by one, to be disarmed and searched. Bob Brown was recognized by several who looked at him in surprise. He grabbed one of the men who had been in his barracks. "Have you seen Simon Cooper?"

"He is dead," the guy, an English-speaking Spaniard, replied. "One of the first to get hit. Your *amigo* Coureur is probably alive. I saw him knocked down, but he seemed to be wounded."

Jonas Blane walked up. "Which one of you sons of bitches ordered those villagers into the line of fire?"

"It was Commandant Dekker," the Spaniard said.

"Which one is he?" Jonas asked in a cold voice.

"He was shot when he wanted us to make a last stand."

"Show me his body."

The Spaniard, with his hands still in the air, led Jonas and Bob around the group to the other side of the crowd of prisoners. Paul Dekker, the front of his uniform soaked in blood, lay on his back staring up at nothing with dead eyes. Jonas glanced at Bob. "Is he the one?"

Bob nodded. "Yeah. He's the field commander. He wasn't a headquarters weenie. He was the take-charge guy in combat."

"Well," Jonas said, "the son of a bitch died while he was in charge, didn't he?"

"Y'know something, boss," Bob remarked. "That's the way he would've wanted it."

Jonas sneered. "Well, ain't that just too sweet?"

CHAPTER TWENTY-THREE

D.R. OF THE CONGO
OPERATIONAL AREA
26 MAY
1550 HOURS LOCAL
1350 HOURS ZULU

The wounded civilians had been treated by the medics, and while they were grateful for the kind treatment, the people harbored a sullen resentment against the counterinsurgents. As far as they were concerned, both sides were responsible for the atrocity that had maimed and killed their friends and family members. It was the same old story for the Congolese villagers, who had been caught in the middle of civil wars, rebellions, and invasions. They had paid the ultimate price in suffering more times than they could count.

Captain Tshobutu made arrangements to have ambulances come from Mjikubwa to pick up the more seriously injured civilians. This was done by having Carlito Grey use his Shadowfire radio to make commo with the Sixth Parachute Infantry Battalion at their nearby garrison. From there word went to certain intelligence elements in the Congolese National Government. It was they who contacted the *gendarmerie* with no other information except that there were confirmed injuries at the village of Mwitukijiji, and that medical evacuation was urgently required.

While all that was going on, the mercenary prisoners were herded into a group with their arms tightly bound behind them for the forced march back to the base camp. The Congolese paratroopers were extremely rough with the foreign EPWs, giving bruising blows with rifle butts as they prepared them for the hike. Two of the most energetic guards were Privates Nagatu and M'buta. Although they were not the soldiers that the mercenaries were, the two kids let the Europeans know who was in charge. They bellowed orders at them in Swahili, punctuating the commands with hard kicks to shins and the backs of calves. All mercenaries who were WIA and could not be classified as walking wounded were shot out of hand where they lay. The lucky ones were unconscious; the less fortunate, who were aware of what was going on, saw the end coming.

The five Unit operators did nothing to interfere with the less than merciful treatment. When on missions in foreign countries, they were required not to intervene in local customs and traditions no matter how distasteful. Such actions could stir up serious resentment and not only jeopardize current operations but any further cooperation with the government concerned.

Another thing to take into consideration was that the mercenaries were foreign invaders, hired to come in to topple the national government. The paratroopers were members of an elite battalion, well trained, patriotic, and loyal to their officers and country. Some of their friends had been killed and wounded in that day's actions, and those casualties lessened any inclinations to show kindness to the Europeans who had shown up to do mayhem for the almighty Euro. Consequently, the foreigners had gone from soldiers of fortune to soldiers of misfortune.

When captors and captives left the village, the Americans fell back to the rear of the formation to follow. Jonas Blane glanced over at Bob Brown. "I noticed you walking around checking out the mercenary KIAs."

"Yeah," Bob said. "I was looking for a kid I met there. A Brit by the name of Simon Cooper. He was AWOL from the Parachute Regiment. I'm afraid Simon didn't make very wise decisions in his life. I found him out where Charlie Grey and Sergeant Katungo had been. He got stitched from chest to belly." He reached into his pocket and pulled out a piece of bloodstained paper. "Simon had written down his parents' address. I suppose he hoped that if he was killed they would be informed. From the way he spoke of his mother and father, they sounded like decent people. I'm thinking of writing them and letting them know what happened to their son."

Jonas reached over and grabbed the paper, wadding it up and throwing it away. "You remember one thing, Sergeant Brown. You were not—I say again—*were not* here! Is that clear?"

"Right, boss," Bob said. "It was just that I kind of liked him. I thought an anonymous letter might be a closing for them."

"Stupid idea!"

"Right, boss."

COUNTERINSURGENCY BASE CAMP
27 MAY
0900 HOURS LOCAL
0700 HOURS ZULU

Lieutenant José Peira sat in the chair in Captain Tshobutu's hut. Jonas Blane and Tshobutu stood in front of him. Bob Brown leaned against the captain's desk, watching the interrogation of his former squad leader. The Portuguese's face was bruised, and one eye was almost swollen shut from the beatings he had received from the Congolese paratroopers during the march from the battle site. When he had first been brought into the hut, he had prepared himself for pure torture, but now realized he was going to go through a simple, primary interrogation.

Jonas handed a bottle of cognac to the EPW, and Peira took a swallow. "Thank you."

"It looks like you and your comrades have been getting some pretty rough treatment," Jonas said.

"It is a violation of the Geneva Conventions," Peira said through battered lips. "The document gives us rights as prisoners of war."

"You are not covered by that agreement," Jonas said. "Keep in mind that you're not a member of the armed forces of any recognized sovereign government. You are a mercenary by choice, which was a bad one by the way."

"What about you?" Peira asked. "You are an American like Ted Durant."

"Who the hell is Ted Durant?" Jonas asked.

Bob interjected, "That was my cover name when I joined the mercenaries."

"I'd forgotten about that," Jonas said.

Peira snuffed through his broken nose, looking up at Jonas. "What is your status here, *americano*? I do not think you are legal either."

"I'll ask the questions," Jonas snarled. "If you show me any disrespect, I'll close your other eye."

Peira was a man with very little hope, and he hung his head in despair.

"We know the way mercenaries operated through the INTSUM given us by Brown," Jonas said. "What we're really curious about is the real chain of command of the outfit called Commando Nyoka. In other words, the higher echelons. Who is this guy by the name of Baroudeur?"

"He was the commander of the Europeans," Peira said.

"We know that," Jonas snapped. "Who is he working for? We need names, understand? And places along with times and dates."

"None of us knew much about Baroudeur or who he worked for," Peira said. "He and Krashchenko were old friends in the French Foreign Legion. The field commander Dekker knew them from the Legion too. That's all I can say. And you won't find anyone else who can tell you more."

"You were the only surviving officer," Jonas pointed out. "It's logical that you should know more than the volunteers."

Peira shook his head. "We knew nothing except that a Spanish petroleum survey company provided transportation for us and a base of operations in Gabon."

"Brown has already told us all about that," Jonas said. He sighed, looking at Bob. "You were right. Nobody can trace these guys back beyond Baroudeur and Krashchenko."

Bob nodded his agreement. "There's that Spanish petroleum outfit, but I'd bet my left nut that they have their asses covered with layers of masking screens and outright misinformation. Each avenue of investigation will lead to a dead end."

"I'm afraid you're right," Jonas said.

Tshobutu took a deep breath. "It will take months or years to get to that hard-core consortium or whatever they call it."

"It could be they'll never be compromised," Jonas said. He gave his attention back to Peira. "There is one thing you can tell us that we want to know for sure. Who was responsible for herding the civilians back into the village? Who placed them in the line of fire?"

"The order was given by Dekker," Peira said. "I heard him issue it, but I was not in the group that went after them." He took a deep breath. "Let me give you an honest opinion. The people behind this insurrection are powerful—do you understand that? They have a big organization with unlimited finances. Eventually we would have had artillery and tanks. But you moved too fast for us to get fully organized."

"It's obvious there's nothing you can tell us," Jonas said.

"That is something we both know now," Peira remarked.

Tshobutu shrugged, then turned to the guard at the door. "Take the prisoner back to the others."

Peira stood up. "What is to happen to us?"

Tshobutu gave him a cold look. "Justice. That is what will happen to you. Justice." Then he repeated the word in Portuguese for more emphasis: *"Justiça!"*

OVER NORTH AFRICA
28 MAY
1600 HOURS LOCAL
1500 HOURS ZULU

The old company plane of Petróleo Español-Africano flew across the airspace of Algeria, its course set for southern France. The cargo area in the aft end of the fuselage was empty after making a supply run to the station at Gabon. The front end, where a dozen close-packed seats were situated, had only two passengers: Karl Baroudeur and Vlad Krashchenko. Both men were dressed in civilian suits and had brought only a single suitcase each for the trip to Europe.

Baroudeur looked out the window at the sparse landscape of North Africa. "Down there is where the Legion had its real glory days. Eighteen-thirty-one to nineteen-sixty-two. That is when I would have liked to have served rather than Bosnia and those places in modern times."

Krashchenko shrugged. "What difference does it make?"

"It makes a big difference," Baroudeur insisted. "Those were real Legionnaires in those days, let me tell you! Discipline was what it was supposed to be, and the whole *esprit de corps* was nothing like the Legion we knew. All those modern kids with their rock and roll that serve now would not make pimples on the arses of the *anciens*. Do you remember what is written about old General Négrier and the words he spoke to the legionnaires under his command in Indo-China back in the nineteenth century? 'You have become soldiers in order to die; thus I shall send you where you will die.' " He grinned viciously. "Now that is what I call military discipline!"

"I am through with soldiering," Krashchenko said. It was like a declaration.

"Bah!" Baroudeur said. "You are only downhearted because of this setback. We did the best we could with what we had. We were forced to fight with one hand tied behind our backs. On the next job we will have better preparation."

Krashchenko made no reply; he just stared straight ahead.

D.R. OF THE CONGO
COUNTERINSURGENCY BASE CAMP
30 MAY
0900 HOURS LOCAL
0700 HOURS ZULU

Captain Edouard Tshobutu's paratroopers stood in formation, each section properly drawn up separately under its leader. A color guard stood to the front with the battalion standard and the national colors of the Democratic Republic of the Congo bearing a large gold star and six smaller ones on a blue field.

Sergeant Major Samuel Katungo ordered the assembled troops to present arms. At that moment, Jonas Blane, Tshobutu, and Sublieutenant Pierre Kintuba marched to the front of the formation. Tshobutu ordered the men to assume the position of at ease.

"Soldiers of the *Sixième Bataillon Parachutiste d'Infanterie,* you have emerged from this campaign victorious!" he began. "It was a hard fight, and many of our comrades sacrificed their lives to defeat the traitorous dogs and foreign bandits who sought to conquer our homeland. We will be returning to the battalion to take up where we left off when we marched out of our home garrison to participate in this crusade. I regret to inform you that there will be no medals for the brave deeds you have performed nor memorial services for the dead. And no expressions of gratitude shown to us who have survived. However, there will be promotions, I assure you." He paused to note the men were pleased with the raise in ranks. "We have had the honor of fighting beside brave comrades who came from afar to support us. I cannot tell you where they are from. It is obvious, however, that they are Americans, and that is all you will ever know about them. Commandant Blane now wishes to speak to you on behalf of Captain Gerhardt and Lieutenants Brown, Grey, and Matoskah."

Jonas stepped forward and accepted a salute from the captain, then turned to the assembled unit. "Men of the Sixth Parachute Infantry Battalion, we have been honored to serve with you. You have proven your courage and fidelity beyond all doubt. Like you, we will receive no accolades or recognition for what was accomplished in this struggle. And like you, we will return to our normal duties until we are once again called to arms. We wish you farewell and hope that you will always remem-

ber us as we remember you—with respect and camara-
derie."

Jonas turned and once more exchanged salutes with
Captain Tshobutu. Then he marched off the bucolic drill
field to join the other Unit operators waiting for him on
the sidelines.

The operation was over. Almost.

MELILLA, SPANISH MOROCCO
PETRÓLEO ESPAÑOL-AFRICANO, S.A.
CORPORATE HEADQUARTERS
1330 HOURS LOCAL
1230 HOURS ZULU

The Consortium's marshals of the staff were all there:
Jean-Paul Fubert of France; Francisco Valverde, Spain;
Pietro D'Amiteri, Italy; and Heinrich Müller-Koenig of
Germany. Their guest, retired general Philippe Dubois,
had just delivered the official report of the insurgency
attempted in the nation they referred to as the European Congo.

Everyone was silent at the conclusion of this report of
a failure in plans. After a moment, Fubert got to his feet
and walked to the wall, where a large map of Africa was
positioned. He studied it, then slowly turned around. "It
is my opinion that our mistake was the employment of
mercenaries."

"I agree," General Dubois said. "We should have
made use of a combination of a small advisory team of
our brotherhood along with specially trained indigenous
agents-provocateurs."

The German Müller-Koenig spoke up. "As I recall,
that is what you suggested when this operation was first
proposed, General Dubois. It is now painfully obvious
that we should have listened to you."

The old soldier was not resentful. "Let us not dwell

on decisions made in the past. We must look to the future and apply the examples learned in the European Congo."

"You are most understanding, General," D'Amiteri said.

Valverde had other things on his mind. "I am concerned about the surviving mercenaries. How much information do they have that might prove hurtful to us?"

"That is not a matter of concern," Dubois said. "After being marched back to collect their dead in Mwitukijiji and bury them, all were summarily executed by Captain Tshobutu. They now rot in a common grave in the jungle."

"Were they not at first interrogated as prisoners of war?" Fubert asked.

"Of course," Dubois said. "But they had nothing to offer in the way of intelligence."

"That is something else you should be commended for," Fubert said.

Valverde had another worry. "What about the Congolese general?"

Dubois smiled. "You must be referring to Captain Marcel Lulombe, who appointed himself major general. There is nothing to worry about. Mssrs. Baroudeur and Krashchenko saw to it that he did not survive."

"What about those two surviving legionnaires?" Fubert asked.

"We will have further use for them," Dubois said. "They are intelligent men in their own right. Had they enjoyed the benefit of better birth and family, both could have gone much further in the world than the Foreign Legion. They have a great potential to benefit our efforts in the future, believe me, messieurs."

Fubert walked away from the African map to the other side of the room, where one of the entire world was displayed. "Eh, *bien,* I think it is time to open discussions for our next venture. Any suggestions?"

Valverde and Ameiteri raised their hands.

MARSEILLE, FRANCE
HOTEL SOFITEL VIEUX-PORT
1 JUNE
0900 HOURS LOCAL
0800 HOURS ZULU

Peter Luknore stood out on the balcony of his suite, sipping a cup of coffee after breakfast. Inside, his valet, Farouk, packed the master's luggage for the drive back to Switzerland. Luknore's dislike of airports, with all the authorities, crowds, and lists of undesirables, had not abated a bit, and he would continue to travel overland in his old but well-kept Lincoln limousine. He journeyed quite comfortably, accompanied by his personal staff of servants. And, of course, they stayed at only the finest hostelries during those journeys.

The recruitment of mercenaries was over, and a phone call from Bern indicated that 100,000 euros had been deposited to his bank account. Luknore really didn't need the money, but his old friend General Dubois had asked for him to take on the task as a personal favor. And he had also grown quite bored with the quiet life of retirement in his mountaintop chalet in the Alps. It had been good to get back with those rough fellows of the illegal military community for a few weeks. Old emotions were stirred, and he was stimulated by the intrigue and risk. But now he felt a certain spiritual and physical fatigue, and he was glad to be going home. At seventy-two years of age, he was in a world that had changed greatly from his younger days as first a legionnaire, then an OAS agent, and finally a successful arms dealer. This foray had smoothed out the jagged edges of nostalgia and hindsight, and he was now content to accept his life as it had evolved.

Farouk appeared on the balcony. "You are packed, M. Luknore. The bellmen are on their way up to pick up your bags, and Vincent has called me on the cell phone. The car is in front."

"Very well," Luknore said. "Lead the way." He followed the efficient valet off the balcony and through the suite and out into the hall

Watson the secretary was waiting for him. He nodded respectfully. "Good morning, sir. It appears we are all ready for the drive home." He fell into step with his employer as both now trailed after Farouk. They stopped at the elevator, and Watson remarked, "As per your instructions, I have already made arrangements for the donation of your remuneration for this latest endeavor to the nunnery of the Sisters of Charity and Mercy in Bergspitze."

"Excellent, Watson," Luknore said. "They will put it to good use in one or more of their many humanitarian projects."

"Indeed, sir," Watson agreed as the elevator arrived.

CHAPTER TWENTY-FOUR

Orange is a city of the former Roman Empire with a colorful history. Old ruins of those days long gone include an ancient amphitheater built at the beginning of Christianity in Europe. Other sights of antiquity are also available for the pleasure of historians and tourists alike. Additionally, the community is the garrison town of Quartier Labouche, home of the French Foreign Legion's First Foreign Cavalry Regiment. As an army town, there is more than simply the presence of active-duty troops to be seen occasionally in the area. Veterans and retirees of the Legion also live in the community near the military post. Many of these old guys remained in the vicinity of their former outfit for the main reason that they had no place else to go after their years of service. New identities can hide old sins, but not in the places where they were committed, thus these *anciens* found comradeship and comfort being with their own kind, hidden by both time and Legion *noms de guerre*. They had their favorite bars and activities, and enjoyed tossing back a few drinks while swapping lies about the good old days when a legionnaire was a legionnaire, unlike these softies currently serving in the contemporary regiments.

Bar Le Cafard in the city was a favorite hangout of those old boys. The establishment's name means "beetle" in French and refers to a mental illness suffered by legionnaires in the old days at isolated posts in the hinterlands of North Africa. The austere conditions caused these soldiers to be plagued by loneliness, sexual frustration, boredom, and suicidal depression or homicidal rage. Many of the sufferers acted as if they were brushing bugs off themselves when in the throes of the sickness, thus the name. Most sought relief from the malady through heavy drinking, which was tolerated because it offered at least a semblance of relief from the mental and spiritual torment of the malady.

The walls of Bar Le Cafard were decorated with photographs, drawings, news clippings, and old recruiting posters that went back to the days right after World War II when France's struggle with the Viet Minh in Indo-China began. The vets who served in that struggle were now in their eighties and prone to the symptoms of advanced age, but a few still made appearances to drink *vin rouge* and cognac. There was no loud talking as in the watering holes where the current class of legionnaires raised hell; but now and then an old marching song would erupt from the aged drinkers, and everyone would join in on such melodies as "Le Boudin," "Contre les Viets," "Le Fanion de la Légion," and others. They were sung in time to the Legion's slow marching cadence—somber, reverent, and with a great deal of sentimentality and nostalgia.

9 JUNE
1530 HOURS LOCAL
1430 HOURS ZULU

Karl Baroudeur and Vlad Krashchenko met in the
foyer of their apartment house to share an afternoon of
relaxation. They had pretty much physically recovered
from the campaign in the Congo, and their moods had
risen to a subdued contentment. Several visits to a rather
well-to-do brothel, regular hot showers, excellent meals,
and a couple of drunken binges had smoothed out the
emotional knots left over from the defeat. Now they felt
refreshed and were ready to visit the Bar Le Cafard for
some casual drinking and conversation with their own
kind: *les anciens de la Légion Étrangère.*

The pair strolled down the street, dressed casually in
sports shirts and slacks, their bare feet shod in stylish
sandals. Krashchenko wore a straw Panama hat, looking a bit like a weird old geezer on vacation. As the pair
made their way toward their destination, they failed
to note that a man was surreptitiously following them,
maintaining his distance in a skillful manner yet keeping
them in sight.

When Baroudeur and Krashchenko entered the bar,
they nodded to the listless waves of greeting given them
by old men who were already half snockered and con-
tentedly locked into the alcoholic hazes of habitual tip-
plers. Baroudeur went to a table and sat down while
Krashchenko picked up a couple of aperitifs from the
barkeep. Then, as an afterthought, he ordered two hot
jambon-et-fromage on croissants. Krashchenko joined
his old buddy and settled down to what was planned to
be a pleasant afternoon drunk.

Baroudeur, in a good mood, raised his glass, giving the
old Legion toast about watching out for the dust: *"Attention à la poussière."* He took a sip, glancing at the door
when a young man entered the bar. At first he was sur-

prised to see a guy that age come into an oldsters' hang-out; then his surprise increased when the man seemed familiar.

"Durant!" Baroudeur suddenly exclaimed.

Krashchenko looked up in time to see Bob Brown pull the Beretta 93R automatic pistol from his waist-band. The silencer on it seemed ominous, and the first round fired hit Baroudeur in the forehead. Krashchenko went for his own weapon, a .32 Derringer in an ankle holster, and was rewarded with a bullet to the face that blasted out the back of his neck, blowing flesh and blood all over a couple of *anciens* behind him. Bob swung back to Baroudeur and fire twice more, very fast. The victim jerked violently, then slid out of his chair to the floor.

The other old men in the bar, being combat veterans, immediately scrambled under their tables, without no-ticing Carlito Grey and Lance Matoskah in covering po-sitions at the back door.

Bob turned and rushed out to a waiting car with Jo-nas Blane driving while Mack Gerhardt sat in the front passenger seat. Bob jumped into the back, and Jonas hit the accelerator, speeding down the street. Carlito and Lance took a separate route of escape in their own au-tomobile.

Now the mission was really accomplished.

Epilogue

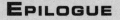

Fort Griffith, Missouri
The Cave
12 June
0815 hours local
1415 hours Zulu

The small briefing room was crowded that morning. Besides Jonas Blane, Mack Gerhardt, Bob Brown, Carlito Grey, and Lance Matoskah, the CIA controller-at-large Delmar Munger and Booker Cartwright of the State Department were also present. The man in charge of the session, Colonel Tom Ryan, stood at the podium located in front of the large map mounted on the front wall.

The tactical debriefing had taken place the night before between the colonel and the operators, with each firefight, patrol, and other field activity discussed, dissected, and critiqued. Colonel Ryan was well aware that hindsight was twenty-twenty, and he always hated like hell to pick apart past actions after the furor had died down. It seemed patently unfair to judge the performance of men who had been forced into quick decisions during dangerous situations when instantaneous responses had to be made; but it was a necessary evil of leadership. By being picky and critical, the lessons learned from those times of terror and panic would be firmly planted in the subconscious of those involved. Thus they would be ready for the next occurrences when lives were in danger and the line between victory and defeat was thin and wavering.

But now a new day had dawned, and the grousing, resentment, and angry outbursts were over and done with. It was the hour of going over the big picture. Ryan gave his Unit operators one of his lopsided grins. "Mission accomplished. That's it, plain and simple. You whipped their asses, and you got a right to be proud of yourselves. The Democratic Republic of the Congo is back to normal, sort of, and the powers-that-be are checking things out so that the local situation doesn't go to hell again."

Jonas raised his hand. "We never heard what happened to the mercenaries after we left."

"They are no more," Ryan said. "The Congolese National Army dealt with them with maximum prejudice. No trials, of course."

Jonas nodded. "I don't like it, but I can't say I'm surprised."

The colonel glanced at Bob. "Did you make any friends among those guys?"

"Yes, sir," Bob replied. "There was this kind of mixed-up English kid who had a lifetime of making bad decisions. And a French-Canadian who was there to make enough money to open a hunting-and-fishing lodge up in the boondocks of Quebec. Most of those guys were attracted by the euros."

Lance Matoskah asked, "What about the insurgents from the National Army?"

"The NCOs were broken to the ranks, and all were transferred to a labor battalion in deepest, darkest Africa," Ryan replied. "I don't know what they'll be doing there, but draining swamps while up to their asses in crocodiles comes to mind."

"Does that include the officers, sir?" Lance asked.

"They got special treatment," Ryan said. "All were cashiered. Then they were sent to their own specially assigned part of the muddy, steamy jungle. They were provided with rudimentary tools, cheap building material, seeds, and other items, such as clothing, some sticks of furniture, and all the crap they need for bare survival. Those poor bastards will spend the rest of their lives barely existing in that primitive environment. Their wives were given a choice to either go with the husbands or divorce them. Most if not all chose divorce, and I suppose they gathered up the kiddies and went home to Mama and Papa."

"Have you heard anything about Captain Tshobutu and Lieutenant Kintuba?" Mack inquired. "They were a couple of sharp officers—I'll give 'em that. And Sergeant Major Katungo was one hell of a leader too."

"You must be referring to newly promoted Lieutenant Colonel Tshobutu and Captain Kintuba," Ryan said. "And I've been informed that Katungo has been made a chief warrant officer. They are all back in their old outfit, which has been expanded into a battalion combat team that now includes a heavy-mortar battery and an armored-reconnaissance platoon."

"Glad to hear that," Jonas said. "But what I'm really curious about is that Consortium or whatever it's called. Has any more intelligence come out about that bunch?"

"I've learned a lot more about 'em," Ryan said. "It's new to me, but not to the intelligence community." He glanced over at Munger, then back to Jonas. "They've been active for about fifty years, but were actually formed before the end of the Second World War working quietly and steadily to gather their strength. Most of the members are French, Spanish, Germans, and Italian, and they have big bucks and lots of connections in high places. Nobody is sure how the organization works or where they're operating from. But this thing in the Congo has caused a lot of worry. A covert operation suddenly blossoms into an active insurrection, and when it is stopped, there are no smoking guns, clues, or hints about who started it. The only thing left is a bunch of indigenous losers who were sucked into the scheme through bribery and lies."

"There's gotta be some way to tie them into it," Bob Brown insisted.

Ryan shook his head. "The only way they are connected to incidents is not by evidence, but by the lack thereof. That leaves a lot of holes."

"Do you think we'll be hearing from them again?" Jonas asked.

"From the way they operate we probably won't even be sure it is them," Ryan said. He paused. "Okay. Let's keep this program rolling. Delmar Munger has a few words for us."

Munger, carrying a small portfolio, got up slowly and walked defiantly to the front of the room. He stopped and gazed in triumph at the five operators. "I am authorized to speak for both the Central Intelligence Agency and the United States State Department this morning. I want to impress that on you. I might also mention that as of late last night I received information gleaned from a report sent in by the chief CIA operative in the Democratic Republic of the Congo. This intelligence is the result of interviews of survivors on both sides of the fracas as well as visits to the sites where much of these occurrences went down. So you listen good, because I'm standing here in front of you with the facts. *Facts!* And lying or arguing on your part is not going to contradict anything I say."

Ryan glared at his men. "I will not—I say again—*will not* tolerate any wise-ass remarks from any of you, no matter what Munger says! Any bad reactions on your parts will be handled by me personally. There're all sorts of dirty work details that can be tended to around here while you mull over the error of your ways."

Munger opened the portfolio. After a brief review, he looked at Jonas. "Will you give me an oral outline of your program to win the insurgent Congolese over to your side?"

Jonas had been ordered how to respond to any such inquiries. "I didn't have a program, per se, I spoke to individual insurgents and mercenaries when the opportunity presented itself."

"Describe such an incident," Munger said.

"I'd see an insurgent and I'd walk up and say, 'Howdy do. Do you want to join our side?' "

"That was it?"

"Pretty much," Jonas said.

"How many of those individuals elected to cross over?"

"Let me think," Jonas said. He assumed an expression of deep thought, then began counting on his fingers. After a moment he said, "None."

"That was the best you could do, even though you were aware that the Secretary of State had issued specific instructions that a concerted effort was to be made to win these people to our side?"

"Yes."

Munger glowered. "What about civilians in the area? Did you speak to any of them?"

Bob Brown raised his hand. "Mr. Munger! Mr. Munger! I spoke to a young civilian girl from Mwitu-whatever. It was during the time I was inserted into the mercenaries."

Munger made some notes. "All right, Brown. What did you say?"

"I told her to get on home."

Munger frowned. "What the hell was that all about?"

"Well, a couple of those guys were trying to rape her, so I stopped them and told her to get on home."

"I'll give you that one, Brown," Munger said hesitantly. "That was an act of kindness that would make her sympathetic to our cause."

"Could I get a letter of commendation from the State Department, please?" Bob said. "It would look ever so good in my two-oh-one file."

Colonel Ryan, fighting down the desire to burst out laughing, interjected, "Never mind, Sergeant Brown. I'll write one for you myself."

Munger slapped his hand down hard on the podium. "You cowboys think you're real smart, don't you? Well, I'm not playing your crazy game—got it? So let me read you the riot act. All the after-action studies on this operation make it abundantly clear that no Congolese were persuaded to join your efforts. You completely ignored explicit instructions you were to carry out. And this was in direct defiance of the United States Government."

"Mr. Munger, it would appear that administering such a program was impossible under the circumstances in the field," Ryan said. "When they lost the helicopter it cut down their ability to move freely and rapidly through the OA. There was not enough time to conduct psychological warfare on top of everything else. And you seem to be forgetting that they were serving with native-born Congolese. That has to count for something."

"Not to me," Munger said.

"I am giving my men orders not to discuss the subject further."

"Oh, you are?" Munger said with a grin. "All right, Colonel, then let's get to a spicier subject, shall we? Let's discuss the wanton slaughter of civilians during the last battle."

"Now we're getting somewhere," Jonas said. "Here's the skinny on that tragedy, Mr. Munger. During a complex attack and retreat maneuver to draw out enemy armor, the insurgents were stopped and turned back. Their field commander, a citizen of France through his service in that country's military, ordered his men to go to the place where the people had withdrawn to safety, and drive them into a position between both forces. He next ordered those under his command to open fire on us, using the civilians as human shields. This information I got from postoperational interrogations of EPWs among the mercenaries."

"Dozens of these civilians were killed or wounded, were they not?"

"Yes," Jonas replied.

"And how many of your men fired into them?"

"None," Jonas said. "We already had two enveloping factions maneuvering into position, and those of us in the center ceased fire and waited until the pressure was taken off."

"Are you sure none of those Congolese paratroopers with you cut loose during that confusing, turbulent situation?"

"I am positive."

Munger smirked. "Really? Who performed the autopsies on the dead, Blane? I understand the enemy troops were using Russian rifles of a different caliber employed by you and those paratroopers. Which caliber struck the poor innocent civilians? So I ask you again, what about autopsy results?"

"There were no autopsies and you know it," Jonas snapped.

"Then all we have is your word that your force did not shoot down any innocent villagers while they cowered and begged for their lives," Munger said.

Now Colonel Ryan lost his cool. "You watch your goddamn mouth, Munger! Sergeant Major Blane turned in an official after-action report about that incident stating that he had ordered his men to cease fire when he perceived the location of the civilians. And that's good enough for me."

"Well, it's not good enough for the CIA or the State Department, Colonel Ryan!" Munger growled. "And you're in some pretty deep yogurt yourself too. Who ordered the gangland hit on those two Frenchmen in Orange?"

"I'm not required to make a report to the CIA regarding the incident," Ryan said. "You'll have to refer to my upper echelons to deal with that situation."

"That's very handy, isn't it?" Munger said, uttering a rhetorical question. "Especially when your upper echelons are on a level that seems impenetrable. And it's all balderdash, Colonel! Let me remind you that there is still a United States Congress with a powerful committee that oversees all intelligence and special operations. The CIA and State Department most certainly plan to go to them to complain about the methods your operators applied in this particular crisis. And this time, they'll call you in and wring you dry. Your outfit will be disbanded, and you and all these goddamn pirates of yours will be slammed back so deep into the federal prison system they'll have to pump in fresh air and sunshine to 'em. Your goddamn days are numbered, Ryan!"

Ryan spoke calmly. "When you get back to Washington, ass face, pass on this proverb to those politicos. It goes, 'You can't argue with success.' "

Munger grabbed his portfolio and slammed it shut. He gestured to Booker Cartwright, and the two men left the room, leaving Ryan and the others alone. No one said anything for a moment. Then Jonas Blane stood up. "These are problems that are just starting."

"You're right about that," Ryan agreed. "This isn't the end of this little song and dance."

Bob Brown shrugged. "Say, Colonel, how about joining us in our team room for a beer?"

"Yeah," Ryan said. "I could sure as hell use one about now. It looks like my ass is gonna be back up in front of a bunch of goddamn politicos."

Carlito Grey winked at Lance Matoskah as they followed the others out of the room.

GLOSSARY

AAR: After-Action Report
ACOG: Advanced Combat Optical Gunsight; a 4x32 scope.
Afghan: Currency of Afghanistan—43.83 = $1.
AFSOC: Air Force Special Operations Command
Agent Provocateur: An individual who infiltrates groups and movements to sway members toward a certain style of behavior.
AGL: Above Ground Level
AK-47: 7.62-millimeter Russian Assault Rifle
AKA: Also Known As
AKS-74: 5.45-millimeter Russian Assault Rifle.
Angel: A thousand feet above ground level, i.e., Angels Two is two thousand feet.
AP: Armor Piercing or Air Police
APC: Armored Personnel Carrier
AS-50: .50 caliber semiautomatic sniper rifle with scope.
ASAP: As Soon As Possible
ASL: Above Sea Level
Assault position: Last site of cover and concealment before reaching the objective.
Asset: A person who, for various reasons, has important intelligence to provide operators and/or teams about to be deployed into operational areas.

AT: Antitank

AT-4: Antiarmor Rocket Launchers

Attack Board (also Compass Board): A board with a compass, watch, and depth gauge used by subsurface swimmers.

ATV: All-Terrain Vehicle

AWACS: Airborne Warning and Control System

AWOL: Away Without Leave, i.e., absent from one's unit without permission.

Bastion: Part of a fortification or fortified position that juts outwardly.

Battle rattle: Combat gear carried on the body by troops.

BDU: Battle Dress Uniform

BOHICA: Bend over. Here it comes again.

BOQ: Bachelor Officers' Quarters

Boots-on-the-ground: This refers to being at a specific location, ready to get down to the business at hand.

Briefback: A briefing given to staff by a Delta Team regarding their assigned mission. This must be approved before it is implemented.

BS: Bullshit

PX: Post Exchange, a military store with good prices for service people.

C4: Plastic explosive

Cammies: Slang for attire manufactured with a camouflage pattern.

CAR-15: Compact model of the M-16 rifle.

CAS: Close Air Support

CG: Commanding General

Chickenshit: An adjective that describes a person or a situation as being strict, unfair, or malicious.

CLU: Command launch unit for the Javelin AT missile.

CO: Commanding Officer

Collective: A lever on a helicopter that determines the pitch of the aircraft, i.e., the higher the pitch, the greater the lift.

Cone of Fire: The pattern of scattered hits from the single fire burst of a machine gun. The bullets do not follow the same trajectory because of the weapon's shaking, variations in ammo, and atmospheric conditions.

CP: Command Post

CPU: Computer Processing Unit

CPX: Command Post Exercise

CRRC: Combat Rubber Raiding Craft

CS: Tear gas

Cyclic: A joystick on a helicopter that determines the horizontal movement of the aircraft.

Dashika: Slang name for the Soviet DShK 12.7-millimeter heavy machine gun.

DASR: Department of the Army Security Roster

Det Cord: Detonating Cord

DJMS: Defense Joint Military Pay System

DPV: Desert Patrol Vehicle

DZ: Drop Zone

E&E: Escape and Evasion

Enfilade Fire: Gunfire that sweeps along an enemy formation.

EPW: Enemy Prisoner of War

ERP: Enroute Rally Point. A rally point that a patrol leader chooses while moving to or from the objective.

ESP: Extra-Sensory Perception

ETS: End of Term of Service

FLA: Field Litter Ambulance

FLIR: Forward-Looking Infrared Radar

Four-Shop: Logistics Section of the staff.

FRH: Flameless Ration Heater

Front Leaning Rest: The position assumed to begin push-ups.

FSB: Russian acronym for the Federal Security Service, the organization that was the successor to the KGB after the fall of the Soviet Union.

FTX: Field Training Exercise

G-1: Administrative Section of a brigade staff or higher.

G-2: Intelligence Section of a brigade staff or higher.

G-3: Operations and Training Section of a brigade staff or higher.

G-4: Logistics Section of the staff a brigade staff or higher.

GHQ: General Headquarters

GI: Government Issue

GIGN: *Groupe d'Intervention de la Gendarmerie Nationale.* French antiterrorist group made up of members of the *Gendarmerie* police.

GPS: Global Positioning System

GROM: *Grupa Reagowania Operacyjno Mobilnego.* Polish antiterrorist group made up of volunteers from the commandos and combat swimmers.

HAHO: High-Altitude High-Opening parachute jump.

HALO: High-Altitude Low-Opening parachute jump.

Hamas: Palestinian terrorist organization that has been voted into office in Palestine. Their charter calls for the destruction of Israel.

HE: High Explosive

HEAT: High Explosive Antitank

Hezbollah: A militant Islamic terrorist organization located in Lebanon. It was organized in response to the Israeli occupation, and is still active.

H&K MP-5: Heckler & Koch MP-5 submachine gun.

Hootch: A simple shelter structure one generally must crawl into.

Hors de combat: Out of the battle (expression in French)

HSB: High-Speed Boat

IFV: Infantry Fighting Vehicle

Immediate Action: A quick fix to a mechanical problem.

Interpol: An international police organization of more than one hundred national law enforcement members.

INTREP: Intelligence Report

INTSUM: Intelligence Summary

IR: Infrared

IRP: Initial Rally Point. A place within friendly lines where a patrol assembles prior to moving out on the mission.

ITPIAL: Infrared Target Pointer Illuminator Aiming Laser

JCOS: Joint Chiefs of Staff

JSOC: Joint Special Operation Command

K-Bar: A brand of knives manufactured for military and camping purposes.

KD Range: Known-Distance Firing Range.

Keffiyeh: Arab headdress (what Yasser Arafat wore).

KGB: Russian organization of security, espionage, and intelligence left over from the old Soviet Union, eventually succeeded by the FSB.

KIA: Killed in Action

KISS: Keep It Simple, Stupid—or more politely, Keep It Simple, Sweetheart.

KSK: *Kommando Spezialkräfte*. German military organization responsible for special operations outside of Germany.

LBE: Load-Bearing Equipment

Light Sticks: Flexible plastic tubes that illuminate.

Limpet Mine: An explosive mine that is attached to a metal surface.

Locked Heels: Describes when a serviceman is getting a severe vocal reprimand while standing at a strict position of attention.

LZ: Landing Zone

M-18 Claymore Mine: A mine fired electrically with a blasting cap.

M-60 E3: A compact model of the M-60 machine gun.

M-67: An antipersonnel grenade.

M-203: A single-shot 40 millimeter grenade launcher.

MATC: A fast river support craft.

Medevac: Medical Evacuation

Merc: Mercenary

MI-5: United Kingdom Intelligence and Security Agency

Mk 138 Satchel Charge: Canvas container filled with explosive.

MLR: Main Line of Resistance

Mossad: Israeli Intelligence Agency (*ha-Mossad le-Modiin ule-Tafkidim Meyuhadim*—Institute for Intelligence and Special Tasks)

MRE: Meal, Ready To Eat

Murphy's Law: This means that if something can go wrong, it most certainly will.

NCO: Noncommissioned Officers, i.e., corporals and sergeants

Nom de Guerre: French for "war name."

NVB: Night-Vision Binoculars

NVG: Night-Vision Goggles

NVS: Night-Vision Sight

OA: Operational Area

OAS: *Organisation Armée Secrète*. Terrorist organization of disaffected French military who objected to the granting of independence to Algeria.

OCONUS: Outside the Continental United States

OCS: Officers' Candidate School

OER: Officer's Efficiency Report

One Shop: Administrative Section of the staff.

OP: Observation Post

Operator: Operational member of the Unit.

OPLAN: Operations Plan

OPORD: Operations Order. This is what an OPLAN morphs into.

OPSEC: Operational Security

ORP: Objective Rally Point. A location chosen before or after reaching the objective. Here a patrol can send out recon on the objective, make final preparations, reestablishing the chain of command, and other activities necessary either before or right after action.

OTC: Operator's Training Course

Passive Systems: Protection provided by camouflage, dispersion, concealment, deceptive measures, and similar warning and defensive systems.

PDQ: Pretty Damn Quick

PLF: Parachute Landing Fall

PM: Preventive Maintenance

PMC: Private Military Company

Poop: News or information.

Posse Comitatus: The use of American federal armed forces as law enforcement inside the boundaries of the United States.

POV: Privately Owned Vehicle

P.P.P.P.: Piss-Poor Prior Planning

PT: Physical Training

Puhtee: An Afghan rolled stocking cap that can be worn in many ways

RAPS: Ram Air Parachute System; parachute and gear for free fall jumps.

RHIP: Rank Has Its Privileges

RIB: Rigid Inflatable Boat

ROE: Rules of Engagement

RON: Remain Over Night. Generally refers to patrols.

RPG: Rocket-propelled Grenade

RPM: Revolutions Per Minute

R and R: Rest and Relaxation, or Rest and Recuperation.

RRP: Reentry Rally Point. A site outside the range of friendly lines, to pause and prepare for reentry.

RTO: Radio Telephone Operator

Run-flat tires: Solid-rubber inserts that allow the vehicle to run even when the tires have been punctured.

RV: Rendezvous Point

S-1: Administrative Section of a staff below brigade level.

S-2: Intelligence Section of a staff below brigade level.

S-3: Operations and Training Section of a staff below brigade level.

S-4: Logistics Section of a staff below brigade level.

SAMIL: South African Military

SAS: Special Air Services. An extremely deadly and superefficient special operations unit of the British Army.

SAW: Squad Automatic Weapon—M249 5.56-millimeter magazine or clip-fed machine gun. This is the Belgian Minimi machine gun originally manufactured in 1982.

SCUBA: Self-Contained Underwater Breathing Apparatus

SERE: Survival, Escape, Resistance, and Evasion

SF: Special Forces

SFOB: Special Forces Operational Base

Shahid: Arabian word for martyr (plural is Shahiden).

Shiites: A branch of Islam; in serious conflict with the Sunnis.

SITREP: Situation Report

Snap-to: The act of quickly and sharply assuming the position of attention.

SOCOM: Special Operations Command

SOF: Special Operations Force

SOI: Signal Operating Instructions

SOP: Standard Operating Procedures

SPA: Self-Propelled Artillery

SPECOPS: Special Operations

SPECWARCOM: Special Warfare Command

Spetsnaz: Russian Special Forces unit of various branches.

Stand-to: Procedure of being on alert or ready for action.

Stick: A line of parachutists who exit the aircraft through the same door.

Stick: A word used in the French Foreign Legion to describe a punishment in which the palm of the hand is used to strike the back of the head of a clumsy, inattentive, or misbehaving legionnaire.

Sunnis: A branch of Islam; in serious conflict with the Shiites.

T-10 Parachute: Basic static-line-activated personnel parachute of the United States Armed Forces.

Taliban: Militant anti-West Muslims with extreme religious views; in serious conflict with Shiites.

TDy: Temporary Duty

Thermite Grenade: An incendiary cylindrical device containing a thermite mixture capable of burning through and/or welding steel or iron.

Three-Shop: Operations and Training Section of the staff.

TO: Table of Organization

TOA: Table of Allowances

TOC: Tactical Operations Center

TO&E: Table of Organization and Equipment

Two-Shop: Intelligence Section of the staff.

U.K.: The United Kingdom (England, Wales, Scotland, and Northern Ireland)

UN: United Nations

Unass: To jump out of or off something.

USAF: United States Air Force

USASFC: United States Army Special Forces Command

USSR: Union of Soviet Social Republics—Russia before the fall of Communism.

VTOL: Vertical Takeoff and Landing

WARNO: Warning Order

Waypoint: A location programmed into navigational instrumentation that provides directions to a specific spot on the planet.

WIA: Wounded In Action

WMD: Weapons of Mass Destruction; nuclear, biological, etc.

Zulu: The time at 0 degrees longitude, i.e., Greenwich Mean Time.

ABOUT THE AUTHOR

Patrick Andrews is an ex-paratrooper who served in the 82nd Airborne Division and the 12th Special Forces Group of the U.S. Army. As an "army brat" during his boyhood, he attended schools in Oklahoma, Arizona, Alabama, and North Carolina. Later the family moved to Wichita, Kansas, where he completed his education, then enlisted in the service. After release from active duty, Mr. Andrews became a professional writer, living in California and Florida. He now resides in Colorado on the front range of the Rocky Mountains with his wife, Julie, and two indolent cats.

BURN NOTICE:
THE FIX

by
TOD GOLDBERG

First in the brand new series based on
the critically acclaimed USA Network
television show!

Covert spy Michael Westen has found himself
in forced seclusion in Miami—and a little
paranoid. Watched by the FBI, cut off from
intelligence contacts, and with his assets
frozen, Weston is on ice with a warning:
stay there or get "disappeared."

The *New York Times* bestseller and gripping personal story behind *Black Hawk Down*.

IN THE COMPANY OF HEROES

by
Michael J. Durant
with Steven Hartov

Piloting a U.S. Army Special Operations Blackhawk over Somalia, Michael Durant was shot down with a rocket-propelled grenade on October 3, 1993. With devastating injuries, he was taken prisoner by a Somali warlord. With revealing insight and emotion, he tells the story of what he saw, how he survived, and the courage and heroism that only soldiers under fire could ever know.